After graduating in Chemistry & Physics from London University, Mike Walsham worked in pharmaceutical research for a few years before joining a well-known international computer company in sales and marketing.

He worked in the computer industry mostly in the UK, but also for over eleven years in several African countries, such as: Ethiopia, Zambia, Botswana, South Africa.

During his time in Zambia between 1973-75, Mike and others drove from Lusaka and through Tanzania to successfully climb Kilimanjaro. He obtained a Private Pilot's Licence in 1974 at the Lusaka Flying Club and went on to be an instructor.

He has a strong interest in music, particularly Jazz, as well as stamp collecting and Hornby Dublo trains. He has a keen interest in classic cars having owned his first Triumph TR4A in 1965 and selling his last one in 2020. As a result of working abroad, he enjoys travel, especially to places of historical interest in Europe and Africa. He is thoroughly committed to his family—four children, nine grandchildren—and to his local C of E church.

From 2007, for about seven years, he wrote articles for his local Parish News on subjects such as: the Ark of the Covenant, the Knights Templar, the Cathars, the Battle of Agincourt, the Scramble for Africa, the C of E Cathedral in Johannesburg.

A keen sportsman who still plays squash and walks, with a strong interest in most sports, particularly at international level. He was a crew member on a 42ft yacht in 2002 sailing from Menorca to Split, Croatia. In 2004, again a crew member taking a 44ft yacht from Southampton to Split.

His close relative's involvement in WWII stimulated him to write historical novels based to some extent on the relative's experiences in the Intelligence Services and the Royal Navy.

To all those people on the Atlantic convoys and the escort ships who gave their lives in trying to supply arms, military personnel, and food to the war-ravaged British population from 1939-1945.

To all those who worked in resistance movements during WWII and who gave their lives setting Europe ablaze in the name of democracy and freedom from tyranny.

Mike Walsham

OUTWITTING THE ENEMY

AUSTIN MACAULEY PUBLISHERS™

LONDON * CAMBRIDGE * NEW YORK * SHARJAH

A CIP catalogue record for this title is available from the British Library.

ISBN 9781398473058 (Paperback)
ISBN 9781398473065 (Hardback)
ISBN 9781398473072 (ePub e-book)

www.austinmacauley.com

First Published 2022
Austin Macauley Publishers Ltd®
1 Canada Square
Canary Wharf
London
E14 5AA

To the people managing the Western Approaches Command Centre Museum in Liverpool and those who have worked tirelessly over the years to open up the bunker for the general public to appreciate its significance in the Battle of the Atlantic.

To my wife, Sandra, our four children and their families.

Chapter 1
Sunday, 3 November 1940

As the train slowly drew into Victoria Station, Andrew wondered what the parts of London near his flat would look like. When he was attending the Naval Training course on the Hamble, everyone was updated with the day and night-time bombing raids of London and other major cities. The BBC, however, restricted what it put out over the wireless broadcasts to the nation so as not to lower the morale of the citizens.

The train came to a halt. Andrew took his case and kitbag down from the luggage rack, stepped on to the platform and walked with all the other passengers towards the exit. There were many men in uniform—probably on leave—so he didn't look out of place in his leading seaman's outfit with his kitbag over his shoulder. He handed in his ticket and walked out of the station into the dimly lit concourse. The station clock indicated that it was just after 7 o'clock. It felt strange to him that he was going to his Service flat for the first time since late July.

The streets were unlit. He passed buildings that were still smouldering from the last lot of bombing by the *Luftwaffe*. He unlocked the entrance door, went inside to the hallway, put his bag down and wandered around the downstairs' rooms. All the windows were covered in black paper; there were barely any lights on. One of his flatmates was in the kitchen preparing himself something to eat.

"Hello, Andrew," said John. "You've been away quite a while. Is everything going alright on the course?"

"Yes, very well, thank you. I've not been completely out of touch with what the Nazis have been doing to London, but it really is very bad, isn't it?"

"Soon after you left London, attacks by the *Luftwaffe* were mainly to destroy the RAF's fighter planes and to render their airfields unusable. They threw everything at us with hundreds of bombers supported by numerous Me109 fighters. Our boys flew so many sorties, day after day. We frustrated them so much that they then turned to bombing cities and manufacturing sites. From mid-

September there were daily bombing raids at day and at night for over fifty consecutive days. The East End and the London Docks have been regularly bombed with many hundreds of people killed and thousands made homeless. You are lucky you missed all the action!"

"I didn't really miss everything as we were aware of waves of bombers coming over in mid-September to bomb Portsmouth and Southampton; that's just up the road from where I was. I take it that the buildings used by the Service personnel haven't been bombed or damaged in anyway?"

"Not that I'm aware of, Andrew. But you must have heard that the Houses of Parliament were badly damaged? By a stroke of luck, the Church House—you know, the headquarters of the Church of England nearby—was struck, but it survived relatively unscathed. This impressed Churchill so much that he had it refurbished and requisitioned it as an annexe to the Palace of Westminster. Both Houses secretly moved there less than two months ago; there they will stay until the end of the war. Not only that, Buckingham Palace has been bombed several times while the King and Queen were in residence. Fortunately, they were not injured, although a few of their servants were hurt. The PM wanted them to leave the country—somewhere like Canada—but they flatly refused.

"Sorry, old boy, here am I prattling on while I'm preparing my meal and forgetting to ask if you would like something."

"No thanks, John. I might have a sandwich later."

He left the kitchen and took his things up to his room. He unpacked everything, changed out of his seaman's uniform into something more casual and sat down at his desk. For nearly an hour, he pondered over his meeting with Charles scheduled for the following morning: *what has he planned for me this time?* he thought to himself. He wasn't coming up with any bright ideas, so as he didn't feel hungry, decided to go to bed early.

Even though it was a damp morning, he walked to Charles's office in St James for his meeting scheduled for 10:30 a.m. As he reached the door, the brass knocker looked as if it had had an extra polish. He knocked firmly and went into the reception hall.

"Hello, Mr Williams. Good to see you again."

"Miss Jones, how I've missed you these last few months," he said with an engaging smile.

"Come now, you are flattering me. Please sign the register; Mr Compton-Browne is expecting you."

Andrew went up the stairs two at a time, knocked on Charles's door and went inside, just as he said 'enter'.

"Very pleased to see you again, Andrew," as Charles put out his hand to welcome him."

"You've still got Miss Grumpy, I see."

"She's a very efficient woman; reliable too. Don't you be too quick to criticise her. Anyway, I heard you did well on the first of your naval officer training courses. I got a glowing report from the captain in charge."

They both sat down as Charles started asking many questions about certain aspects of the course.

"Well done, all very interesting. On something quite different, you may or may not be aware of all that's been going on since you left in July. One of the most significant things from our perspective is that Mr Churchill—on 22nd July—set up an organisation called the Special Operations Executive, or SOE. I am reliably informed that the person given responsibility for setting up the SOE, is due to move their headquarters to two large flats in Baker Street early this month. The PM has ordered the SOE director to 'set Europe ablaze'.

"The main *raison d'être* of the SOE is to recruit agents and train them in espionage and sabotage, as well as to assist local resistance movements. Many will be sent to operate behind enemy lines, or in neutral countries where the Germans are making a nuisance of themselves. This organisation seems to me to be the direct result of General de Gaulle's development of the French resistance group, also known as the Free French Forces."

"But, to a large degree, isn't that what the SIS agents do today already?"

"Not quite, Andrew. You might remember from our discussions early last year—after you had signed the Official Secrets Act—that the Secret Intelligence Service, the SIS, or the Service as we tend to refer to it, has been in operation since before the First World War. We have had agents in most European capitals under the guise of Passport Control Officers at each Embassy. So, we like to think that we are old hands at intelligence gathering. Any information sent back from the Embassies' officers usually comes in the diplomatic bag which is then passed on to the appropriate section head.

"Now that we are at war with Germany, we have already recruited and trained more agents in order to carry out special activities in Europe—similar to the one that you and George carried out in Germany in March. The chief of the

SIS, C, who is also my boss, has viewed the SOE group with a fair amount of mistrust and suspicion, perceiving them as a bunch of amateurs."

"That sounds a bit harsh, when we are trying to achieve the same goal," Andrew remarked.

"It does, but before too long, I'm sure we will exchange information for our mutual benefit, and to the benefit of the war effort. My goodness, is it really after midday? It has been such a while since we've seen each other, let me take you to lunch; we can continue our discussions in the afternoon. Would that suit you, Andrew?"

"A good idea, Charles. I'm feeling a bit peckish."

They had a very enjoyable meal at one of Charles's clubs, not far from his office. On their return, Andrew thought Charles looked rather serious as they sat down opposite each other.

"One of the main reasons I asked you to come in today is to tell you what we're doing about German agents that have been captured—mainly those operating in this country. In the Great War, the Ministry of Defence acquired a house on Ham Common, near Richmond in Surrey. It was used for treating our officers who were suffering from shell shock.

"Soon after the outbreak of war in September 1939, it was taken over by MI5 and is referred to as Camp 020. MI5 and the SIS use this establishment for the interrogation of German spies. A multi-lingual army officer runs the show who swears that torture is never employed, as it seldom produces accurate information. A method used very successfully in getting quality information out of these chaps is with the use of 'stool-pigeons'. One of our 'fake prisoners' would be placed in a cell with a captured spy who would think he was a fellow German agent. The cell would be bugged so that an interrogator would listen in on their conversations. This has found to be a very useful tactic in yielding very valuable information; and, believe it or not, a few have been 'turned' to become double agents."

"Hang on a minute, Charles, I can easily see where this is leading to. You are thinking of asking me to be one of these so-called fake prisoners; is that correct?"

"Look, I cannot insist on your doing this, but it does have the support of C and the Foreign Office. C thinks you are an ideal candidate to help the Camp 020 officers. C has spoken to the chap in charge and he is willing to give you a try.

Obviously, it will certainly be a bit different from any of your other activities, so what do you think?"

"As you say, very different from anything I've done before. I have to tell you, however, that when we were escaping through Germany last March, it did cross my mind how we might be treated by the SS—had we been caught—as well as how we would react to their interrogation methods. Three weeks, you say?"

"I actually said a few, but three will do for now. Are you up for it?"

"I'll give it my best shot. Do I stay in the flat and go down daily?"

"No. That's not very practical. You will have to live down there so that you are on hand twenty-fours a day to work with the leader and his small group. I will contact the colonel's superior and inform him of your agreement to participate. I'm very pleased you are willing to be involved. Assuming you are accepted, I will arrange for a car to collect you and take you to Ham Common. I'll confirm all this on the phone on Friday evening."

"Before I leave, I would like to go to visit my wife and young son; I haven't seen them since May."

"That's a good idea, but do arrange to be back at your flat on Friday afternoon. It would be best if I phoned you after you've returned, at around 6:30 p.m. If everything is agreed with the colonel, I'll be able to give you further instructions."

"I don't have to wear or take anything special, do I? I'm assuming it will be quite casual?"

"Absolutely, Andrew. These spies will be in cells and brought into a special room for interrogation one at a time. You certainly won't be needing a suit! If that's all, I'll confirm everything to you on Friday evening?"

"Charles, I had better get back to the flat and give my wife the good news. I'll leave tomorrow morning."

They both stood up. Charles wished him an enjoyable time at home. He also told him he would find the colonel an interesting character.

Andrew phoned his wife in the evening, at a time when he knew Alfred would have been put to bed. She was very pleased to hear he was coming home for a few days; she hoped they might get out for a drive or a walk, even if the weather was very wet as it was at present.

Andrew was up early on Tuesday morning. He decided to wear his naval seaman's uniform as he thought he looked rather smart in it and his wife would like it too. He left the flat just after 10:30 a.m. and ran to Victoria station in between the heavy rain showers. He bought his ticket with the clerk telling him that there should be a train at 11:20 a.m.: Nazi bombing permitting, the man joked. He grabbed a very ordinary mug of tea from the main tea room before setting off for the train. He arrived at his destination just after midday and took a taxi to his house. Just as he was paying the driver, his wife came running out of the house, closely followed by his dog, Max.

"It's wonderful to see you, Andrew. It seems ages since you were last here." They embraced, he kissed her on the cheek just before Max jumped up and nearly knocked them both over.

"Steady on, Max," as Andrew bent down and took his black Labrador's head in his hands.

"Where's Alfred?" he enquired.

"I put him down for a nap, but I'll go and get him once you are indoors."

They went into the hall, Andrew put down his kitbag and briefcase. Max jumped up and down, running around in circles making funny noises in his excitement at seeing his master again.

"Do you want to go up and change, Andrew, while I get you a drink? Gin and tonic or a glass of wine? I have a white open, but you'll probably prefer red?"

"Yes, red please. I'll be down in a couple of shakes to help you choose one," Andrew replied.

"We don't have a lot of choice, but I'll leave it to you."

Andrew dashed upstairs to the main bedroom, but suddenly remembered he should make less noise as Alfred was asleep in his nursery. He peered around his son's door at his cot noticing that he had grown quite a lot, looking rather podgy since he last saw him in May; all those fair-haired curls too. He tiptoed into his own room, unpacked the few things he had and changed into some casual clothes. He went down stairs to the hall and was greeted again by his excited dog.

"What will you have to drink, dear?" he shouted to his wife from his position in front of the cocktail cabinet.

"I'll have some of the white wine that's on the floor of the larder, please."

Andrew opened a bottle of red that he found in the bottom of the cabinet and took two glasses out to the kitchen. He found the white wine, poured the red and white out, handing the white to his wife.

"Cheers, dear," he said, as they touched glasses.

"Nice to have you home again, Andrew, even if it is only for a short while. There's a cottage pie in the oven and cabbage about to boil on the top. You watch over it all while I go and get Alfred up. He'll be a bit shy to begin with, so you'll just have to be patient with him."

Andrew remembered from his trip home in May that Alfred was rather reticent towards him, but by the end of those few days, he was beginning to get quite used to his father's presence. He was brought back to the present when he noticed the cabbage boiling away, so he turned the heat down a bit. Within some minutes, his wife came into the kitchen carrying Alfred. Andrew turned and gave him a great big grin, as he squeezed his cheek, but not too hard.

"Wow, he has certainly grown. I see he's wearing the dungarees that I bought for his first birthday too."

"He's been wearing them for the last couple of months. He likes them so much it's difficult to get them off him to have them washed," as she put Alfred down to stand on the floor whilst she got on with the lunch.

"I've laid the table in the dining room, so please see that I've put everything out that we might need. I have fruit preserve for pudding and I have managed to make some home-made ice cream."

Andrew bent down to Alfred and tried to coax him to go with him to the dining room, but he moved towards his mother and clung to her leg, all the time looking at his father. Andrew took no notice, but went out of the kitchen and out of his sight. Instead of going straight to the dining room, he quietly went back to the kitchen door out of Alfred's view, he squatted down so his head was about three feet from the floor. Slowly, he brought his head around the door and said 'boo' not too loudly. Alfred chuckled back, as Andrew disappeared from sight. He repeated this game one more time. This time, Alfred ran over to the door just as his father was going to go 'boo' for a third time. He grabbed his father's ears, gave him a broad smile and ran back to his mother.

"I think Alfred is more confident than when you were last here," his wife said. Andrew went to the dining room, and, as he expected, everything was on the table that should be. He noticed Alfred's long-legged chair and wondered where his wife might have bought it.

Alfred ran into the dining room, followed by his mother, who was carrying everything on a tray.

"Please can you put Alfred into his chair, Andrew, and put his straps on so he doesn't try to climb out. When you've done that, the wine is still in the kitchen."

Andrew did as he was asked and they sat down to their lunch. He noticed that Alfred's small portion of lunch was in the dish that he used to use when he was a small boy.

"My goodness! Where did you find that dish?" he said, as he pointed at Alfred's meal.

"I found it amongst some of the things your mother gave us before we moved here. He's very attached to it. As you might remember, one unscrews the metal plug and pours in hot water so that his meal keeps warm. Alfred insists on using it for every meal."

After some twenty minutes, Andrew cleared all the plates away and took them to the kitchen. He returned with the fruit compote and the ice-cream for his wife to dish out. At the end of the meal, Andrew took everything from the table and washed up all the dishes, while Alfred was read a story in the lounge by his mother.

"It's not raining at the moment, so why don't we go into the garden. You'll be able to see all the vegetables that we're growing. Alfred will show you his new wheelbarrow that he uses to bring the freshly picked produce from the garden. Mr Charlwood, the gardener, who comes most Wednesdays, made the wheelbarrow for Alfred. We might see him tomorrow. I'm sure he would be pleased to see you."

They all went outside, together with Max, who was very excited to be out of doors.

"You take daddy down the garden, Alfred, and show him your wheelbarrow. I'm going to the hall stand to get the camera."

Andrew followed his son down the garden as he ran towards the vegetable area, closely followed by Max.

Alfred grabbed the handles and walked a little unsteadily towards his father, but grinning as he got nearer.

"Can you come up here, Alfred, towards the front door, as I'd like to take a picture," his mother asked.

Alfred seemed to understand. His mother positioned him facing the house with his hands on the handles. Andrew held the dog as his wife took the picture just as the sun broke through the clouds for a few moments. Alfred got bored of standing still so he tried to run around the front garden, but he lost his footing as he turned to look at his father and fell down.

"Don't cry old chap," his father said, as he moved quickly over to help him to his feet and brush some loose bits from his legs. But Alfred wasn't used to anyone else helping except his mother, so he ran over to her, crying as he went.

"While you attend to Alfred, I'll go and look at the rest of the garden with Max," Andrew told his wife.

After about thirty minutes, the clouds came over again, depositing more rain, so they all quickly went indoors. Alfred had soon got over his fall and played quite happily with some of his toys with his father in the lounge. It got dark very early, so they drew the curtains and had to put the lights on to see what they were doing. They had some tea after 4:30 p.m. and then Alfred was taken upstairs to have his bath.

"Have you spoken to Doreen, Brian's widow, recently?" Andrew asked his wife on her return to the lounge with Alfred, at about 6 o'clock.

"I'm sorry to say that I haven't; probably not since mid-June, after the memorial service."

"Once Alfred's in bed, I would like to give her a call to find out how she's getting on. Is that alright with you, dear?"

Andrew picked Alfred up and bounced him on his knee, at the same time reciting a couple of nursery rhymes. He seemed to enjoy it and didn't want his father to stop.

"We'll go for a nice walk tomorrow with Max. Would you like that?"

Alfred seemed to understand, looking around for Max, but he wasn't there. After a few more minutes, Andrew passed his son to his wife for her to take him up to bed. They waved at each other as he was carried from the lounge. He knew his wife would read him a story before coming back down to the lounge, so he went over and switched on his radiogram, selected a few records and put one on the turntable. He played Fats Waller—one of his favourites—who's piano playing he particularly admired. Andrew played the piano well, but didn't come anywhere near to how Fats played.

"That's a good selection, Andrew. Haven't heard 'Two sleepy people' for a little while. Can you get me a drink, please, before you telephone Doreen? I'd like a gin and tonic."

Andrew poured himself some red wine as well as his wife's drink.

"Cheers," he said, as they touched glasses. Andrew was plucking up courage, wondering how he should start the conversation with Doreen. He went out to the hall only to be met by Max who thought it was to be his lucky moment and go out with his master. Andrew rubbed his dog's head and told him to lie down.

"Hello, Doreen; it's Andrew. Sorry I haven't been in touch for a while, but I've been away. Did you get my letter that I sent in June?"

"Andrew, it's so good to hear your voice. Yes, I did get your letter, it was very kind of you to write. I found it very helpful, so soon after Brian's memorial service."

They chatted for a good ten minutes. Andrew then asked if she would like him to come over to see her, as he was on leave for a few days. She said she was alright, as her sister was staying with her till the end of the week. They spent a few more moments talking over some old times together, including a few that made Doreen laugh. He was disappointed not to be going to see her, but he accepted her suggestion for another time.

"Doreen seems to be getting on quite well," Andrew told his wife when he returned to the lounge. He explained that she had her sister staying, so he wouldn't be going to see her during this leave. They decided to have a snack supper as they listened to a selection of records. Conversation seemed to Andrew to be a bit easier and more light-hearted than on his previous leave.

Chapter 2
Wednesday, 6 November 1940

Andrew and his wife both woke up quite suddenly to hear the rain falling heavily on the windows. He put on his bedside light and found it was 6:30 a.m., it was still very dark. *Not much of a walk with Max today, if it stays like this*, he thought to himself. Just at that moment, there was a noise of Alfred shouting from his nursery.

"Shall I go, or will you?" Andrew said quietly.

"I had better go. He's more likely to expect me, even if he was quite relaxed with you yesterday."

Andrew got up to go downstairs to make a cup of tea. He saw Max in the hall staring up at him with an expectant look on his face. He opened the front door for him to go out, but when he saw the rain coming down, he refused to budge.

"You'll have to go out at some time, whether it's raining or not," he said to Max, as he touched him on the head.

He made the tea, put everything on a tray and took it upstairs. Alfred had been changed and was sitting up on the bed when Andrew appeared.

"Did you remember to bring a biscuit for Alfred?" Andrew was asked.

"Oh, no. I wasn't aware he had anything before his breakfast."

"I'll get one of those hard ones that he had yesterday; it helps with his teething," she said, and dashed down stairs.

They enjoyed this special time together, with Alfred gurgling away and trying to put words together that only his mother seemed to understand.

The rain had eased off after breakfast, so Andrew put on his waterproof clothes and cap. Max was very excited as he realised his master was going out and he would be going with him. They left the house, took the path on the other side of the road and went into the farmer's field. Andrew had trained Max so well that he needed no lead and would obey his commands. Even though Andrew hadn't taken his gun, Max ran up and down the fields looking for rabbits, or pheasant; anything that could have been shot under different circumstances.

Some fifty minutes later, the rain started again, so the two of them ran most of the way back to the house. Andrew took the towel from the hall and dried Max as well as he could in the porch. He took off his wet outdoor clothes and went into the lounge to see Alfred playing with some of his toys.

"I don't know if you've noticed, Andrew, but he seems to have a tendency to use his left hand a lot."

"That's not a problem for me, but if my mother finds out, she'll want him to change and use his right hand. You know what she's like," he remarked.

"So far, she's not even seen him since he was born. Strange woman that, not wanting to see her first grandchild, and a boy at that."

The morning went well for the three of them. The rain stopped again in the afternoon, so Andrew went to the garage to tinker with his treasured Type 43 Bugatti. He was dying to take it out, but only if the weather cleared up a bit. He cleaned the plugs, added some engine oil, checked the tyre pressures and cleaned all the bodywork with the chamois leather. He started it up and gave it a good run inside the garage; it all sounded just fine.

He went indoors for drinks before supper and decided to listen to the 6 o'clock news. One of the interesting items was that Franklin Roosevelt had been re-elected president of the United States for an unprecedented third term. The news bulletin highlighted the fact that at least the USA might continue to support its allies, even if they didn't actively enter the war—not yet anyway.

The weather was much brighter the next morning, so after a light breakfast, Andrew took Max for a good walk. By about midday, he 'got permission' to take the Bug' out for a run. He thought he would go to one of his favourite pubs on the way back and see if it was any busier than it was during his previous visit in May. He drove about twelve miles until he reached the Crawley bypass where he could give the car a real run. It didn't take long for him to be going over 80 mph; he felt wonderful, the car was so responsive. He changed down when entering the roundabouts, but he was still going fast. The car handled beautifully. If only there wasn't a war on, he could do this sort of thing much more often, and go further afield. He drove into the carpark of the Crooked Billet a bit too quickly and skidded to a halt in front of a chap reversing his Austin 7 out from a parking space. Andrew just smiled and gesticulated an apology, but it wasn't received too well. The driver got out of his car and walked purposefully towards Andrew.

"What did you think you were doing, driving so recklessly into here like that?"

"I'm very sorry, but I haven't had the chance to drive this car for nearly six months; I got a bit carried away, sir," Andrew said, noticing that the man was probably in his fifties or sixties.

"Just a minute, don't I remember you from a previous occasion when you drove this car into the carpark of the Red Lion, sometime in July last year, wasn't it? I was getting out of my car and you came in rather too quickly then. You must really take more care; you could knock someone over."

"You are right, but what an extraordinary coincidence," Andrew replied, as he got out of his Bug, shook the man's hand and smiled.

"I seem to remember saying to you last time we met that, if I were to be knocked down by any car, yours would be the one I would choose," the man said, laughing as he got back into his car. Andrew waved at him as he drove off and disappeared inside the pub. He looked around and could see only half a dozen people. He smiled at the barman, ordered his pint, but the man made no eye contact with him, nor did he try to enter into any conversation. He took his drink and went to sit at the table near the window. He started to reminisce about the times he'd been in the Crooked Billet with Brian: *Times have really changed, so what will these places be like when the war finishes?* he thought to himself, *assuming we win, of course.*

After about thirty-five minutes, he'd had enough, he left the pub and drove home. Just as he put the car away in the garage, it started to rain heavily. He went through the back door into the kitchen to find his wife preparing lunch. He put his hands on her hips as she stood at the stove.

"What delicacy have you got here?" he said as he kissed her neck.

"It's not easy to make anything special with all this rationing, but I do get a few extra things from the butcher every now and then. He let me have some liver when I knew you were coming home, so it'll be liver and bacon with mashed potatoes."

"Wonderful," Andrew replied. He went out of the kitchen to get a bottle of red wine.

"We'll eat in the kitchen, Andrew," she shouted to him. "How was the pub?"

Andrew returned with the wine and proceeded to open it.

"It was so quiet. How can they make the place work and be profitable? It's so depressing, and the weather doesn't help. I think I'll light a fire in the lounge this afternoon. Shall I go and fetch Alfred from his cot, dear?"

"No, thanks, I'll do it; he might need changing. You keep an eye on the lunch."

They all had a relaxing time during the early part of afternoon with the open fire roaring away. Alfred played with his toys and let his father join in every now and again. Andrew looked out of the window, saw that the rain had stopped and stood up.

"Not sure how much time I have before it rains again, but I ought to take Max out for a bit of a walk."

His wife agreed, saying that she would make some tea at 4:30 p.m. As soon as Andrew entered the hallway, Max got up sensing that his master was going out. He managed to keep him still as he put on his collar, but he was very excited. Andrew put on his boots and heavy rain gear and led Max out of the front door. Once out of the garden, they crossed the road and walked towards the large hedge which gave them some shelter from the wind. After some fifteen minutes, it started to drizzle again. Andrew looked at his watch to see it was already 4:10 p.m., and getting dark, so he called Max, turned around and walked briskly back to the house as the rain got heavier.

"I'm back dear," he shouted from the hall, as he tried to get most of the water from Max's coat with his own special towel in the porch. After some minutes, he told Max to get in his basket so he could attend to his own wet clothes. Once his shoes, cap and coat were off, he skipped upstairs to get into a change of clothing.

"Are you coming down for some tea, Andrew?" his wife shouted up from the hall. "I've laid it in the kitchen as I shall give Alfred his meal at the same time."

"I'll be right down, dear; just changing out of my wet clothes," he replied.

After some ten minutes, Andrew was down in the hall. He felt Max around his shoulders to find that he was reasonably dry, but Max rolled onto his back hoping for his tummy to be rubbed by his master, which it duly was for a few moments. Andrew walked through the lounge to the kitchen to see the table laid for tea. Alfred was sitting in his high chair, he turned and grinned at his father. He made some strange talking sounds to him as he showed his father his piece of toast.

"Are you going to eat that all up?" he said, but Alfred dropped it on to the floor. He looked over the arm down at the toast, expecting it to be picked up for him.

"It's one of his new games, Andrew. If it's not picked up, he will refuse to eat any more of the others."

Andrew sat next to his son, stared at him and pulled his cheeks in and out so as to make a funny sound. Alfred laughed loudly for a few seconds, but then looked down at the toast on the floor. He wasn't going to be fooled that easily.

"Help yourself to bread and jam, Andrew. The jam is home made with fruit from our garden."

Andrew did as he was ordered, with Alfred watching what he was doing. Andrew cut the piece of bread into soldiers and passed one to Alfred, who snatched it from his father's hands and dropped it to the floor, not far from the piece of toast.

"So that's your game, is it, young boy?"

Andrew bent down, picked up the two pieces, waved them in front of Alfred's mouth and promptly put them in his own mouth. Alfred let out a scream as he started to cry.

"Oh, Alfred, never mind; Daddy's only teasing you," said his mother, as she came and sat at the other side of him.

"Does he often have these sorts of tantrums?" he asked his wife.

"Not too often, but he's growing up. Young children will always try to find out where they stand with adults, particularly their parents. Unfortunately, you haven't had much time to see him developing, as such you probably think he's been spoilt, but he has only got me to bring him up. I'm not blaming you, but you are away at war and have only had a chance to come to see us a very few times since he was born."

"I didn't say or imply anything, but his behaviour sometimes surprises me; that's all."

No more was said. Andrew didn't want to cause a scene, especially as he was leaving the next afternoon. He had no idea when he would be back home again. Tea time was a bit protracted as each of Alfred's parents tried to entice him to eat more of his food—even if it had already been on the floor a few times. They all had had enough just after 5:45 p.m. Andrew agreed to clear the table and wash up everything while his wife took Alfred for his bath.

"Here we are," Andrew's wife said, as she reappeared in the lounge with a smiling Alfred just after 6:30 p.m. Andrew took Alfred from her, placing him on the carpet in front of the fireplace. He stood up and waddled over to his mother with his hands in the air to keep his balance. She turned him around and told him to walk back to his Daddy, who was now seated in his armchair. Alfred looked reluctantly at his father, but did make the effort as his father called him over and opened his arms to welcome him.

"Now, that wasn't too bad, was it?" said Andrew, as he ruffled the child's fair curly hair; but Alfred turned and walked quickly back to his mother. This exercise was repeated several times over the next fifteen minutes that delighted Alfred as he gurgled with laughter.

"Time for bed, Alfred," said his mother, as she picked him up and brought him over to Andrew for his 'goodnight' kiss. He waved at his father as he disappeared from the lounge. While he was on his own, waiting for his wife to return, Andrew made himself and his wife a drink. He knew he had to prepare himself for some awkward and probing questions.

"All settled upstairs, dear?" Andrew enquired, handing the drink to her, as she collapsed on to the sofa.

"Just what I need. Thank you, Andrew."

"Cheers to our little family," he said, and went over to 'clink' her glass.

"So, Andrew, when do you think you will be back again? Too much to expect you here for Christmas, I suppose?" as he went and sat down in his chair.

"I guessed you would ask about where I might be going next, but even I won't be sure until I return to London tomorrow evening. But you can be reasonably certain of one thing: I won't get any more leave this side of the New Year. We are at war, you know?"

"So, another Christmas on my own, I suppose?"

"You could always go and spend some time with your sister in Twickenham. I'm sure she would enjoy having some company with her husband away at sea. She might even ask your father over, so it would make a nice family Christmas occasion. On the other hand, you could ask them both down here. It would make life easier for you—Alfred would then be in his own home and you wouldn't have to mess Max about either."

Silence fell over the room as both of them thought more about the situation.

"What time do you have to leave tomorrow, Andrew? Not too early, I hope?"

"I am expected back in London at about 5 o'clock, so I ought to catch the train about an hour before. I shall then be able to take Max for a good walk in the morning—raining or not."

Andrew's wife put her glass on the side table and got up from her chair.

"I'll go and make a few sandwiches. Is there anything in particular you would like as a filling?"

"Nothing special, thank you; whatever you have most of will be fine," he replied.

Andrew felt the atmosphere was starting to get a bit frosty.

"I'm going to let Max out into the garden, dear," he shouted to his wife as he left the lounge for the hall. Max greeted his master and seemed to guess that he would be let out. Andrew opened the front door to find that it had stopped raining. He noticed the sky was clear as he stepped outside after the dog. He walked down the path at the side of the house, stopped just by the conservatory and peered down towards the vegetable area. He couldn't really see anything, but he saw distant flashes to his left that suggested London was being bombed again. *Poor buggers in the east end of London and the docks*, he said to himself, *getting another drubbing from the Luftwaffe.*

After some ten minutes, he thought he ought to return inside. He called Max who came running up to him, obviously feeling better for the exercise! Once in the hall, Andrew dried Max and stepped into the lounge just as his wife appeared with a tray. He went over to the radiogram and selected a couple of records from the cabinet. He thought it might cheer his wife up a bit if he played something she liked; he found an Artie Shaw tune.

"That's nice," she said. "Do you remember us dancing to this a couple of years ago? How different things were then."

Andrew said nothing, even though he recalled the time very clearly. He also remembered Monique playing some similar records when he and Gerhart were staying with her in Pesmes in April. They had sabotaged a train in Nazi Germany that was carrying tank parts to the assembly plant. They had been escaping from the Germans through France. It seemed a lifetime ago. He was brought back to the present by his wife telling him to help himself to the evening snack from the tray. He refilled his wife's glass and sat back in his chair.

"Shall I play it again, or would you like the other side?" he asked, as he walked over to the radiogram.

"Perhaps play it again, but have your sandwiches first."

He did as was suggested, sat down and they discussed the time when they heard the music over two years ago. Inevitably, they spoke about being with Brian at the time and how much they will miss him.

The evening passed quickly and easily and, before they knew it, the grandfather clock in the dining room struck 10 o'clock. Andrew collected all the things from their snack and took them to the kitchen. He went back to the hall and let Max out for a final time before shutting up the house. They went upstairs, looked in on Alfred to find him just as he had been left over three hours earlier.

Andrew woke up at 6:30 a.m. It was still quite dark, but it wasn't raining. He pushed Max out of the front door and followed him in his dressing gown and slippers. He couldn't help thinking about when he would be back home again. After about ten minutes, he returned indoors with Max, went to the kitchen and made a pot of tea. When he got upstairs with the tray, Alfred was sitting on the bed next to his mother.

"Did he sleep through the night?"

"Yes, he did, but he was a bit wet when I fetched him a few minutes ago."

"Does he need something to drink?"

"No, thank you; I have something here that I brought up last night."

They spent over three quarters of an hour playing with Alfred and having their tea, by which time it was quite light outside. Andrew said he would have just a quick breakfast of toast and marmalade as he wanted to get out with Max and give him a good walk.

By 10:30 a.m., he was ready to go out with Max. They walked briskly across the road and down the side of the field. As usual for Max, he went on the far side of the hedge hoping to chase rabbits on to his master's side, but nothing appeared. After some forty-five minutes of crossing several fields, Andrew thought it was time to turn back. The clouds were beginning to gather again, so he broke into a run for the last fifteen minutes.

"I'm back," he shouted, as he rushed into the hall, closely followed by Max.

"Did you get caught in any rain?" a voice enquired from the kitchen.

"No, we were lucky, but it's very wet under foot," he replied, as he rubbed Max down with his towel.

"I've made a light lunch and we'll have it in the kitchen with Alfred in twenty minutes."

"That's fine," replied Andrew, as he went upstairs to change: he thought he would have lunch in his uniform. He packed the few things in his kitbag and brought everything down to the hall. He went to the kitchen to find Alfred already in his highchair, playing with his food.

"Oh, you've already changed into your uniform," his wife said, with some surprise in her tone.

"I thought it would be best," he said, as he took a piece of Alfred's toast. There was a shout from the boy, so Andrew thought it would be a good idea to put it back on his plate. His wife said nothing.

"Do take a seat, Andrew," as a plate of cottage pie arrived in front of him.

They chatted during the meal and Andrew finished his meal before the others. He looked at his watch to find it was already 2 o'clock. He got up from the table saying that he was going to call for a taxi to collect him at 2:40 p.m.

"The sun's out at present, so can I take a photo of you in uniform before you leave, Andrew?" as she collected the camera from the work surface.

He agreed. He carried Alfred out to the garden and Max followed, thinking there was to be some fun outside. Alfred was held by Andrew as the photo was taken, then another was taken with Andrew on his own.

"That'll do, dear," Andrew said, "the taxi will be here very shortly."

He walked through the front door, collected his kitbag and briefcase and came back into the sunshine. The taxi arrived as Andrew picked up Alfred, embraced his wife and ruffled the top of Max's head.

"I hope to see you sometime in the New Year, but I can't be certain when," Andrew said, as he disappeared through the front gate. His wife took Alfred's hand, returned indoors followed by Max.

Chapter 3
Friday, 8 November 1940

Andrew arrived back at his flat in good time to change out of his uniform into some casual clothes before his call from Charles at 6:30 p.m. He made himself a black coffee and took it back to his room, as he still had nearly an hour to spare.

He had nodded off when he was suddenly brought back to the present by one of his flat mates knocking on his door.

"You are wanted on the phone, Andrew."

"I'll be right down," he replied. As he walked to the door, he looked at his watch. "Thanks, Mike."

He went down to the hallway and picked up the receiver.

"Hi!"

"Hello, sorry if I'm calling a bit before time. Did you have a good three days with your family?"

"Yes, thank you, although the weather could have been better."

"Good to hear that. Can we meet at my office at 10:30 a.m. tomorrow as I have a few things to discuss with you?"

"No problem, I'll be there."

The phone went dead, so he returned to his room to finish his coffee; it was cold, so he poured it away into the basin. He wondered if he would be accepted to go to the interrogation centre near Richmond, or would he be required somewhere else? He was rather excited about being involved with spies from the other side.

The following morning, Andrew walked briskly to Charles's office just as it started to drizzle. He used the brass knocker to signify his arrival. The receptionist opened the door and ushered Andrew inside with a warm greeting.

"Good morning, Mr Williams. I trust you are well? Please sign the register and go straight up to Mr Compton-Browne's office."

"Thank you, Miss Jones, I'm very well."

Andrew raced up the stairs, knocked on the door and went straight into Charles's office.

"Hello Andrew," Charles said, as he stood up, shook Andrew's hand firmly, at the same time pointing to the chair at the front of the desk. "I know it's rather unusual calling you in on a Saturday, but this is very special.

"I have been having lengthy discussions with C and he's been in contact with the Foreign Office and other members of the War Cabinet. In view of all the bombings on London and other places over the last few months, we firmly believe that the *Abwehr* have spies around the country—mostly in London— passing messages back to their superiors. Coded messages have been intercepted by our people as they pass information back to Germany. Some of those agents have been captured and they are being held at our interrogation centre near Richmond. I know you are keen to participate in this exercise and everyone believes it's very important, but I need to ask you one more time about your involvement."

"As I have said previously, I will give it my best shot."

"That's good news. I will forward your acceptance up the line. I will phone you on Monday at 7:30 p.m. with further instructions. It is very likely you will be collected from your flat on Tuesday morning, but I won't know the time until just before I speak to you. The driver will have fresh documents and other papers. Is that clear?"

"Yes, Charles. Thank you. I'll hear from you on Monday evening."

Both men stood up, shook hands and Andrew left Charles's office.

Andrew spent most of the rest of Saturday and early Sunday washing, drying and ironing some of his clothes. He put out the things he thought he might need on top of the chest of drawers, placing his passports and identity papers into his satchel. He'd been told that he would be using his agent name, so he would try to ask Charles when he spoke to him later in the evening, but it might be too sensitive a question over the phone. If he were in agent mode, he hoped he wouldn't be the one where he wore a moustache, as it was sometimes very difficult to keep on.

At 7:30 p.m., the phone rang. One of his flat mates answered it and called Andrew from his room. They never gave their names when answering, nor did Charles or other people in the Service give theirs, in case it was tapped.

"Hello," said Andrew.

"All is on for tomorrow, just as we arranged at our meeting. The driver will be at your flat at 8 o'clock and he will have everything else you need with him. As I have said, you might be at Ham for as much as one month. You should have an interesting time with a slightly eccentric colonel, who conducts his interrogations in a very particular way. During that period, I might need to speak to you, or you might have to be recalled to London, but that would only happen under exceptional circumstances."

"That's all understood," Andrew said.

"Just one more thing: I would like to write a letter to my wife. I will give it to the driver so that he can take it to you for security clearance. Will that be alright?"

"That's fine, Andrew. Be sure to say nothing specific about where you are or what you are doing. Leave the envelope unsealed and we'll arrange for it to be sent from somewhere like Gibraltar. Good luck," and the phone went dead.

He went up to his room and sat down to write the letter to his wife. He found a piece of paper and dated it 28th November 1940. He asked after his son, Alfred, as well as his friend, Brian's, widow. He explained that he was now away at sea and didn't know when he would be back for some leave. He hoped she would keep in touch with her sister and that good news had been received about their brother-in-law, who was also away on a ship somewhere. He said he was enjoying his job aboard ship and working with a good lot of blokes. He told her to look after herself and their son during his absence. He addressed the envelope, folded the paper, placed it inside without sealing it. *Job done,* he muttered to himself. He'd had a light meal earlier, so he thought it would be best to go to bed and rest.

Andrew slept fitfully on Sunday night, but he was still well prepared for the driver's arrival, even if it was 6:30 a.m. He rechecked his suitcase's contents, made sure again that his pistol was in the secret bottom compartment of the case, that he had all the necessary documents and papers in his satchel. He went and made another cup of black coffee, took it back to his room and sat in front of his desk. Before he knew it, there was a knock on the door that startled him. He looked at his watch: it was exactly 8 o'clock. He put on his jacket, picked up his case and went to the front door.

"Hello, Mr Williams. I've come to take you on a drive," said the man who stood on the step.

"Thank you, Don," Andrew replied to the man that usually drove C to his appointments.

Don gave Andrew an envelope that contained his papers, put his case in the boot, with Andrew in the front seat—the place where he always tried to insist on sitting. The journey was easy as they went over Kew Bridge, up Queens Road in Richmond, then down past the entrance to Richmond Park and on towards Ham Common. The sentry stopped them to look at their papers and check their names against his list of permitted entrants.

"Thank you, gentlemen. Please proceed down the drive to the main door," said the guard, as he handed their documents back.

On their arrival at the main entrance, a man came out and greeted them. Don gave Andrew his suitcase, shook his hand and watched him disappear inside the house before driving off.

"Would you please sign the register, Andrew. My name is Colin, I work with the Colonel. I'll take you to your room on the first floor where you can unpack. I'll see you in the lounge in ten minutes," he said as he pointed to a door to their right.

Andrew put his clothes away in the wardrobe and chest of drawers then pushed the suitcase under the bed. His papers were in his small satchel that was over his shoulder; he put his jacket back on. He went downstairs into the lounge where Colin was talking to two other men. He introduced Andrew to each of them. They helped themselves to tea and biscuits and sat down on the chairs that had been placed around a table.

"We welcome you to Camp 020, as we call it. I need to put you in the picture about what we do here and how the Service thinks you can be of assistance to us," Colin said. "We perform a very necessary function for the Intelligence Service. At present, we have seven men in individual cells who have been captured mostly in the London area. We know you were involved with the *Schwartz* people and you went with the police to the house in Maida Vale. The Service suspected it was used as a London centre for *Abwehr* agents which turned out to be the case. Three men were subsequently captured and they are being 'hosted' by us here."

"That's very interesting," Andrew remarked, after he had finished his tea. "I'm curious to know where and how you found them?"

"Very careful and thorough work by the Service and the police revealed the names and whereabouts of two of them, the third man was one of those that attacked you near Victoria: the one whose shoulder was not broken," Colin said, with a chuckle and a smile.

"Well I'm blessed! Will I get a chance to break his shoulder as well?" Andrew joked, as they all smiled.

"That won't be necessary. Anyway, even though we aren't subject to the Geneva Convention rules here, the Colonel insists that using torture or physical violence against those suspected of spying does not yield the required results. In some cases, we use 'stool-pigeons' as fake prisoners, so that the suspected agent thinks he is a fellow agent. The cell is usually bugged with listeners sitting in a nearby room, eavesdropping on their conversations. This is where you come in, Andrew."

"What? You want me to be a fake German agent?" Charles had told him how he would be involved, but he deliberately reacted for effect.

"That's the idea, yes. It came to the mind of the Service people—your boss, Charles, in particular—after your mission to Germany to sabotage the railway line in March. You will be known as Artur Selmer, your own agent name. We will use your Danish passport and identification papers—but not the German ones that allowed you to drive railway engines, of course. This afternoon, I will go through the role we want you to play, but you'll know very little about the German agent, nor will he know anything about you."

"But if I'm supposed to be working for the *Abwehr*—and so is he—isn't it possible we could be aware of each other's existence?"

"No, that will not be possible. You will have been working for the outfit operating out of Denmark and he in London for its headquarters in Berlin. You will see, it will work. Shall I show you around the buildings and then go for an early lunch?"

Chapter 4
Tuesday, 12 November 1940

It was in the early afternoon—3 o'clock to be precise—that Colin and Andrew agreed to meet in the lounge, together with a colleague of Colin's. He explained for Andrew's benefit, about one of the things they were trying to achieve with the prisoners during their 'holiday' at the Ham establishment. Occasionally, one or two had shown an interest and an aptitude in becoming spies for the British, so that—for all intents and purposes—they could either be turned or become double agents. Several men had already been 'turned' and were back in Germany or France working on behalf of the Service.

He explained it was for that purpose that Andrew was being asked to join the team. He told him he would play the role of a Danish fisherman that had been based on the west coast of Jutland. He had been persuaded by a senior German officer from the invasion force to spy on British ship movements. He would report any sightings to a contact in southern Norway. Unfortunately, in early November, he was sighted by a British destroyer whilst some way out in the North Sea. He tried, in vain, to escape, but that raised the crew's suspicion, so he was captured. He had plenty of incriminating evidence on him to indicate that he was spying and relaying information back to his contact in Oslo. He was brought back to England, eventually ending up here a few days ago.

"Does that sound a good enough summary of your situation?" Colin enquired.

"Yes, I suppose it does. Presumably I must speak German to the fellow prisoner or should I speak German with a Danish accent?"

"German with a Danish accent would be better, but you will understand German perfectly. That is the case, isn't it? You are supposed to understand only a smattering of English so you are to speak hardly any English."

"You know very well that I speak those languages! What clothes do you want me to wear or will you provide them?"

"Most of the prisoners wear what we have given them, so you will be given the same. We have already been sent your measurements, but you might not get the correct size. Be aware that you will be manhandled into the cell quite roughly, to make it look authentic. We are hoping the German agent will be interested enough in accepting our offer of becoming a double agent. He has already been here for two weeks. All our prisoners are in solitary confinement most of the time. This might be our last chance to 'turn' him."

"How long can I expect to be in the same cell with this man?"

"It very much depends on how well the two of you get on together and how the other chap cooperates with the interrogator; that will be the Colonel, of course. He has some very interesting methods that he is renowned for."

"Just one thing I need to tell you: I had quite a nasty injury to my left arm in June. It has healed, but there is a scar. I will make up some cock-and-bull story about how I got it, should he notice it."

"That's not a problem. You won't be placed in your cell until sometime Wednesday evening or Thursday morning; we can't tell you what time. Unfortunately, it is possible that the Colonel might take advantage of your injury. If the arm gets bad again, we do have a doctor and a nurse on site."

Andrew tried not to think about what might happen during the interrogation process; it didn't excite him. He began to wonder why he had agreed to get involved in this exercise in the first place. He didn't expect to be treated just like a captured spy, but he thought it must be the only way they can go further with this other man—a sort of last resort.

"Have you any more points you wish to raise?"

"No, but it seems as though I'm going to be treated in the same way as any of your prisoners."

"Almost exactly, yes. We have found it works. The real prisoner will relate to someone like you better as both of you will have had similar treatment. I need to mention that the two of you will be interrogated separately."

Colin called the meeting to a close. He suggested he take Andrew to see where the cells were, but neither should speak as the inmate he will be with might recognise his voice when he's placed in his cell. Once back in the hallway, Colin mentioned the times of meals and asked him to join him for supper at 7:30 p.m.

Andrew went back to his room and lay on his bed with his hands behind his head. He found himself dropping off to sleep. He was dreaming about Gerhart and himself being in the German *gasthaus*. Instead of escaping their clutches, they were caught by the *Gestapo* and taken to a camp where they were stripped and tortured. He woke up in a cold sweat; for some reason, his wounded arm was hurting. He looked at his watch: it was 7 o'clock. He took his sponge bag to the bathroom next door and washed his head and face. He looked in the mirror. He thought he looked like he'd seen a ghost. He brushed his hair and returned to his room; he changed into different trousers and a clean shirt. In the hallway, he heard people talking; he could smell the food. He followed the sounds and smells into the dining room. Colin introduced Andrew to three other men, as well as the doctor and the nurse. The meal was quite wholesome, bearing in mind the war was on. Conversation flowed easily, but nobody talked about themselves—just the war. With most of France overrun by the Germans, and the heavy bombing raids over London and southern England, they all wondered when the *Wehrmacht* would invade, even though the *Luftwaffe* was not yet in control of the skies. The meal finished with a not very hot mug of Camp coffee that Andrew only half finished. He felt he needed to get some proper sleep, so he excused himself and went to his room.

Andrew awoke at 6:30 a.m. and saw it was a fine day. He followed Colin's recommendation of taking a walk around the gardens in the afternoon, making sure he wasn't near where the cells were. He didn't feel very hungry at suppertime, but he felt he should make an effort. After all, he thought that if he's taken to the cell in the night, he had no idea when he would get anything else to eat. He went to bed at the same time as he did the day before.

He slept very lightly as he expected someone to come to his room at any minute. At around midnight, there was the distinct rumbling sound of many aircraft that woke him. He carefully looked through his drawn curtains to see enemy planes heading for London with the beams of searchlights trying to locate the planes for the anti-aircraft guns to fire at. A few were dropping bombs with several exploding near the outer extremities of the grounds of the house. Eventually, morning came, but still nobody. He got up as usual, spending the day in the same way as the day before. The same people were at supper. If they were aware of what was going to happen to him, nobody said anything, nor did they mention the Colonel. This process went on for another day.

Just as he was getting himself comfortable in bed on the Friday, the door swung open. Two men threw back the bedclothes and shouted at him in German—using his agent name—to put on the clothes that they had thrown at him. He managed to put on the trousers, the shirt and the long coat before he was dragged down the stairs. He was taken out of the house to the entrance of a large side building. One of the men unlocked the door as the other one pulled him inside.

"Artur, you are to be put in one of these cells," one of the men shouted, continuing in German. "You will stay in here until we have time to interrogate you. Do you understand?"

"Yes," replied Artur in German, as he was flung towards the bed.

He wasn't sure what time it was as one of the men had taken his watch from him before leaving his room. His toes hurt from being dragged around without any socks or shoes, but the guard had thrown some gym shoes into his room before closing the cell door. He looked around the cell with great difficulty, the single, bare lightbulb in the centre of the ceiling was not on. He could just make out a metal framed bed with a blanket on it. He stumbled into a bucket and knocked it over with a loud clatter. He stood still trying to get his eyes used to the darkness. He just managed to make out a basin in the far corner with a dripping tap. He saw a high-backed chair near the end of the bed with a table beside it. He managed to make out a window high up on the wall opposite the door he had come through: it was covered with black paper to keep out the light.

He thought he would lie down under the blanket as he was starting to feel cold. He lay down on what he reckoned was a straw mattress, rolling the blanket around himself as if he were in a cocoon. There was no pillow, but he closed his eyes hoping he might sleep; he couldn't stop shivering.

He must have dozed off because the next thing he knew was the noise of the cell door opening.

"I've brought you some bread and water," said a man's voice he didn't recognise, in German. Artur said nothing; he lay still pretending to be asleep, wondering if the man was going to make him sit up and eat, or even throw the water into his face, but he did neither. The man had a dimly lit torch to help him put the water and bread on the table, but for some reason he didn't shine it on Artur. He heard him cough as he left the cell and lock the door.

Artur thought back to the time he was brought to the cell. He was under the impression he would be put in a cell with a German spy and not be interrogated as an individual. He was confused; perhaps it was just an error by the man who spoke. He decided to get up and drink some of the water, so he got out of bed and managed to find the glass on the table. *Ah, that feels better,* he said to himself, as he consumed all the water. He went back to his bed and went to sleep.

"Wake up, Artur," a man said who had entered his cell, at the same time putting on the light. "I've brought you some porridge."

Artur had been surprised by the man waking him, but he had no idea for how long he had been asleep, if indeed he had been. As the man left the cell, Artur got up. He looked at the steam coming up from the bowl on the table; he decided to go and eat some of the porridge while it was still warm. *Not bad really,* he mumbled to himself, *but a bit lumpy.* He had nearly finished when the cell door opened.

"We're taking you to another cell, Artur," the man said, in German. "You don't need to finish your meal. Put on the gym shoes and follow me."

Chapter 5
Saturday, 16 November 1940

Artur was led by the man out into the corridor. They turned left past two doors. At the third one, another man was waiting with a bunch of keys. He opened the door, walked inside gesturing for Artur to follow him.

"This is Artur Selmer," he said to the prisoner, in German. "Artur, this man's name is Herr Heinrich Knipp. You will be companions for a while."

Heinrich stood up. Both he and Artur gave the Nazi salute, at the same time saying *Heil Hitler*, just as Artur had been instructed. The man locked the door as he left the cell. There was an extra chair in Heinrich's cell, so they both sat down and smiled at each other. There was a great deal of similarity between these two men: height, hair colour, blue eyes, stature, age.

"They brought another man into my room two days ago," Heinrich remarked, in a strong accent from around the Munich area.

"I think he's the boss here. He's tall and has a monocle over his right eye. He told me to stand to attention and call him 'Commandant'; I had to remain that way till he left.

"How long have you been here, Artur?"

"I was brought in a couple of days ago," Artur replied, in an accent that suggested he came from near the border with Denmark.

They exchanged information for the next half an hour about the state of the war and how Germany very much seemed to have the upper hand.

"So, where were you picked up, Heinrich?"

"I was near one of the main airfields in Kent watching men attending to the British fighters with my binoculars. I'd spied on many airfields in Kent and Sussex over the previous few weeks. One of the security guards patrolling the field saw me. I had been facing south and I think he saw the sun reflecting off the lenses; it was very careless of me. I ran towards a nearby barn, but the guard ran quickly and brought me down. I was taken back to the main building where I was asked questions by a senior air force officer; I was told to hand over my papers and my binoculars. He spoke very little German and I pretended to speak no English, but I understood everything he and some of the other men were saying. After a short while, he used his telephone. He said to the person on the phone that I had been captured for spying on the airfield. After he had finished the call, he told me that someone would be coming to collect me; until he arrives, I would be kept in isolation in a secure place."

"How long were you there for, Heinrich? Did they beat you up?"

"I was probably on my own in the room for well over two hours. They brought me some water and a sandwich, but nobody touched me. Eventually, two people collected me in a car and brought me here. I've been here now for over two weeks. As I said, I was interrogated by the 'Commandant' in this cell five days ago. Early yesterday morning, however, I was taken to another cell which had a much brighter bulb in the centre of the room. I was again told to stand to attention; I was in that position for several hours as the Commandant and a guard looked on, but they said nothing. How about you, Artur? Where were you found?"

"I was on a small fishing boat in the German Sea. I am a Danish man who also speaks German."

"I had noticed your accent was slightly strange!" Heinrich remarked with a grin.

"I am a fisherman and I sail out of the harbour on the east side of the small island of Romo that lies off the west coast of Jutland in Denmark. A member of the *Abwehr* came to the island from Esbjerg in the middle of October. He spoke to a few fishermen trying to find someone who spoke German, as well as Danish. Most of them were anti-German, but I agreed to spy on behalf of them. My missions are to watch out for British ships sailing north towards Norway and the Norwegian Sea. I would report my sightings by radio on my short-wave transmitter back to my *Abwehr* contact in Oslo; he would then alert the *Luftwaffe* at airfields further up the Norwegian coast. Unfortunately, after about seven days, one of the escorts must have been very suspicious of my boat's presence as, in almost next to no time, a British Motor Torpedo Boat crew captured me, took me to a port on the east coast of England—Hull, it was called—and impounded my fishing boat there. I was brought down here earlier this week."

Artur wasn't sure if he had said too much, but at that moment the cell door opened.

"Stand up to attention," the man said commandingly in German. Artur presumed he was the colonel who was accompanied by two other men; the cell door was closed behind them.

"I would like to remind you that you're here in a British Secret Service interrogation centre and we expect to get the whole story from you. Do you understand?"

"Yes, Commandant," the two replied in unison.

"Selmer, you will be taken back to your cell. We will interrogate Herr Knipp and then you."

One of the men grabbed Artur's arm and led him to the door, but not before he had winked at Heinrich and given him the thumbs up. He didn't think any of the men saw his gestures.

Back in his cell, Artur wondered what the interrogators would be doing with Heinrich; hopefully, he would get back to see him before too long. He lay on his bed with his hands behind his head, thinking about what might happen next and dozed off. He was awoken by the cell door opening:

"A bit of lunch for you," the man said, as he put it on the table and removed the dish with the unfinished porridge; he went back out of the door. Artur looked at it thinking it didn't look very appetising, but he knew he had to eat it anyway. When he'd finished, he lay back on the bed again as there was nothing else to do: no books, no paper and pencils. He remained isolated in his cell for the remainder of the day; nobody came to interrogate him.

The next two days followed the same pattern for Artur: porridge, two hours with Heinrich, back to his own cell for some lunch and then isolation for the remainder of the day. On the Tuesday, however, Artur was not taken to Heinrich's cell until the afternoon. He wasn't sure if he should ask the guards about the change, but he resisted the temptation.

"So, what happened this morning, Heinrich?" Artur asked after the guards had left his cell.

"I had a visit from the Commandant yet again this morning. He told me that if I didn't give him more information about my contacts back in Germany, as well as those I was working with over here, spies like me have been known to be shot by firing squad or hanged."

"Did you say anything to him?"

"No, I didn't make any reply. We were both silent for a good ten minutes. He then said that I could possibly escape death if I could be persuaded to work for the British, become a sort of double agent."

"What did you say to that suggestion?"

"I told him that I would have to think about it, and would like to discuss the offer with you first."

"Do you think you could do it, Heinrich? How would your seniors react if you suddenly returned to Germany when you're supposed to be in England?"

"It would be a problem if I went back, but as I'm expected to be here, I would be given a new identity, I suppose. I usually make my reports to someone in London who relays them to the *Abwehr* centre in Koblenz. But, as I've not been in touch for nearly two weeks, they probably think I've been captured, or even killed."

"Believe it or not, I have been made the same offer. I am attracted to the idea as I have strong feelings about how the *Wehrmacht* stormed through Denmark in April, on their way to Norway. At that time, we only had a small army and we presented the Nazi war machine with very little resistance.

"Where do you operate from in London? I suppose there are a few of you that live together somewhere?"

"We used to be in a house in an area of London called Swiss Cottage," Heinrich replied, "but with me being captured, the others will probably have found somewhere else and tried to lie low."

Artur wondered how long the group had been in London. Could any of them have known about the Germans that lived in Maida Vale until June, such as the Schwartz'? He guessed the Commandant or his fellow interrogators would have been eavesdropping on all their conversations, so it was up to them to ask any further questions.

"You only have two options as I see it, Heinrich: you either get shot by the firing squad or you agree to be an agent for the British. If you want to be considered being a British spy, you would have to give the Commandant details of the people working with you in London, the places where you all lived and names of those receiving information back in Germany."

"I realise that Artur, but I'm only twenty-seven years old and I don't have strong enough feelings for the Nazi party, particularly after the needless bombing of London and other places over the last few months."

"Then your choice is simple, even if you are going to drop your colleagues in the shit."

"I have an idea what the British interrogators might swallow. It just depends how much they want me to work for them."

Artur guessed what Heinrich might have in mind, but he wasn't going to say anything at this moment. While he was thinking things through, the cell door opened and he was ushered out of Heinrich's cell and back into his own. He thought he had done the best he could, under the circumstances. It now depended on how seriously the Commandant wanted to turn Heinrich.

He had lain on his bed and must have dropped off as the next thing he knew was the guard coming into his cell with a small amount of supper. It hardly looked worth eating, but he ate it anyway.

The following morning, two guards came to Artur's cell. He didn't know what time it was, but he hadn't been brought any breakfast. He was taken past the other cells, to another part of the house and into a comfortable room. The Commandant sat in one of the armchairs and Artur was told to sit in the chair next to him. The conversation proceeded in English after the guards had left.

"We're quite pleased with the attitude of Herr Knipp; he seems receptive to the idea of working for us, but there's a long way to go yet."

"From what he's told me," Artur said, "facing a firing squad or being hanged doesn't fill him with a lot of enthusiasm, especially as he's not a strong Nazi supporter. You probably already know that anyway. I don't think he has the slightest idea that I'm not a German spy by the way."

"We feel he wants to do something with his life, Artur. I think you've played the role very well. It would be very helpful, however, if we could get an address of where they lived, some names of his fellow agents and his contacts in Germany to pass on to the Service."

"I told him that, but I don't think that's going to be very easy. I could always mention the Schwartz, see if he has heard of them and take it from there."

"OK, Artur, that's a good idea, but do be very careful."

The Commandant rang a bell that was on the coffee table. Two guards came into the room and were told, in German, to take Artur back to his cell. Each guard took an arm, led him down the corridor and into his cell. Artur saw he had been left some porridge on the table; he assumed it must have been there some while as it was cold—he ate it anyway. He was left on his own for the rest of the day, and the next day, but was taken to Heinrich's cell by the guards on Friday morning.

"How are you getting on, Heinrich?"

"Apart from a guard coming in with the occasional meal, I've not seen anyone or even been visited by the Commandant for over two days. This isolation is starting to get me down, it allows me to think too much about the alternatives that lie ahead."

"What do you do when I'm not here, Heinrich? Do you walk around the cell or do any exercises?"

"No, I don't do anything except lie on my bed until food comes. Otherwise, I try to sleep. I think about my parents and my sister back in Germany. My parents are not members of the Nazi party, but some of my friends are staunch supporters: two of them in the SS."

"How was it that you became an agent when you aren't a Nazi party member?"

"One of my two friends in the SS said he was related to a lady called Erika, who was the wife of the head of the *Abwehr* based in Berlin. She arranged for me to have discussions with a junior staff member of the *Abwehr* in my home town of Weinsberg, a bit east of Heilbronn."

Artur nearly choked when Heinrich mentioned Heilbronn. It was near the place he and Gerhart had stopped for fuel for their motorbike nearly nine months earlier, after they had sabotaged the railway line NE of Stuttgart. He tried to remain calm, hoping Heinrich hadn't noticed the slight reaction he thought he might have displayed.

"The *Abwehr* man contacted me and we met in a café on the outskirts of town. He asked me about my family, how I was able to reach Erika, my feelings about the Nazi regime and so on. He was particularly interested that I had a good command of the English language."

"He presumably liked what you had to say so did you have to sign anything or go on a training course?"

"I had a very limited amount of training, nor did I have to sign any documents. I was given the name of a man in London who would provide me with a Ration Book and details of the airfields I was to spy on. All other documents—including new identity papers—would be provided by the central *Abwehr* office in Berlin."

"What was your agent name and who was your contact in London?" Artur enquired, hoping he wasn't being too inquisitive. "I'm only asking as it might be the same person I had to refer to, if I got into any difficulties and had to land my boat in England?"

"It was to have been a woman, but she had been shot several months earlier. The cell operated out of a house in Maiden's Dale, I think it was."

"Don't you mean Maida Vale, Heinrich? That's where my contact was," Artur said.

"That's the name, Artur."

"I can't remember the name of the person who replaced the woman, can you?" Artur asked, still searching for more details.

"Kurt Weismann. His English name was Fred."

"Did you manage to contact him after you were caught at the airfield in Kent?"

"As I said earlier, nobody will know in London or in Berlin what has happened to me," he said rather curtly. "I usually have to report every week to London. Anyway, they left Maida Vale very quickly for Swiss Cottage and probably will now be somewhere else."

At that moment, a guard came into the cell. He said Artur's time with Heinrich was ended. Artur was pleased with the move as he felt he had asked quite enough questions for now. He was taken to the same comfortable room at the other end of the house where he was told to wait for the Commandant.

Chapter 6
Friday, 22 November 1940

The Commandant came into the room, but didn't apologise for keeping Artur waiting for over half an hour. They spoke in German this time.

"We seem to be getting somewhere with this man," the colonel remarked.

"I have decided to let him be on his own for a few days. He is very nervous about being in isolation, as he said to you. I will go to his cell at irregular intervals and during the night just to try and get under his skin. I won't ask any questions, but will get him to stand to attention for many minutes and then leave him. When you are next taken to see him, we are hoping he might give us more names. You'll have to make up some story about what has been happening to you during your absence from his cell. Are you happy with that, Artur?"

"Of course. Could you possibly let me have some reading material: a book or magazines?"

"I'll arrange that for later this afternoon; I'll bring them to you myself."

The Commandant rang the bell, the guard came in and Artur was escorted back to his cell. He reckoned he had done a good morning's work, but thought Heinrich was starting to get rather irritated with Artur's questioning. In the middle of the afternoon, the Commandant brought a copy of Thursday's Daily Sketch, The Thirty-Nine Steps by John Buchan and two copies of Motor Sport magazine—March and September 1940. He told Artur to put them all under his mattress before the guards came in with his food, to make sure they didn't think he was getting special favours.

"You've definitely earned these," he told Artur, with a broad smile, as he handed the items over to him.

For the next few days, Artur read the magazines over and over again. Just for a moment, they made him wish he was back home where he could take his favourite Bugatti out for a spin.

Shortly after he had finished his porridge on Monday, the guard came in telling Artur he was taking him to spend some time with Heinrich. Artur wondered how he would be, would he be pleased to see him?

"Hello, Heinrich," Artur said, as he gave him the Nazi salute.

Heinrich was lying on his bed, he didn't get up when Artur was brought in, but just turned his head.

"Are you alright, Heinrich?"

"I don't feel so good. The Commandant kept coming into my cell since I saw you last time. He came in every night several times, got me to stand to attention for what seemed like ten or fifteen minutes, then left without saying anything. I couldn't get any decent sleep. He came during the daytime also, making me stand to attention for even longer. He walked around the cell and sometimes stood behind me. He suddenly would shout my name, saying he wanted names of my contacts."

Heinrich swung his legs over the side of his bed; he looked up at Artur through his tired eyes.

"I don't know if this helps, Heinrich, but I have decided to tell the Commandant everything: all my contact names, what my real name is etcetera. I am told I could work for the English as well as the Abwehr. He has promised to take me back to my boat. I will take it back to Romo island, send some outdated information about the British Fleet to my Oslo contact and disappear into Germany."

"My goodness, that's a brave move, Artur. Are you sure about it?"

"I have already spoken to the Commandant. He will give me a new name, identity papers, a Ration Book and so on. I will be reporting to someone in the British Secret Service and be sent on a short, unarmed combat course."

"But you will be betraying those for whom you were working. Won't you have a conscience about it? Won't it be very dangerous when the *Abwehr* find out that you've tricked them?"

"I am reliably informed that good spies don't have a conscience, but it's still your decision to work for the British or not. As I said, I have made my mind up. I will need to contact the man in London to tell him that I am alive after all. I will just lie low for a while so my boat can be prepared for sailing at sea again. What was the name and number of the man in London as I've forgotten?"

Heinrich brought out a scraggy piece of paper from under his mattress.

"Here it is. Read them and memorise them."

"It helps me remember things if I read them out loud," Artur said, as he read out four names, two phone numbers and an address in Swiss Cottage. Heinrich then put the paper back from where it came.

"Thanks, Heinrich. That's very helpful of you."

Within a short time, the guard entered the cell. He took Artur's arm telling him that it was time for him to return to his own cell. He knew he would remember the details Heinrich had given him; he was also certain the Commandant would have eavesdropped on them. What interested him most was Heinrich's contact in Koblenz was a woman: he said her name was Fraulein Marta Schwartzman.

Later that afternoon, Artur was taken from his cell by a guard to talk to the Commandant in the room that they had used before.

"We are very pleased with the details that Herr Heinrich has given us, Artur," he said in English after the guard had left them. "We overheard your conversation and wrote all the details down that you read out; they are just what we hoped for, so we've passed them to our main contact at the Service in London."

"I would like to mention, Commandant, that I recognised the name Fraulein Marta Schwartzman. You might not be aware that I was sent to Munich on a mission last November. I was accompanied by a woman who had been in the Service for over five years. We were sent to witness the assassination of Herr Hitler as he gave his annual speech in the Beer Keller."

"I remember hearing that Hitler escaped by a matter of minutes before the bomb went off," the Commandant added.

"That's correct, but Fraulein Schwartzman was very badly injured and, by all accounts, she died on the Munich hospital operating table that night. Her real name was Miss Maggie Pearce. My agent name was Baron Albert von Schwartzman; she was supposed to be my sister, Fraulein Magdalene Schwartzman."

"My goodness," the Commandant remarked, "what an extraordinary coincidence, if it really is the same person."

"I'm certain that if my boss, Charles, hears the name he will believe, as I do, that this Koblenz woman is the same one that worked for the Service. People in the Service will have to make extensive investigations, via their contacts in Germany, to get to the bottom of this."

"Very interesting, Artur, that she has only changed her first name, but kept her English agent surname."

After a further fifteen minutes of discussions, the Commandant rang the bell, the guard came in and was ordered to take Artur back to his cell. As soon as they had left the room, the Commandant went to the phone on the desk to ask the switchboard operator to contact Artur's boss in St James.

"Hello, Charles; this is the Commandant speaking from Camp 020."

The two of them exchanged several sentences about the war effort, the relentless bombing raids on towns around Britain by the *Luftwaffe* and the unlikelihood of there being a German invasion in the near future.

"It's good to speak to you, Charles, but, as you can probably guess, I'm calling about Artur Selmer, who has been with us for two weeks now. I want to tell you that using him as a stool pigeon with one of our Nazi spies has worked well. He has obviously developed a good rapport with the German; they seem to have trusted each other. The German has eventually given us names, phone numbers and so on, and has expressed an interest in becoming a double agent."

The Commandant then talked about Fraulein Schwartzman being in Koblenz working for the *Abwehr*.

"That's extraordinary," Charles remarked. "We were led to believe that she was dead after the explosion in Munich last November."

"Exactly what Selmer said. I strongly suggest you do some serious digging and get one of your chaps in Germany to look into it."

"I'll get on to it straight away. When I get confirmation of her being alive and working for the *Abwehr* in Koblenz, I'll let you know.

"How much longer will you be wanting Artur for as the Admiralty and I want him to complete his naval officer training? There's the second part of a course starting next week that we thought he should attend, if possible."

"I don't see why that's not possible, Charles. I don't think we'll get anything more of substance from the German, but I'd like to keep him for a couple more days, just in case."

"That's fine by me. I'll arrange for a car to collect him on Thursday morning, about 10 o'clock. You don't need to tell him about the arrangements until sometime Wednesday."

"Will do, Charles. Thanks for letting Selmer stay here; he's been very helpful to us and a pretty good experience for him. Bye for now."

The Commandant rang off. He turned from his desk to stare out of the window. *Is there really anything more Selmer can get out of Heinrich?* he thought to himself. He didn't think so, but it would be worth trying over the two days left.

When Artur returned to his cell, he thought over the details that Heinrich had given him. He was greatly puzzled by the knowledge that Fraulein Schwartzman, or Maggie Pearce as the Service knew her, was actually still alive. The man in Munich, 'Sparks', who arranged for Maggie to be taken by ambulance to the hospital and organised her burial, must either be working for the *Abwehr* or was duped by them about her death. Artur thought it was most likely to be the latter. As there was nothing else that he could do about it for the time being, he lay on his bed to read through the Motor Sport magazines for the umpteenth time—the book by Buchan didn't really interest him.

Artur was suddenly aware of the guard entering his cell with some supper: he must have nodded off. He quickly put the magazines under the blanket, but said nothing to the guard. As he was eating his rather unexciting meal, he started to wonder how many more days he would have to stay at Camp 020.

The following afternoon, a good two hours after he had finished his uninteresting lunch, a guard came in to take him to Heinrich's cell.

"Heil Hitler," they said to each other, just before the guard left the cell.

"The Commandant came to see me this morning," Heinrich mentioned.

"Did he have anything to say to you?" Artur replied, also in German.

"He was quite pleasant to me, even if I did have to stand to attention, as on previous occasions. He wanted to know if I had changed my mind about giving him details of my contacts and their details. I asked his permission to stand easy so I could get a list of what I thought he wanted. I handed the piece of paper that I showed you to the Commandant. He told me he was pleased to see that I was now cooperating and would pass the information on to his seniors in London. He then left my cell."

"Did he say when he would be coming back to see you?"

"No, he didn't. I expect he'll need to hear what the people in London will say first."

Artur knew very well that he couldn't tell Heinrich that he had had a meeting with the Commandant the previous day and that he—plus another interrogator—had eavesdropped on all their discussions and already knew the details on the piece of paper. He needed Heinrich to feel that he was his confidant, in case he could recall any more names.

"It would appear, Heinrich, that you might have moved a step closer to being thought of as a possible double agent. You will remember telling me about your contact in Koblenz whose name was Marta Schwartzman? Did you have any other people you could contact, if Marta was for some reason unavailable?"

"Not in Koblenz, no. You must understand, Artur, that most of what I had to report was to the person in London; he would then usually forward it to the *Abwehr* centre in Koblenz. Only on one occasion, just after the middle of September, did my London contact tell me to report directly to Marta. That's when she told me that *Unternehmen Seelöwe* had been cancelled. It meant that the Luftwaffe were no longer going to bomb airfields in Kent and the South of England, but overfly to London and other cities." Artur knew about the invasion plans and that it was called Operation Sealion in the German Service.

"By the way, what were the names of the two men in the SS, one of which got in touch with Erika in Berlin?" Artur asked, not being sure if he was making the questions too direct.

"Why do you need to know, Artur? You are starting to sound like the Commandant," Heinrich said, rather angrily.

"Sorry, my friend, I was just curious, that's all."

They fell silent for a while, with Heinrich pacing the room, at the same time occasionally glancing at Artur, who just sat on his chair, watching Heinrich. After a few minutes, the cell door opened. The guard came in to tell Artur that he was taking him back to his cell. Once they were outside Heinrich's cell, the guard said he was under instructions to take him to the Commandant's room first. They went to his room where Artur was told he would join him soon.

"Good afternoon, Selmer," the Commandant said in English, once he'd closed the door. "Please take a seat. It appears that Herr Heinrich is starting to get a bit angry with all your questions, don't you think?"

"It would appear so. It's interesting that he's not asked me for the names of any of my contacts, although he believes I know the same contact as his in London."

"Agreed," the Commandant said, as he moved to look out of the window, but it was already getting dark.

"I am of the opinion that you have probably reached the end of your usefulness with Heinrich. When I spoke to your boss, Charles, yesterday, he is keen for you to finish here. He wants you to finish your naval officer training on a course starting on Monday. He will send a car for you the day after tomorrow at 10 o'clock."

"Goodness me! There's certainly no rest for the wicked. I assume the car will take me straight to Charles's office?"

"That's what I understand."

The Commandant told Artur that he thought Heinrich would end up being a good double agent, but he thought he would have to change his behaviour and be very much calmer in certain, difficult situations.

"I don't think it will be necessary for you to go to Heinrich's cell again, but I shall tell him you have been considered to work for the British and have left the interrogation centre. You will be collected from your cell late Wednesday afternoon and taken to the room you used when you first arrived here. You are invited to have supper with us, as well as breakfast the following morning. We don't want you returning to Charles in an undernourished state, do we?"

"That's very kind of you, sir."

As on previous occasions, the Commandant rang the bell for the guard to come in. He was instructed in German to take Artur back to his cell. Once he got back, he sat on his chair, wondering if he would have another chance to meet up with Heinrich—he wasn't very happy with the way the last meeting ended up.

The next day went slowly; he wasn't told to go to see Heinrich. The following morning came and went too.

Late in the afternoon, the guard came to take Artur back to the room in the main part of the house that he first used. He was pleased to be changing into his own clothes after he'd had a good bath. At 7 o'clock, there was a knock on the door.

"Come in," he said.

A man entered Artur's room informing him that supper would be served in the main dining room at 7:30 p.m.: he would be joining some of the staff. Artur was semi-prepared: just needed to put on a tie, brush his hair and put on his shoes.

As he came down to the hallway, the Commandant saw him and beckoned him into the dining room. After he had introduced him to three of the Commandant's colleagues, he asked him what he would like to drink: beer or wine?

"I would prefer a glass of red, sir, if you have some?"

"Coming up right away. We have a bottle already open from lunch time."

As Artur was handed a glass, he directed him to a place at the round table so that they were sitting next to each other. During the meal, the Commandant was very complimentary about Artur's contribution at Camp 020, particularly how easily he seemed to relate to Herr Knipp to the extent that the prisoner might well be used as a double agent. The rest of the conversation revolved around the state of the war effort and how the Royal Air Force had managed to stop the *Luftwaffe* from ruling the skies over the South East of England.

When coffee was served, Artur looked at his watch to find it was close to 10 o'clock. He excused himself, thanked the Commandant for his hospitality saying he would like to return to his room for a good night's sleep in a more comfortable bed than the one in his cell. As they all stood up to wish him a good rest, they gave him an understanding smile and a nod.

The following morning after a sizeable breakfast, Artur packed his suitcase and waited in the hall for the car to arrive. As it drew up, the Commandant appeared, picked up his case and walked with Artur outside to the waiting car. He wished Artur well and once again thanked him for his time at the interrogation centre. He said he would be sending his report to his boss in the next few days.

At around 11:30 a.m., the car drew up outside Charles's office in St James. Artur thanked the driver, took his case from the backseat, went up the steps into the reception area.

"Nice to see you back, Mr Williams," the receptionist said, as he signed in. "Mr Compton-Browne is expecting you; please go straight up to his office."

Andrew knocked on Charles's door and went in.

"Welcome back to London and the Service, Andrew."

"It's good to be back, Charles. I see you still have 'Miss Grumpy' on reception duty," Andrew remarked with a smile.

"Don't you mock her, Andrew; she's a very efficient woman," he replied, as he ushered him to a chair by his desk.

"So, Andrew, did you find the last few weeks useful experience? I understand from the Commandant that you made a significant contribution at the interrogation centre, although I await his report before making too many comments," Charles said with a smile.

"It was a tough assignment, not physically, but more from the mental point of view. It would appear that I developed quite a good relationship with the German spy Heinrich Knipp. He could become another double agent after some further training."

"You no doubt heard about *Fraulein Marta Schwartzman*—alias Miss Maggie Pierce?"

"Yes, I was told that she was in the *Abwehr* based in Koblenz when we thought she had died in Munich."

"Someone is working on her," Charles said, "to establish exactly what happened after the explosion in the Munich Beer Keller last November. 'Curiouser and curiouser', as Lewis Carroll said in his Alice in Wonderland book! More of that will no doubt emerge over the coming weeks.

"For now, I need to talk about the next part of your naval training. There's a course starting on Monday up in Scotland at Inveraray. It is a Combined Operations shore-based training centre, that is to say for Army, Navy and Air Force personnel. It trains men in the use and handling of assault and landing craft, amongst other things. You can expect to be there for two months, after which you will be sent down to HMS *King Alfred* based in Hove. It is normally a ten-week course, but I'm reliably informed that you will be discharged at the end of March, after eight weeks."

"At least it doesn't sound like a whole lot of classroom work," Andrew retorted, with a sigh of relief.

"Quite so, but at least you'll come out with a commission at the end of it all."

"Miss Jones has all your joining instructions, money for the train fares and some pocket money. You ought to travel in your seaman's uniform, but make sure you take plenty of warm clothing as a cold winter is forecast."

"Thanks for nothing, Charles. I might need to buy a couple of sweaters when I'm up there so do I use my own money?"

"There should be plenty of cash in the envelope you'll be given. If there's no more to discuss, I suggest you get on your way and prepare for a few months away. Do call me if you really need to, otherwise I'll see you in my office on Monday 31st March at 10:30 a.m."

Both men stood up and shook hands. Andrew collected the envelope from Miss Jones and left for his flat.

Chapter 7
Friday, 28 March 1941

It had been a long and exacting four months of training. The eight weeks in Scotland had severely tested all the trainees, mainly because of the exceptionally cold and snowy conditions. Six of the trainees were removed from the course as they couldn't deal with the exacting standards set by the instructors. Fortunately, on the banks of Loch Fyne and being near the west coast, the frost and snow was not quite as severe as it had been elsewhere in Scotland and the NE of England, but two other recruits had to withdraw as a result of frostbite.

Andrew was pleased with his results at Inveraray. He was commended on his performance by the captain in charge for his positive attitude during all aspects of the courses, in particular for his willingness to help those with less aptitude and experience than himself. It surprised him somewhat as he believed he didn't suffer fools gladly, or those that didn't want to play the game. After all, that's what it was really: a game.

He was thinking everything through as he relaxed on the train from Brighton to Victoria. He was very pleased to have completed the three-month course on HMS *King Alfred* in Hove in only two months. His boss, Charles, and a senior man from the Admiralty, had presumably persuaded the men in charge for Andrew to join the course one-month after it had started. It meant he received his commission at the end of the course with everyone else. He wasn't really very surprised, bearing in mind the considerable experience he had gained from his mission on the British battle cruiser to Northern Norway to bring back King Haakon and the Norwegian cabinet last June.

He thought the course at Hove had been very well run. It was a real eye-opener to find that the enormous underground carpark at the Marina—together with the large swimming pool complex—had been requisitioned by the Admiralty in September 1939. He learned that their conversion had provided several different parts of a ship including the officers' mess, trainee accommodation and a ship's handling simulator. Other areas had been altered for the wardroom, classrooms and even a chapel for use by the ship's chaplain.

Andrew was brought back to the present when he realised the train was slowing as it entered Victoria station. He took his kitbag and suitcase down from the luggage rack. He thought he looked very smart in his new lieutenant's uniform that had been made especially for him at the branch of Austin Reed's in Vallance Gardens—over the road from HMS *King Alfred*.

He put on his new naval hat as he stepped down on to the platform. He looked at his watch once he was through the barrier: it was 3:15 p.m. He took a taxi to his flat and rushed to the door as it was raining hard. Nobody else was around so he went straight upstairs to his room. It seemed strange to be back after four months away on courses. He quickly changed into some casual clothes, hung his uniform up in the wardrobe and went downstairs to make himself a coffee. He sat at the small table in the kitchen sipping his black coffee, staring out of a small section of the window that wasn't obscured by the cross-hatching of tape over the window. *I wonder what the Service have in mind for me next?* he thought to himself.

After some minutes, Andrew finished his coffee, returned to his room and finished putting his belongings away. He decided not to write a full report for his boss covering the four months of naval officer training, but just a list of important topics covered and how he felt he had done in each of them. He hoped Charles would be impressed, but knew a more complete report would be sent to him by the captain in charge in due course.

Over the weekend, Andrew walked for several hours around the areas close to his flat enjoying the early Spring air. He spoke to people outside Buckingham Palace who told him that bombs were dropped early in March. By all accounts, a German plane had flown along The Mall and dropped a single high explosive bomb that hit the North Hall. A few hours later, a wave of bombers dropped more incendiaries, this time on the forecourt. He could easily see the mess they had made, but thankfully they hadn't hit the Palace itself, nor injured the King or the Queen.

Monday morning arrived. He walked to Charles's office and went into reception.

"Hello, Mr Williams. You've been away quite a while," Miss Jones commented. "Welcome back."

"Thank you," Andrew said with a smile, as he entered his details in the book.

"Please go up; Mr Compton-Browne is expecting you."

Andrew knocked in his customary way and went into Charles's office. They greeted each other warmly.

"I'm not going to say what I usually do about 'Miss Grumpy', but she seems to be much more relaxed and friendly than when she first came here."

"It's funny you should say that as I had noticed a difference too. Apparently, she used to live in London's East End before the war, but she and her brother managed to find accommodation in Holland Park at the end of 1939. With all the bombing that's been going on, she's pleased to be out of that area, although she does worry about her neighbours and friends who still live there. That's probably why her demeanour has improved.

"Some coffee, Andrew? Black as usual?"

"Yes please."

Charles served the coffee, went around his desk to his chair as Andrew pulled his chair in front of the desk.

"I've produced a summary of the areas covered on the courses for you," Andrew remarked, "but not a full report as you will no doubt get that from the captains of the two establishments in the fullness of time," as he pushed two sheets of paper across the desk.

"I must congratulate you, Andrew. I have had nothing but good reports from the men in charge of the courses. You are now a real Royal Navy lieutenant," Charles said, with a loud chuckle.

"But, strictly speaking, I'm only a temporary sub-lieutenant," Andrew stated.

They laughed and reminisced about Andrew's time on the British battle cruiser when everyone—including the admiral—thought he already was a full navy lieutenant!

"I need to tell you about a few things that have been going on, not only recently, but since de Gaulle made his broadcast on 18th June to the people of France, and to French people everywhere, on the BBC. He invited French soldiers, engineers and other specialists in Britain and elsewhere to contact him. He made a second broadcast four days later of a similar message that was apparently heard by more people than the first one. Of the 100,000 soldiers temporarily on British soil, only 7,000 stayed to join de Gaulle, whereas the rest returned to France, but, guess what, they were immediately captured and made prisoners of war."

"I remember the speech as I was working with Spears and de Gaulle in putting the final draft together."

"Yes, of course," Charles said, "but one of the significant results was made apparent to the Service a few months later. Residents and fishermen in Brittany heard both speeches and were fearful of having to work for the Nazis. So much so that many of them sailed their fishing smacks and crabbers to ports in Cornwall, such as Penzance, Newlyn and Looe.

"We sent a chap from the Service—someone of my level—to Newlyn to speak to some of the fishermen about how they might help us bring back RAF pilots and crew members who had been shot down over France. This they've been doing, as often as they can, very successfully ever since. What has helped significantly is the attitude of the many residents living near the Breton coast in setting up safe houses. A network has been established in north-western France that leads these airmen to these safe houses. It's a very risky business because the *Wehrmacht* are crawling all over the coastal areas—Brittany in particular. If any residents are caught giving assistance to our chaps, they have been known to be shot in front of the rest of the village. If the airmen are found, they are sent to prisoner of war camps in eastern Germany.

"Whenever RAF men do return to England, they are quizzed as to the whereabouts of these houses in Brittany. Where possible, coordinates of these places are distributed to squadron leaders in the South of England for possible future use.

"On another topic altogether, the Service and the Foreign Office have received accounts of a large amount of building work going on around the Loire estuary at St Nazaire. Coded messages have been received from one of our contacts near that part of France about this activity. We are asking you to go to the St Nazaire area to find out what's going on. We believe U-boats will be kept there for forays against the Atlantic convoys. If that's the case, the War Office want to destroy these facilities.

"You will travel down to Cornwall to meet our man in Newlyn. He will arrange for one of the French fishermen to take you to a port on the Brittany coast—the destination has yet to be finalised."

"That sounds interesting, Charles. How soon do you need me to go?"

"We have much to organise first, but you will have all the identity papers and documents showing you to be a fisherman whose come down from Boulogne to work with a chap that keeps his crabber near Portsall, on the NW coast of Brittany."

"I hope I won't be wearing a false moustache? I had terrible problems with one when I was in Dunkirk?"

"No, that won't be necessary, but we will give you a brown dye to darken your hair and eyebrows; it will be a better product than the stuff you used before as it won't make your hair so greasy. The fisherman at Newlyn might only take you part of the way, you'll then transfer to another boat that will go back to France. You won't know if you will be transferring to a second boat until just before you leave Newlyn.

"As far as clothing is concerned, any of yours that have labels will need to be marked as though they are French. People in our team are already working on the identity papers you'll need. As soon as you can, take any clothes that you might choose to have in your suitcase or kitbag to our Broadway office where they will be vetted and relabelled where necessary. It might seem a bit over the top, but we can't take any chances. After all, we are at war."

"For how long do you expect me to be away? It might have some bearing on what I pack?"

"Two or three weeks, maybe more. You will only take a bare minimum. The woman in the first safe house will supply you with a shirt, a dark, locally knitted polo-neck sweater, a pair of trousers, two pairs of socks, a raincoat and some shoes."

"So why do I need to take anything? How does she know my sizes anyway?" Andrew retorted.

"We have erred on slightly larger sizes for the clothing; the socks and shoes will fit. It's very important you have comfortable footwear as you might have to walk quite a lot. If your cover is blown or you are suspected of not being a fisherman, you might need to run—good-fitting shoes are essential in those situations. We anticipated you would agree to going so details have already been forwarded to the woman at the safe house.

"I need to tell you that in February, SOE set up a mission called Operation Savanna. It involved a number of de Gaulle's Free French paratroopers being dropped near Vannes. The plan was to kill as many German Pathfinder pilots as possible by blowing up the bus as they were being transported to the nearby airfield at Meucon: the pilots are responsible for spearheading night raids on Britain, hence the importance of the mission.

"Once on the ground, the men quickly discovered that their plans were hopelessly out of date: the pilots were now being driven in twos or threes by car! The number of weeks of delay to the operation's execution rendered it a failure, but a major benefit was that they brought back much valuable intelligence about life in occupied France: curfew laws, transport regulations, examples of identity papers and so on. All this has been very helpful to us in setting up yours and other Service missions."

"If my geography of France is correct, I will have to pass very close to Vannes on my way to St Nazaire. I will therefore have to take great care getting to St Nazaire, but even more so when in the vicinity of Vannes."

"Exactly so, Andrew. One of the SOE men went on to Paris to work with the French resistance, whereas the rest were rescued off the coast near Les Sables-d'Olonne by one of our subs to be brought back to England."

"Once I've successfully completed my mission, how am I expected to get back to England?" Andrew enquired.

"Nothing has been organised. We were not sure how long it might take, so you'll have to find your own way back—maybe by the same route you take to get to France. You'll have to use your own initiative."

"When do you expect me to go down to Newlyn?"

"As I have said, take any clothes you might need with you to the Broadway office as soon as you can. Ask for Mrs King, she'll make any label changes she feels are necessary. I want you to return to my office on Wednesday at 4 o'clock to collect your clothes, documents and currency for the mission.

"Our man in Newlyn is called Tony; you will find out how to contact him by making yourself known at The Swordfish Inn. I'll tell him you will be arriving in Newlyn on Friday, early in the evening. The train journey is over ten hours, so you'll have to leave London on an early service to get there by the evening. You may not be aware that the Germans have been bombing the Cornwall and south Devon towns and ports quite regularly over the last nine months. It is possible that if there is another raid in the next few days, the train might be delayed, but Tony will be alerted to that, should that happen.

"Oh, by the way, with your being away for so much of the last five months, I forgot to tell you that, after I received the captain of the battle cruiser's report, I was sent his citation recommending you for the Distinguished Service Medal. It was written in glowing terms about how you saved his ship from almost certain severe damage—or even from sinking—when you shot down the Stukas. It was endorsed by the admiral so I'm sure you'll receive this most prestigious of awards."

"Thank you, Charles, but as I've said all along, I was only doing my duty as an officer on the king's ship."

"Well, hopefully you will accept the award with good grace for a job well done. Additionally, King Haakon has created a special Norwegian decoration to be awarded to all those assisting with his and his cabinet's safe exit from Tromsø. You are included in the list, near the top as it happens. Many congratulations"

"I'm speechless, Charles."

"Sorry not to have told you earlier, Andrew. Anyway, I think you ought to be on your way so you have time to get your things to Mrs. King."

They both stood up and shook hands, Charles with a particularly broad grin on his face.

Chapter 8
Monday, 31 March 1941

It started to rain in the afternoon as Andrew came out of the Service flat carrying his kitbag. He had taken Charles at his word: he packed only a few items. He decided to hail a taxi to the Broadway offices as the rain became heavier.

"Good afternoon," Andrew said to the commissionaire as he entered the Broadway building and into the reception area.

"Hello, I've come to see Mrs King," he said to the receptionist with his customary engaging smile. She dialled a number.

"Mrs King asks you to take the lift to the third floor. Turn left out of the lift and her section is at the end of the corridor."

"Thank you very much," he said, as he signed the registry book, gently touching her hand and giving her a wink.

Andrew knocked on the door at the end of the corridor and walked in. He looked around the room and an attractive middle-aged woman waved at him beckoning him over to her desk.

"So, Mr Williams, I hear you are off to France for a while and you need me to make your clothes look like they are French."

"That's right, Mrs King," as Andrew handed over his kitbag.

Mrs King tipped out the kitbag's contents onto her desk, at the same time separating items into different piles.

"You've not got very much, Mr Williams; are you sure you won't need more than these things?"

"Apparently not; someone in France is to give me more items. Anyway, please may I leave these with you to see what you can do? If it's alright with you, please could you return my clothes to Mr Compton-Browne's office in St James before Wednesday afternoon?"

"Not a problem, Mr Williams."

Andrew thanked Mrs King, giving her a big smile as he turned and walked to the door. He suddenly thought, as he walked out of the lift on the ground floor, if he could see Helen before leaving for France.

"Please could you phone C's secretary, Helen? Tell her that Andrew Williams is in reception," Andrew asked the receptionist.

There was some conversation for a few moments, after which the phone was passed to Andrew, telling him not be too long as the line had been very busy. Andrew nodded.

"Hello, Helen? It's Andrew Williams. I have to be rather quick, but would you be free for a drink after work on Wednesday? We could meet at the same pub that we met at before? Shall we say 6 o'clock?"

Andrew smiled as he received Helen's reply, said he looked forward to seeing her again. He passed the receiver back to the receptionist, thanking her for using her phone.

As the rain had abated, he walked back to his flat thinking of what might be in store for Wednesday evening. When he arrived in his room, he wrote a short list of extra things he thought he should be taking on his next mission. He removed a package from behind his shoes at the bottom of the wardrobe that contained his pistol plus boxes of ammunition. He checked and cleaned the pistol thoroughly, filled the chamber with bullets putting it—plus the box of ammunition—in his bedside table drawer. He knew he would be getting fresh identity papers and passport, but he wrote them down on the list anyway. After rummaging through his clothes for nearly fifteen minutes, he felt in need of a strong coffee so went down to the kitchen.

"Hello," said Mike, as Andrew walked into the kitchen.

"Do I understand you're off somewhere soon?"

"Yes," Andrew replied, with some surprise in his voice. "I leave early Friday morning."

"I've just returned from a successful mission to Norway. I joined some chaps from the SOE, as well as a number of commando units. SOE had been secretly told there was an armed trawler at Stamsund that had these German Enigma cypher machines on board. Before it sank, we managed to retrieve two machines and some code books that are now with our codebreakers at Bletchley Park."

"My goodness! That sounds like quite a scoop. What did the powers-that-be have to say?"

"It's early days, Andrew, but it could be of considerable significance in protecting our Atlantic convoys from the German U-boats."

Nothing further was said by either man; Andrew made his coffee and returned to his room. *Bloody U-boats*, Andrew muttered to himself. *Let's hope I get some positive evidence from St Nazaire so the RAF boys can bomb the hell out of their prized subs.*

In view of what Charles had said to him about the probability of doing a lot of walking when in France, Andrew used his time wisely on Tuesday and Wednesday morning to walk many times around St James and Hyde parks. It rained most of Tuesday, but he knew he had to go out; he needed to be sure that he could walk six-plus miles without sustaining any ill effects, regardless of the weather. He felt a bit stiff after he had finished on Wednesday lunchtime so he decided to have a hot bath before heading for Charles's office.

"Hello, Mr Williams," Miss Jones said in a friendly manner. "I've given a parcel that arrived an hour before you did to Mr Compton-Browne, plus an envelope."

"Thank you. I'm glad they have arrived," he replied, as he signed the reception book. He knocked and went into Charles's office on the 2nd floor. They greeted each other in the usual manner, then each sat at opposite sides of Charles's desk.

"Well then, Andrew, are you ready for this important mission?"

"As ready as I can be. I've been thinking about it a lot over the last few days. I hope I can live up to everybody's expectations and get the information you all need," Andrew replied, looking at the items on the chair under the window.

"I suggest you have a good look in the envelope."

Andrew went to the chair, picked up the envelope and brought it back to the desk. He emptied the contents on to the desk: identification papers, French Francs, a small map and a code book slid out.

"There are two items that you should also take with you," Charles remarked. He opened his desk drawer, then placed a sheathed knife and a small, rectangular leather case in front of Andrew.

"These are the two essential objects: the first is the F & S fighting knife; it is relatively new, being made by the Wilkinson Sword company; we are lucky to be given a few of them. The second is the leather case containing a miniature camera called a Minox Riga. A few have found their way to England into the Service's hands; they come from Latvia. It is a very advanced design, is easy to use, it can take as many as fifty pictures. It will take pictures of documents as well as objects in the distance."

Andrew took the knife from its sheath and examined the long handle. After a few moments, he took the slim silver-looking camera out of its case, put it up to his eye and pretended to take a picture.

"What you have to do," Charles explained, "is take hold of the left side. When you slide the right-hand side outwards, the film advances so you can take a picture by pressing the button on the top. Closing the camera up again protects the lens and the viewfinder. All very simple, compact and light."

"Fantastic piece of kit. It should prove to be a very useful device."

Andrew then looked at his papers and documents. He saw that he was still going to be known as Artur Selmer, originally coming from a village north of Calais near the Belgian border.

"If you look through your clothes, you will find a tube of dye for your hair and eyebrows. There is also a special oval hair brush: if you hold the top and twist the bottom section, it will unscrew into two parts. The middle of each part has been chiselled out so that the camera can be hidden inside—without the leather case, of course! Try it out."

Andrew placed the camera in the top section of the brush, put the bottom part in place and twisted it clockwise. He then realised that he should have turned it anticlockwise a number of times to close it. The join between the two parts was not visible.

"Ingenious piece of work," Andrew remarked. "It's a pity the brush isn't big enough to take the knife as well," he said with a laugh.

"I do wish to remind you that this mission is not only very important for the possible protection of the British convoys, but also it will require a great deal of courage, care and deception on your part. For once you will be acting totally alone, none of the people you meet will be known to you, you should trust nobody. One thing in your favour is that most of the Bretons you encounter are anti-Nazi and resent the Germans occupying their country. There are, of course, some that are sympathisers."

When Charles looked down at the floor for the piece of paper he had dropped, Andrew had a quick glance at his watch: 5 o'clock. He hoped he would not be late for his rendezvous with Helen.

"I noticed you brought your kitbag with you, Andrew, so I suggest you now put everything in there. When you get back to the flat, do go through it all very carefully. If you have any concerns or questions, please call me tomorrow morning. Do you have anything you want to ask me now?"

"Do you know the name of the lady I shall be staying with in the first safe house in Portsall?"

"No, I don't have her name. Andrew, you must understand that secrecy of your mission is of the utmost importance. So, the fewer people knowing the details, the better. As I've already said, the people of Brittany are risking their lives to assist English and Polish airmen trying to return to England; it therefore follows a plan can quickly change, if a situation arises that warrants it. I see you have put everything in your kitbag, so perhaps you ought to leave and return to your flat."

The two men stood up, shook hands and smiled at each other.

"I wish you a safe trip, Andrew. I look forward to seeing you on your return to England."

Andrew left the room, went down to reception, signed out and disappeared down to the roadway. He thought he had just enough time to be at the pub by 6 o'clock, so long as he took a taxi back to his flat. As the taxi drew up outside his flat, he looked at his watch to find it was 5:40 p.m. *It's going to be a close-run thing*, he said to himself. Inside, he ran up the stairs two at a time, dashed into his room, threw his kitbag into the bottom of his wardrobe, brushed his hair and ran down stairs, at the same time putting on his raincoat. He walked briskly to the pub, went inside and looked around. There were more people than he had expected, but, as he couldn't see Helen, he bought a drink for her and a pint for himself. The clock at the back of the bar showed the time to be 6:05 p.m. The same table by the entrance was available, so he put the drinks down on it.

"Hello, Andrew," a gentle voice said, as Helen touched his neck with her cold hand. He turned to face her, looked into her eyes, giving her a kiss on her cheek.

"I'm so pleased you could make it," he said, smiling like a Cheshire cat.

"I took the liberty of buying you a drink—like the one you had when we last met here." He passed the Vermouth to her; she covered his hand with hers and took the glass.

"Good to see you again," they said to each other in unison, touched glasses and smiled.

"It seems ages since I last saw you, Helen. In fact, it was way back towards the end of June last year."

"I remember it all very vividly," she said, touching him on the arm.

"Have you been away much of the time, Andrew? I half expected you to have contacted me, particularly around Christmas, but never mind you are here now."

Andrew realised that, even though she was C's secretary and she would have known what he had been doing since last July, there was no way he could talk about any of it with her.

They chatted about the state of the war, her sister who lived with her in south London, the bombing of London and other cities.

"I haven't asked you how much time you have this evening, but would you like some supper?"

"It seems rather mean, I know, but I need to catch a train at about 7:45 p.m. My sister is preparing the evening meal as our mother is staying with us for a few days. I hope you don't mind my leaving early?"

"Of course, I'm disappointed, but I quite understand. Have you got time for another drink?"

"That would be lovely, thank you Andrew."

Andrew fought his way to the bar, ordered another round and returned to Helen's side.

"So, how's your brother, Jack?" Andrew enquired, as they touched glasses. "Has he joined the military? He would be very useful being a practicing doctor?"

"He joined the RAF last October, as it happens. He's a flight lieutenant. We're all very worried about his prospects of surviving the war, but if that's what he wants to do, who are we to get in his way?"

"Good for him. Do pass on my best wishes when you next see him."

After some minutes, Andrew looked at his watch and saw it was after 7:15 p.m.

"I don't want to rush you, but you'll need to leave soon if you want to catch that train."

They downed their drinks, went out of the pub where Andrew hailed a taxi.

"Waterloo station, please; this lady has a train to catch."

The driver did as he was asked. In next to no time, they were at Waterloo station. Andrew got out of the taxi, opened the door for Helen, they embraced and kissed lovingly.

"Hope to see you again before too long, Helen," he shouted as she skipped purposefully up the steps. She briefly turned and waved at him then she disappeared into the station. Andrew stood, just watching, for the next few moments. He gave the driver his flat address, entered the cab and fell into the back of the seat as the taxi drove away at speed. Once inside the flat, he went to the kitchen to see what food might be available. As usual: not a lot. As it was still quite early, he decided to walk quickly to Victoria station; he knew the restaurant called the Chez Gaston stayed open till 9 o'clock.

"May I have a pint of bitter please," Andrew asked the barman. "Do you have a menu?"

"Not much choice tonight, sir," replied the barman as he passed a menu over the counter; most of the choices were crossed out. Andrew scanned the remaining items.

"I'll have a portion of chicken pie, please."

"Where will you be sitting, sir?"

"Over by the window," Andrew pointed to a table.

He spent about thirty minutes over two pints of beer and his mediocre meal that was brightened by his thoughts of having seen Helen again. He decided to return to the flat as he had lots to do the following day.

Chapter 9
Thursday, 3 April 1941

He woke at 7 o'clock and went straight down to the kitchen to make himself a coffee which he took back to his room. When he was in the bathroom washing and shaving, he decided to dye his hair at the same time so he would more clearly resemble his picture in his papers.

He left the flat at 9:30 a.m., deciding to take a taxi to Paddington station to save time. He was in a short queue for the booking office, but was soon talking to the ticket clerk. He asked for a single, one-way ticket to Penzance for the following morning. He was told that the first train was at 8:14 a.m., but he'd need to change at Bristol Temple Meads station.

"Is there a through train?" Andrew asked.

"Not till 9:37 a.m., getting to Penzance at 6:53 p.m.—the stopping train only gets in five minutes earlier. I've got to tell you, sir, that we've been experiencing some delays to the Cornish towns over the last few months due to Nazi bombing raids of some of the ports. Hopefully, there won't be any hold ups on the journey tomorrow."

"I'd like to catch the later of those two times, please," Andrew replied, as he handed over some money for the journey and a reserved seat. He took the change, put the ticket in his satchel and thanked the clerk for his kind attention.

When Andrew returned to his room in the Service's flat, he took out his kitbag from the wardrobe and emptied everything onto the bed. He examined the clothing to see that his trousers, two shirts and a sweater, had French labels sown on. He selected all he would be wearing the next day and put them on the chair by the window. He placed the F&S knife, pistol and ammunition boxes in the false compartment at the bottom of the kitbag. He then made a list of everything he would be taking with him and put it in his satchel.

His imagination was starting to make him feel a bit anxious about the new mission, so he thought he would get some fresh air. He looked out of the window: thankfully it wasn't raining. He decided to take a walk around one of the parks. As he walked, he tried very hard to think about the purpose of the assignment: should he commit what he saw at St Nazaire to memory or should he take pictures? He was fascinated by the miniature camera, he couldn't believe that someone could create such a small, but intricate, photographic device.

As it was now past midday, Andrew thought it was time for a drink so he walked to the Shepherd's Tavern in Hertford Street. It wasn't too crowded as he wandered up to the bar and paid for a pint of bitter. He returned to the small table by the entrance and looked out of the window to the street outside. *I wonder when I'll have the next opportunity of drinking in London?* He mumbled to himself.

On his return to the flat, he noticed it was nearly 2:30 p.m. He sat on the edge of the bed looking at his list. He was both excited and nervous about what might happen over the next couple of weeks. He took off his shoes and lay back on the bed with his hands behind his head. His mind took him to France: back to Pesmes with Monique. They were running for all their worth, being chased by German soldiers that stopped every now and then to shoot at them. They ran past a restaurant, round the corner towards the bridge. They slid down the bank at the start of the bridge and hid under the first arched support. Andrew took out his pistol as he heard the soldiers shouting to each other, saying that they'd lost the two French people. Monique crouched behind Andrew as he took aim at the leading soldier of the eight or nine that had pursued them. He knew he didn't have enough ammunition to kill them all, but he felt he had no alternative than to kill the leaders. He fired five rounds killing five of the men instantly. The remaining four soldiers sheltered behind a tree. Andrew murmured to Monique that their best chance was to surrender. They stood up with their hands in the air so the soldiers could see them, but the man at the back shot at them. They fell to the ground; he felt a pain in his chest.

Andrew woke up in a sweat. He found himself face down on the floor in his flat with his chest on his shoes. He knew he had had a nightmare, but it was so realistic. He got up and went to the bathroom to wash his hands and face. He looked in the mirror, saw his tousled, darkened hair and his pale face. *Come on Williams, pull yourself together man; get a grip of yourself!* he said to the image looking back at him. He dried his hands and face, went back to his room to brush his hair. He undid the brush, checked that the camera was still in place and screwed it together again.

The rest of the day he spent down in the kitchen or the lounge. Two of his flat mates came in at about 7 o'clock so they all played cards for a couple of hours. At 9:30 p.m. Andrew excused himself as he needed some sleep. The others knew he was going on a mission the next day so quite understood. They had a superstition not to wish anyone good luck the day before leaving on an assignment so they just said 'goodnight, see you soon'.

Andrew slept soundly until his alarm woke him at 7 o'clock. After dressing and leaving his room, he went to the kitchen for some toast and honey that had been brought back to the flat by one of his mates whose mother had hives. He double-checked his room and his satchel before leaving at 8:30 a.m. He took a taxi to the station noticing he was in good time for the train; he went through the barrier. He had a seat reserved on the platform side of the first-class compartment, facing the engine. There were two other people in his compartment, but apart from nodding his head at them as he put his kitbag on the luggage rack, no words were exchanged

Andrew heard the whistle from the engine, the train started to move forward. It left on time: he was on his way. His mind took him forward to the area near Penzance. He had been told by Charles that the *Luftwaffe* had bombed many towns and airfields in the West Country, particularly south Cornwall. The Germans knew the Royal Navy kept many MTBs—and other naval craft—to protect British shipping in that part of the English Channel. He wondered if Newlyn had been a target?

He found himself nodding off with the soporific movement of the train. He was next aware of the speaker system alerting passengers that they would be arriving at Reading in the next seven minutes—or that's what he thought he heard. The train slowed and then stopped. Not many people were on the platform, even fewer got off the train. After some five minutes, they were off again: next stop Bristol Temple Meads station.

Andrew was fond of a distant relative who lived in the outskirts of Bristol; he hoped her house had escaped the huge number of incendiary bombs that had been dropped around the docks area. He was aware of the *Luftwaffe* concentrating on the harbour and Filton airport since last November, but knew they had often missed their targets and bombed residential areas. As the train entered the station, he could see the devastation of the city: many properties and buildings were still smouldering. He got up from his seat, took hold of the leather strap to let the window down. For some reason, he peered up and down the platform at the people about to board the train—some were wearing gas masks, many were holding suitcases. One young woman wanted to enter his compartment so he opened the door for her, took her large suitcase and helped her up into the carriage.

"Thank you very much," she said, as she stepped inside, at the same time giving Andrew a coy smile. "It is rather heavy," she remarked. "My seat is this one in the corner," as she pointed to the seat next to the entrance to the corridor.

Andrew placed the case on the rack above her seat, at the same time giving her one of his endearing smiles. They were watched by the other two people in the compartment. No sooner had they taken their seats than the engine's whistle sounded. The train gave a sudden lurch then started to move forward. Some people on the platform were waving and blowing kisses to friends or loved ones as the train moved out of the station.

After some twenty minutes, the door from the corridor opened.

"Tickets please," said the inspector with a smile. He took each ticket in turn, looked at it carefully, punched a hole into it and returned it to each passenger.

"The buffet car is now open for luncheon, but as you might imagine, the choice is very limited at present. Our next stops will be Exeter, Plymouth and finally Penzance." The inspector nodded at each passenger as he left the compartment.

Andrew looked at the young woman and asked if she was having lunch, but she declined with a smile telling him that she had brought something with her. Andrew was a little disappointed, so he left for the restaurant carriage on his own. Within forty minutes, he was back in his seat, not really having enjoyed what he'd eaten, but knowing he must eat something as he might not get anything else for some time. All the other three passengers seemed to be asleep, but he found he couldn't for the moment: he was wondering if he should go into agent mode before he meets Tony later today, or maybe sometime tomorrow.

After some while, he noticed the train slowing down. All the others had been woken by the change in speed.

"In case you're wondering, the train stops just outside Exeter to take on water," one of the passengers told them all. "It takes about ten to fifteen minutes, then we continue into Exeter station." They all gave a nod of understanding what he had just said. Sure enough, the engine whistled after about ten minutes to move into Exeter station. Two passengers got up from their seats, took down their suitcases and said 'good bye' as they went out of the carriage door. That left the young woman and Andrew as the only people in the compartment.

"So, do I assume you are getting out at Plymouth?" Andrew remarked, as the train pulled away from Exeter station.

"Actually, no," she replied. "I'm going all the way to Penzance and on to Newlyn."

Andrew looked at his watch, thought for a moment, then turned to the woman who was already looking at him.

"Excuse my asking you, but how will you get from Penzance? Do you have someone meeting you?"

"With any luck," she replied, "I hope to find a taxi as it shouldn't be very late."

"You might not believe me, but that's such a coincidence: I'm going on to Newlyn too. Would it be possible for us to share the taxi? Assuming there are no delays, we should be in Penzance shortly after 6:45 p.m. so a taxi ought to be a possibility before the time of the usual blackout?"

"It certainly sounds like a good suggestion," she replied, as she got up from her seat and went out of the compartment. She returned about twenty-five minutes later: lipstick on, hair brushed, her jacket over her arm. Andrew looked at her approvingly and smiled.

When they stopped at Plymouth, one elderly lady entered their carriage. Andrew helped her inside and placed her case on the rack. The train started with a jolt that made the lady fall towards Andrew, but he held her and gently let her down into her seat.

"Thank you very much, young man. I thought for a moment that I was going to fall between the seats, but you saved me."

"All part of the service," he said, with a smile. He thought she was rather overweight as he watched her breathe heavily.

"I hope you will be kind enough to get my case down when we get to Penzance?" she said, to which Andrew replied that he would be only too pleased to do so.

The train arrived at Penzance a few minutes ahead of schedule at 6:40 p.m. Andrew helped the lady with her luggage and down onto the platform.

"My niece should be here to collect me, but thank you for your kind assistance."

A young woman came up to them, greeted her aunt and led her to the hall and outside to a waiting car;

Andrew followed, as did the other lady passenger.

"Are you familiar with where the taxis are?" Andrew enquired.

"Yes, follow me. Where are you heading for in Newlyn?" she asked.

"I'm going to the Swordfish Inn. Do you happen to know it?"

"Yes, very well. It's on the Strand. I'm staying with my aunt who lives near the end of Tredavoe Lane, so I can drop you off first. What will you be doing in Newlyn? By the way, my name's Jane."

"And mine's Andrew," he said, without explaining what he was in Newlyn for.

Andrew followed Jane to the left side of the station entrance, she waved at one of the three taxi drivers and explained where they wanted to go. The driver looked at his watch explaining that he would have to be quick as he was not supposed to be driving after dark, and he still had to get back home. He drove quickly so that after only a few minutes, they were outside the pub.

"Here, Jane, something towards the taxi fare. Might see you over the next few days, perhaps? You now know where you can find me."

"That would be nice," she replied.

He took his kitbag from the boot of the car, waved at her and walked inside. All the windows were covered in a black cotton cloth with one of the locals ensuring that people came in and out of the pub quickly to limit the amount of light getting out. He looked around at the drinkers who also looked at him. He smiled at some of them as he walked to the bar.

"Is there someone called Tony in here?" he asked the barman.

"He's not here yet, but he should be in by about 7:30 p.m. Perhaps I could get you a drink while you wait for him? What's your name?"

"My name's Andrew and I'd like a pint of bitter please."

"Ah, yes, he told me to expect you sometime about now. Welcome to the Swordfish Inn, Andrew. My name's Phil, by the way," as he poured out his pint and handed it to him. Andrew put his kitbag back over his shoulder and walked away from the bar with his drink. After some fifteen minutes, a man came in through the pub's entrance. He looked about him, then more intently at Andrew. He walked over with a smile.

"You must be Andrew," he said. "My name's Tony. I'm pleased to meet you. I see you have a drink so I'll just get myself a pint."

73

Tony was back with Andrew in a few minutes. Tony had a pewter tankard: he was obviously considered as a local. He seemed older to Andrew than he had expected, but there was no age limit on people working in the Service.

"How was your journey down, Andrew?"

"No problems, quite straight forward."

"Are you aware that Cornwall has been bombed and machine gunned from the air by the *Luftwaffe* almost twice weekly since the New Year? There are several airfields, as well as ports with naval ships, being the targets."

At that moment, the air raid siren went off. Fortunately, the bar wasn't very full, but most people dived to the ground, under tables where possible. There was a silence followed by the droning sound of aircraft coming from the south. They heard the whistle of the bombs as they fell, almost immediately followed by explosions. The pub walls shook, but no windows were broken. Tony and Andrew went outside where they witnessed the fires in the distance. The beams of the search lights lit up the sky, picking out dozens of planes for the anti-aircraft guns to fire at.

"From what I can tell, I think some bombs will have landed near Penzance station; hopefully nobody will be killed this time."

"It's almost as bad down here as it is in London," Andrew remarked.

"On another subject, Andrew: I live in a small house up the road from here, so you will stay with me until you leave for France," Tony mentioned, as the all-clear siren sounded.

"Let's go back in for a second pint before setting off for my place,"

They spent about thirty minutes in the pub, but they didn't speak to anybody else, even though one or two said 'hello' to Tony.

Chapter 10
Saturday, 6 April 1941

Andrew woke up at 7 o'clock wondering where he was. He heard noises coming from downstairs as his memory quickly came back to him. They had spent an enjoyable time in the pub, but he had no idea what time they got back to Tony's. He got up and after going to the bathroom, went down to the kitchen.

"Good morning, old boy," Tony said, with a smile. "I assume you slept well after all those pints we had?"

"I'm not used to Cornish ale: it seems stronger than what I usually drink in London. I don't suppose I could have a coffee by any chance?"

"The kettle's on so just a few moments to wait. If you remember what I said last night, you are due to leave on a fishing boat for France at about 5 o'clock this afternoon. After having coffee and some toast, go upstairs, change your clothes and go into 'agent mode'. From then on, we will be speaking French; you will be Artur Selmer."

Andrew made some coffee, went up to his room and emptied the small amount of clothes from his kitbag on to the bed. He selected a long-sleeved vest and pants, a dark blue, woollen sweater and a pair of trousers. He fastened a spotted scarf around his neck and put on his beret. He looked in the mirror and really thought he looked the part. He went down stairs to greet Tony in the kitchen in his best French.

"That looks fantastic, Artur. The only comment I have at the moment is that it all looks rather too clean," Tony replied, also in French, with a smile.

"You can take your beret off while we have a light breakfast."

By about 9:30 a.m., they were ready to leave the house. Tony had told Artur that they would take a walk down to the harbour, he would introduce him to the skipper, Jacques, who will be taking him to France later that afternoon. They walked along the North Pier where most of the French fishing boats were moored. Tony pointed to one of them. The fisherman on board saw Tony and beckoned them to come on board.

"Jacques, this is Artur Selmer, who will be sailing with you," Tony said in French.

They all shook hands. Artur looked at Jacques intently and saw a steely determination in his eyes. His face was rugged and slightly florid from his days at sea. He guessed he was in his mid-fifties.

"Welcome aboard," he said, as they stepped down onto the deck of the boat. Jacques glanced at Artur, but he couldn't read him very well.

"High tide will be at 3:55 p.m., so we need to leave our mooring as the tide is going out: shortly after 5 o'clock. I assume that will be alright with you, Artur?"

Artur agreed with the time, saying he would be standing on the pier at 4:30 p.m.

"Not sure if you know this, but I'll be transferring you to a fishing boat coming from France around midnight; the skipper's name is Jean-Luc."

Jacques showed Artur around the boat. He explained that they would use the motor for about two to three hours, but would sail for the rest of the time until they met up with Jean-Luc. He mentioned that the weather station had forecasted rough seas in the Channel, but with good to fair visibility. He hoped Artur was a good sailor as things could get a bit tricky. He told Artur that there would be two other men on board: they were the main crew members.

After they had talked for a further twenty minutes, Jacques excused himself as he wanted to prepare the boat for the trip. He thanked them for calling on him as they left.

"What would you like to do now, Artur?" Tony said, continuing in French.

"I would like to check that I have all that I need in my kitbag and my satchel. That will take about half an hour, I suppose, after which I'll get my head down for a couple of hours: it's going to be a long night and an equally long day tomorrow."

"Good idea, Artur. What about food? I can go to the local baker and get some cheese rolls made up; I'll see what else is around."

After they arrived back at the house, Artur went upstairs whereas Tony went out to get some food. Artur had given him his ration book, even if it was in the name of Andrew Williams.

Artur checked out everything he was taking, took off his boots and lay on the bed. He fell sound asleep until he heard a knock on the door.

"Artur, are you awake? It's after 3 o'clock. You ought to get up and have something to eat."

"I'll be down in a few minutes, Tony. Thank you."

Artur went to freshen up in the bathroom. He put more dye on his hair, rubbed it into his sculp and put a small amount on his eye brows. He went back to his room, checked his kitbag and satchel for the nth time and went down to the kitchen.

"Did you have some good dreams or something, you've slept for hours?"

Artur didn't reply, but just grunted.

"Help yourself to whatever you want. I suggest you put a few things into some paper bags so you've got something when at sea. By the way, remember you might not come back here so if anything's left behind, I'll send it up to Charles."

Artur realised he was hungry. Tony had done a good job with the food he'd bought: he told him so. As well as food, he had a couple of glasses of water.

"Have you had enough, Artur?" Tony asked after some twenty minutes. "We ought to be going soon, we don't want to keep Jacques waiting, do we?"

Artur said very little, but put two bags of food in his kitbag, as Tony had suggested.

"I'm ready when you are, Tony."

Tony led the way out of the house towards the port. Artur thought he looked the part in his French clothes and his beret as they walked along the North Pier. He looked at his watch: it was just coming up to 4:30 p.m. He could see Jacques in the wheelhouse with some charts; two other men were fussing about on deck. As they approached the boat, Tony shouted out Jacques' name. He turned, waved with a smile and came out onto the aft deck. Artur shook Tony's hand, thanked him for his help in getting him this far and jumped on board. Jacques greeted Artur warmly as he directed him down into the saloon where he left his kitbag.

"Come back on deck when you can Artur, I need to introduce you to the two crew members and show you the wheelhouse."

Once Tony had called Pierre and Claude over to meet Artur, he showed him all the dials, light switches and the steering area etc. in front of the wheel. He repeated what he had said earlier that they would be using the motor for about two hours after which time they would be operating under sail.

"Have you done much sailing?" Jacques asked, in his broad Breton accent that Artur barely understood.

"Quite a lot," he replied, but lied. He didn't want Jacques to think that he was a complete landlubber. He guessed—rightly or wrongly—that the two crewmen would be doing most of the work: particularly with the sails anyway.

Jacques looked at his watch. He shouted to the two crew that they should be under way: it was 5 o'clock. The two men unhitched the ropes attached to the capstans, pushed the boat away from the pier with the quant pole and brought the fenders in. Tony was still on the pier, but didn't wave them off—another of those strange superstitions of the sea.

They slowly motored their way through the narrow opening between the north and south piers and into the open sea. Before too long, the waves became bigger, but the boat rode them with ease as they were going out with the tide. Jacques had told Artur that the trip to France would take over twelve hours— maybe as much as fourteen—depending on the tide, the weather and the sea.

"Go and speak to Claude who is on the bow deck, he'll be watching out for mines," Jacques instructed Artur, when they were a couple of hours out from Newlyn. "We'll be putting up the sails soon, so I'll have to take the boat into the wind. Just before I do that, I'll blow my whistle once so that you all can get to your stations. There are four sails and it will need all three of you to put them up while I keep the boat facing into the wind."

Artur went to Claude and they talked about some of his experiences crossing the Channel and some of the problems when they encountered German patrol boats. Suddenly, they heard the whistle. Artur followed Claude and did as he was instructed. After some ten minutes, all the sails were up, Jacques brought the boat around to their original heading and cut the motor. The light had faded as there were thick clouds coming in from the south west, but the boat seemed much easier to handle under sail. Pierre took control at 8 o'clock so Jacques led Artur down into the saloon.

"Did you bring any food with you Artur?"

"Yes, Tony made a few sandwiches; he also gave me a large slice of fruit cake that one of his neighbours had made."

Jacques smiled and nodded, as he took food from his own satchel. He boiled some water on the galley stove and made tea for the two of them.

"I don't know anything about you, Artur, but for a fisherman like me to be taking someone to France rather than bringing British or Polish airmen back to

England, you and your mission must be very important. I don't need to know anything about your job, but you need to understand that the men on this boat and those on the one we shall be meeting before too long, are all taking huge risks. This part of 'La Manche' is heavily patrolled by Nazi ships, submarines and the *Luftwaffe*."

"I appreciate what you are saying and what you all are doing for me, Jacques."

"I have to tell you that only a couple of weeks ago in the middle of the night, we were heading for England when we were intercepted by a German MTB. Two of the crew came aboard convinced that we had some English pilots hidden away. More by luck than good judgement, they didn't find them: we had three tucked away in the front of the forward cabin; it was a very near thing. We think someone living in Portsall tipped them off."

"Do you think there are many Nazi collaborators in that area?"

"No, I don't, but you will have to take great care when you get there as you will be easily seen as a non-local."

Claude shouted from the top of the gangway to the two of them that it was getting close to the time of the rendezvous. Jacques got up and beckoned Artur to follow him on deck.

The clouds obscured the moon, but, in some ways, it made it easier to see the flashing light on the boat coming from France. The arrangement had been made for the boat to flash a light for identification: three times at midnight, twice at fifteen minutes past, four times at half past, twice at a quarter to.

Both boats had the minimum requirement of navigation lights: a white one on the mast head, a red one on the port side, a green one on the starboard. Suddenly, Artur saw a flashing light.

"There, a light flashing at about 11 o'clock to our direction, close to the horizon."

Jacques took up the binoculars, looked in the direction Artur had mentioned.

"You are right, Artur, well spotted," Jacques said excitedly. "You have very good eyesight."

They waited fifteen minutes before returning the arranged reply.

"There, look," exclaimed Jacques. "That must be Jean-Luc's boat. Claude, make the expected response. Pierre, turn on the motor, alter our heading to where the light was while Artur and I bring in the mainsail."

Within not many minutes, two men were in the cockpit and two were positioned on the forward deck. The other boat was now clearly visible, as the clouds cleared away from the moon.

"Artur, with your excellent eyesight, scan the sea to port and starboard for any possible enemy craft in our vicinity, while I head for the boat."

"As you say, captain."

Artur scoured the sea on both sides as well as he could. Every now and again, the clouds would reveal the moon which would cast light on the sea. On several occasions, it would give Artur enough time to look more thoroughly. He saw a boat on the starboard side. He took a better look through the binoculars before the clouds obscured the moon for another time. He wasn't sure if it were an enemy ship, but at least it seemed to be travelling away from them.

"We're coming alongside Jean-Luc's boat very soon, so put out the fenders on the port side," Jacques instructed the two crewmen.

Artur watched for a moment, then went down to the saloon to retrieve his kitbag and his beret. As he came back on deck, he heard Jacques and Jean-Luc exchanging a few words. Jean-Luc said he didn't encounter any problems, but that it might be different once it started to get light.

"Artur, the boats are held fast, so you may leave my boat and join Jean-Luc and his crew. I'm sure you will get to France safely; maybe our paths will cross again someday."

"Thank you for delivering me this far. Give my good wishes to Tony and tell him you completed your part of the transfer without a hitch."

Artur shook hands with Jacques, smiled at Pierre and Claude as he clambered up onto Jean-Luc's boat. It was much bigger than Jacques' with a large open area at the aft end, the wheelhouse was in front of the main mast with a door going to a small saloon/cabin below. Without any hesitation, both boats went about under motor power and set off for their respective destinations.

Chapter 11
Sunday, 6 April 1941

Artur had looked at his watch as he placed his kitbag on the seat in the cabin: he saw it was close to 1:30 a.m. Jean-Luc's boat was similar, but larger than Jacques', so he had three crewmen, one of which was only a lad: Jean-Luc's son, Loic. For the first hour, Artur accompanied Jean-Luc at the wheel. They had put up the two large red sails and were riding the waves with ease. The clouds had become thicker and darker since leaving Jacques' boat: it didn't seem to bode well for the later part of their journey to Portsall.

"How long do you estimate it will take to get to our destination?" Artur asked Jean-Luc.

"It very much depends on the storm that seems to be brewing." At that moment, there was a sudden gust, catching them all by surprise. Jean-Luc shouted some orders to the crew, he turned the boat through about 25° so that the wind filled the sails. The boat healed over a long way from the perpendicular, causing items in the cabin to crash to the floor.

While the skipper was struggling to keep the boat on its heading, Artur was told to go to the cabin and secure everything inside the cupboards as best he could. Whilst he was down there, he found some oilskins: he put one on, plus a life jacket. He found four more jackets and decided to bring them up to the crew. Just as he was about to climb up out of the cabin, the boat hit a large wave, throwing Artur off balance. He fell to the floor, sliding towards the back hitting his head in the process on the edge of a cupboard door. He grasped the door, got to his feet and looked about him somewhat dazed. He steadied himself, grabbed the jackets and went out of the cabin. Jean-Luc saw Artur come up.

"What happened to your head, Artur; it's bleeding badly? Are you alright?"

"I'm fine, thank you. Here, put this on," he said, as he handed a life jacket to the skipper. He told Artur to take the wheel while he put it on. He needed nearly all his strength to keep the boat steady, but another large wave caught him unawares. Jean-Luc hurriedly finished putting his jacket on just in time to lend a hand. One of his crew was nearby so he told him to get one of the others to help him to trim the mainsail to under a half, once they had put on their jackets.

"I'll take control now, Artur. You go to give them a hand; make sure you all are attached to the boat using the ties. I don't want anyone going overboard."

The boat was rolling and diving as she went over each wave. Artur attached himself to a tie and handed out two jackets. As soon as Jean-Luc saw Artur and one of the crew were in position, he brought the boat round into the wind, easing the tension on the mainsail. Lowering the mainsail was still a struggle; slowly but surely, they brought the sail to the right position. The boat became more steady; they were pleased to hear the drumming of the motor that was now assisting in the boat's forward movement.

"Now that the mainsail is reduced so much, the boat is a lot easier to control," Jean-Luc said to Artur as he joined him at the wheel. "It's not as difficult keeping her on the correct heading."

The boat continued to be buffeted by the large waves for a further one and a half hours, so their progress was badly affected. Artur continued to look out for enemy ships, but it was only really possible to see anything at a distance when there was an occasional break in the clouds.

"What was your original estimated arrival time in Portsall?" Artur asked Jean-Luc.

"We had hoped to be there by 6 o'clock, but the stormy weather will have knocked us back by at least one or maybe two hours. If we're not moored up by 6:30 a.m., one of the other fishermen will come out looking for us."

Artur thought it was an amazing piece of comradery, but there is war on, he reminded himself. Over the next hour, the waves started to reduce in size, the wind changed from being a south-westerly to a north-westerly. The skipper ordered the crew to raise both sails to their maximum, the motor was stopped and light was beginning to be seen in the East. At this point, they all smiled as they thought the sea Gods were now working in their favour. The next two hours were plain sailing, compared with the hours of the storm.

Artur told the skipper that he could just make out land on the horizon, but Jean-Luc needed the glasses to confirm Artur's sighting.

"Can you make out any prominent places?" Artur was asked after a further thirty minutes.

"There seems to be a tall lighthouse at about 1 o'clock," Artur exclaimed.

"That will be *L'île Vierge*. It's the tallest in Europe; even the Nazis keep it operating to assist their own ships. I'll get a compass bearing on it, draw a line on the chart and work out what our new heading must be."

Jean-Luc altered the boat's direction to the new heading. They were aware that the boat was going through the water more quickly as the wind was now filling the sails. All the crew were near the wheelhouse; they were feeling much happier than they were a few hours earlier. Suddenly, Artur looked to port and, by chance, saw smoke on the horizon—probably from a ship steaming towards them. He quickly drew the others to the possible danger that might be bearing down on them.

"It doesn't appear to be moving," Jean-Luc remarked, as he took a long look through the binoculars. "You may not be aware that from the time Germany took over France in June 1940, many airfields in Normandy and Brittany—and other parts of non-Vichy France—have been taken over and extended. The one at Morlaix, just East of where we are heading for, is used by fighters and bombers of the *Luftwaffe*. My thought is that the ship we can see has been bombed and strafed by aircraft operating out of Morlaix. Artur, you keep watch on that ship and let us know if it gets nearer to us, but with the heading we are on, it should disappear from view before too long, if my theory is correct."

Their boat was making good progress, the weather was cloudy, although the heavy storm clouds had dispersed. After about twenty minutes, Artur reported, with a sense of relief, that the ship was no longer visible.

"The coastline is clearly visible, so get to your stations to bring in the mainsail, but bring in the forward jib in fifteen minutes, when I blow the whistle," Jean-Luc ordered.

They all removed their waterproof gear, replaced their life jackets and moved to their positions. The boat was brought around into the wind as they heard the whistle. They all thought it was a much easier exercise this time and, once completed, the skipper started the engine and brought the boat onto its proper heading.

"We have to watch out for the semi-submerged rocks as we approach the entrance between the two headlands. Fortunately, the chart has them all marked and the tide is in."

After some twenty minutes, the jib was brought in, the engine was reduced to give the boat a speed of about four knots. In next to no time, Jean-Luc saw a fellow fisherman waving from the quay, pointing to a mooring position. The crew put out the fenders on the boat's starboard side as she was brought around next to the mooring. Lines were thrown to the men on the quay who smiled and shouted words of praise at the crew's achievement. Jean-Luc went down to the cabin to complete the log, but there would be no mention of his rendezvous with Jacques' boat, nor that Artur was on board: just a fishing trip as usual.

They all gathered up their belongings, tidied the ropes on the fore and aft decks, checked that everything was secure. The skipper examined the hatches, locked the entrance doors to the cabin and was the last to jump on to the quay. Artur laughed at himself, and the others, as he tried to get his land legs working after the long and bumpy sea crossing.

"Well, gentlemen," Jean-Luc said to his crew, "we have achieved our objective, well done to all of you. I'm sure you would like to return to your homes, but before you do, let me get you a coffee. Madame Claudette's café will be open, I'm sure, even if it's only 8 o'clock in the morning."

"She's been awaiting your arrival for over an hour," one of the other fishermen remarked.

Jean-Luc introduced Artur to the six men that had witnessed their arrival. They shook his hand and welcomed him to the France of the Free French. They all laughed outrageously, probably in relief of being on dry land.

"Are there many German soldiers and military personnel moving about in this area?" Artur enquired.

"More seem to come in each day," one of the men mentioned, as they arrived at the café. "Soon after June last year, the Germans took over as many places as they could along the Normandy and Brittany coastal areas. It meant the *Luftwaffe* were as close to England as they could be for the first phase of the invasion."

"But it didn't work, did it?" Artur retorted with a smile.

"No, but they've changed their tactics to bombing British manufacturing and harbour facilities. Here's your coffee," he said, as he took the mug from Claudette. "Do you want some brandy in it?"

"What a good idea, thank you."

Artur took a sip of his laced black coffee; he felt it warm his whole chest as it went down. It was just what he needed after a long night at sea.

They all talked together very amicably for about thirty-five minutes before Jean-Luc's crew were left to themselves.

"Artur, I must take you to the house where you will be staying; please follow me."

Artur said his farewells to the crew, thanked Claudette for the coffee and followed Jean-Luc up the rue de port. They crossed the road into rue de l'église, knocked on the door of the small fishing cottage and waited.

"Madame Delphine, I believe you are expecting to give accommodation to a man coming from England?" The lady nodded and smiled as Jean-Luc mentioned Artur's name.

"Please come in, messieurs. I'm sorry the place is not very tidy, but I haven't long been awake." She led them into a small lounge that had a square dining table at the far end. She drew the curtains of the window overlooking the road.

"How was your trip, Jean-Luc?"

"It was better than expected, thank you." He had pointed out earlier to Artur that Madame Delphine was Jacques' youngest sister. She had helped as many as nine British pilots avoid the German military in the last four months, before sending them to England from Portsall. Artur said he was impressed. He wondered to himself how she dealt with the Germans that must surely have come looking for them.

"I expect you have already had a coffee at Claudette's, so if you'll excuse me for a moment, Jean-Luc, I will show Artur to his room."

The two of them went upstairs into a small room facing the back garden. There was a single bed, a large wardrobe and a chest of drawers with a towel on it. "I hope you will be comfortable in here, Artur. Jacques told me you wouldn't be staying more than one night before going off somewhere else. By the way, the bathroom is downstairs, next to the kitchen."

"It's very good of you to be putting me up," Artur remarked, as he put his kitbag and beret on the bed. They went downstairs to join Jean-Luc.

"If it's alright with the two of you," Jean-Luc said, "I must go now and see my family, but tell me Delphine, have the German soldiers been to the village during my absence?"

"Not that I am aware of. I must warn you, Artur, that the SS pay us frequent visits here in Portsall and other fishing villages nearby. We believe there is at least one informer here, so do take extra care. With a village like ours, people will be very curious about your arrival and wonder why you are here, especially as you are not in a pilot's uniform."

"I understand," Artur replied, "thank you for the warning."

Jean-Luc made his way to the front door, embraced Delphine and shook Artur firmly by the hand.

"I have been told very little about why you are here, but only when you will be leaving," she said, as they went back into the lounge.

"I'll need to leave tomorrow morning. I believe there is a bus service that goes to Quimper; do you have a time table?"

"There is, but you will have to change in Brest. It will take you over four hours unless someone drives you part of the way. I know someone who often goes that way; I'll go and speak to him while you are resting."

"That's very kind of you," Artur replied with his usual engaging smile. He left the room for the bathroom to attend to the wound on his head then went upstairs. He took off most of his clothes, settled himself into bed, falling asleep instantly. Artur slept for many hours during Sunday, only rising for a meal provided by Delphine at 7:30 p.m.

"We need to talk about your leaving tomorrow and where you want to go to," she said, after they had finished their meal together. "Please tell me your final destination, I will help you if I can: you can trust me, Artur."

"What I told you this morning was not entirely correct: I need to be near to Vannes;" again, he deliberately gave her the wrong destination

"While you were asleep, I went to speak to a man called Gabriel, who drives to Châteaulin almost every other Monday to visit his sick mother; luckily for you he's going tomorrow. He understands the risk, but he is willing to take you. If you are going with him, I said you would be at his house by 8:15 a.m. He'll drop you at the bus station where you can get one that will take you to Vannes. Oh, I nearly forgot: I was sent your measurements by someone in London for me to get you some clothes," she said as she picked up a parcel from the floor beside her chair and handed it to him. "They are not new, but have been washed."

"Thank you for everything, Delphine, you have been most kind. At this moment, I don't know if I will be returning this way to get back to England, but if I do, I'll call here first."

"You will always be welcome," she said, as Artur stood up saying that he needed to get some more sleep before what might be a few difficult days ahead.

Chapter 12
Monday, 7 April 1941

Delphine knocked on Artur's door at 7 o'clock, at the same time telling him that there was breakfast for him in the kitchen. He was immediately awake, thanking her for the call. After some twenty minutes, he was dressed in some of the clothes Delphine had given him and downstairs with his kitbag and beret.

"Good morning, Artur. It seems you slept well?"

"I had a very comfortable night's sleep," he replied, as he smiled at her.

"Please help yourself to bread and jam. Would you like a coffee?"

"Yes, please, black."

He sat down, helping himself to some breakfast. Delphine joined him and knocked his leg with hers as she did so. She apologised, shifting her position as they smiled at each other. He found her very attractive: thought she was in her mid-twenties. He hoped he might return to Portsall, but he thought the chances were probably very slim.

"I will walk you to Gabriel's house: it will take about ten minutes so we'll leave at 8 o'clock," she said as she got up from the table to clear the things away.

Artur saw the clock on the wall showed 7:50 a.m. He thanked Delphine for breakfast as he left for the bathroom. After five minutes, he was in the lounge looking out of the window: he was pleased to see it wasn't raining.

"Are you ready to leave, Artur?" Delphine said from the doorway.

"All ready to go."

They left the house in the direction of the port, then turned right at the first road. It took a further seven minutes to arrive at a small house on the left. Delphine opened the small gate and knocked on the door.

"Good morning, Gabriel. I have brought Artur Selmer," she said, as she stood to one side for the two men to shake hands.

"Pleased to meet you, Monsieur Selmer. If you are ready, we should leave immediately, just in case we get caught up in any road blocks. I don't want to be late at my mother's or she will get worried," he said with a smile. "You know what mothers can be like!"

"I quite understand," Artur replied. He looked at Gabriel as he reversed his black Citroën saloon out of the driveway: he thought he was probably in his late forties, maybe a bit older. Artur said 'goodbye' and 'thank you' to Delphine, stepped into the passenger seat of the car and placed his kitbag between his feet. They both waved as they left her standing in the street.

Once they were out of the village and heading for the outskirts of Brest, Artur asked Gabriel:

"How long do you expect it will take to reach Châteaulin?"

"Just over two hours, but I like to stop at a favourite café of mine—just south of Daoulas—in Le Faou. I also tend to keep off the main roads as the Germans sometimes have roadblocks on the main ones. They're never in the same place, but some of the soldiers can get rather aggressive—not to mention the SS. What is more important is that I don't want to cause any problems for you, especially as you are not known around Finistère."

Artur mumbled his thanks to Gabriel for his concern as he watched the countryside drift by. They passed through Landerneau after just over an hour, followed a narrow, windy road to Le Faou, arriving half an hour later. They drove towards the centre of the village, took the road to the left and parked the car opposite the café.

"Good morning, Gabriel," the young lady said, as they walked inside. "Not on your own today, I see."

"No, this is my friend, Artur. He's visiting me from near Boulogne to visit my mother. He's a distant relative of hers."

Artur grinned at Gabriel's story. He smiled at the woman and greeted her as he looked around to see who else was there.

"You've just missed the Bosch, Gabriel. There were four of them, asking lots of questions, like they often do. Do you want your usual? And what would Monsieur Artur like?"

Gabriel asked for his usual large, white coffee, whilst Artur said he would like a large black. They took their seats at the table by the front window; the coffees arrived after a few minutes. Conversation was slow between them, even after Artur had asked about Gabriel's sick mother: she apparently lived on her own in the large family house.

Artur noticed some activity further up the road only to see some German officers' cars come quickly past the café.

"They seem to be in a hurry," Gabriel commented. "At least they're not going our way. I think we should drink up and be on our way."

They downed their coffees, thanked the lady and went out to the car. Artur was relieved to see his kitbag was still tucked up in the passenger well. Gabriel noticed the time and started to drive faster out of the village

"Does your mother live in the town?" Artur asked.

He was just about to give his answer when they were stopped by several members of the German military after they rounded a corner before entering the village of St Ségal.

"Papers," one of the soldiers said, in German, once Gabriel had wound down his window.

Artur didn't know if Gabriel spoke German, nor did he know if the German soldier spoke French, but he whispered to Gabriel that they should stay in the car until they were forced out.

"PAPERS," the man shouted, pointing his gun at Gabriel's head.

Artur had two sets of papers with him, but he had placed the ones he thought he would be needing in his satchel. He took them out of his satchel without the soldier noticing where they had come from. He quickly checked them and waved them in the air.

"PASS them to me," the German shouted, but Artur pretended not to understand. He wound down his window, again waving his papers near his open window. Clearly the soldier was getting angry: he kicked the front offside tyre twice very hard.

"Where are you going?" the soldier shouted. "Give me your papers."

"We don't speak German," Artur replied very slowly and emphatically in French.

An officer that had been standing at the back of the group watching what was going on, walked forward to Artur's window.

"Your papers, please messieurs," he said in broken French.

Artur passed his and Gabriel's papers to the officer. Artur then smiled at the soldier who was still standing by Gabriel's door.

"Get out of the car, please," the officer said, again in broken French, but Artur stayed where he was; he told Gabriel to do the same.

The officer studied the papers, looked down a list of names on his pad, then back at Artur.

"Why you here, Herr Selmer, and you living in Boulogne?" again in broken French.

"I come to visit my sick aunt with my cousin," Artur replied, slowly in French.

The officer retreated back to his truck with the papers, leaving the other four men guarding the car. He returned to Artur's window after a few minutes.

"I want look in boot," he instructed.

Arthur asked Gabriel for the keys, slowly got out of the car, opening the boot lid with the officer standing next to him.

"What's that?" he said in German, pointing to a large box that had a few holes in the sides. Artur pretended not to understand.

"Open!" he ordered, in German, as he touched the box. Artur had no idea what was in the box, but as it was tied with a coloured ribbon, he thought it must be for Gabriel's mother. The knot was very tightly tied so Artur took a long time to get anywhere. The officer was getting impatient with Artur, so he took his knife from the scabbard hanging from his belt and cut the ribbon in two places, at the same time opening the lid. Artur tried not to appear surprised when he and the officer saw a small kitten staring out at them.

"It's a present for my aunt," he said slowly in French. "It is her birthday soon and she likes cats."

Artur saw the officer smile for a brief moment, close the lid and return to his more usual manner.

"Anything else?" the officer enquired brusquely.

Artur shook his head as the officer told one of the junior soldiers to write down the vehicle's registration number, together with all the details of the occupants from their identification papers. When this was completed, the officer handed their papers back, gave Artur and Gabriel the Nazi salute with the customary '*Heil Hitler*', telling them to proceed. The two of them got back into the car and drove off without responding, or even looking at any of the men.

"I'm glad I had that box with the kitten in it," Gabriel remarked with a smile. "If the officer had looked under the rug, he would have found my rifle and ammunition."

"But why the box with the kitten?" Artur asked. "Surely it isn't really for your mother, is it?"

"Not really. My mother asked me to get one for her neighbour whose cat was run over a few weeks ago."

They proceeded in silence, but each man was relieved that they had got away with their story—maybe not next time, Artur reckoned.

"We'll be coming to the station soon, Artur. The bus station is just around the corner. Delphine said you wanted to go to Vannes, is that right?" Artur nodded.

Gabriel brought the car to a halt at the entrance to the bus station. Artur noticed there were German soldiers at various points, checking people's identity papers. He put on his beret, retrieved his kitbag from the front of the passenger seat well and joined Gabriel at the nearest bus stop: he was looking at a timetable.

"There's a bus going to Vannes at 11:25 a.m.," as he looked at his watch. "If it's on time—and it often isn't—you will only have thirty minutes to wait."

"It's very good of you to bring me here, Gabriel. Does your mother live far away?"

"She lives in St Coulitz. She has a house with a garden going down to the river. She's getting rather frail, the garden's too much for her and she is very nervous about how the Germans are treating France and its people. I've been coming down nearly every two weeks since we threw in the towel in June last year. I keep telling her that if things get worse—which they probably will—I might not be able to come down at all. The Nazis are starting to take our farm produce and grabbing our young men to either work in the armament factories or putting them straight into the *Wehrmacht* as soldiers. My two older brothers have sons and they've been drafted into the German army."

"That sounds dreadful. No wonder your mother's getting nervous. Anyway, Gabriel, I must go to get my ticket and wait for the bus to arrive. Hope your mother's neighbour likes the kitten," he said with a smile. "All the best and thanks once again," Artur shook his hand then strode off to the booking hall.

"There's a bus going to Vannes very soon, please can you tell me if it goes on to St Nazaire?"

The ticket clerk looked at the time table.

"No, it doesn't, you'll need to catch a different bus in Vannes. There's one that leaves ten minutes after yours arrives."

"Please may I buy a return to St Nazaire?" Artur thought it best that he bought a return ticket, even though he was fairly certain he wouldn't be coming back the same way. He handed the clerk some money and took back the change with the ticket.

"Have a good journey, monsieur. Your bus goes from stop number six. Please be aware that the German military and the SS are much in evidence once you get close to Lorient: there's something going on down that part of the coast."

"Thank you. I will take great care."

Chapter 13
Monday, 7 April 1941

Artur saw that Gabriel had already driven off, as he walked to the bus stop where there were several people standing. He tried not to appear too conspicuous, but there wasn't much he could do about his clean clothes: only his kitbag looked out of place for a Frenchman. Nearly ten minutes went by then a bus arrived at the stop: thirteen people got off. The driver and the conductor went to the booking hall, so nobody was allowed onto the bus till they returned.

"Ready to leave in five minutes," the driver said as he climbed into the bus. The conductor followed, ushering people inside one at a time, checking and stamping their tickets.

Artur sat on the right-hand side on the back seat, so he could see what was going on: who got off and—more importantly—who got on. He counted sixteen people on board, including himself. By all accounts, the bus wasn't due to stop many times unless a passenger pressed the bell. Two women got off in Quimper, where the bus waited for five minutes, but nobody got on.

"Next main stop is Lorient," the driver informed everyone, then set off.

After just over an hour, not far from the outskirts of Lorient, the bus was waved down at a roadblock. One of the soldiers knocked on the door for the conductor to open it. Two men of the SS climbed in, walked up the aisle looking closely at everyone, asking only the men for their identity papers and tickets.

All the passengers were near the front of the bus, most being husband and wife except three, Artur thought; it meant the soldiers had to walk half the length of the bus to get to Artur. He greeted them politely, handed over his documents and waited for them to be handed back. The more senior one examined the photo on the identity card, looked at Artur, looked again at the photo, then spoke to the second soldier telling him to fetch the officer in charge. Artur understood what was said, but didn't let the men know. As the man turned to go back down the bus, Artur asked him—slowly in French—if there was a problem.

"All the men on this bus are local to this area and are over fifty-five except for you," the soldier said, in German. Artur said he did not understand, shrugged his shoulders and looked straight ahead of him.

The man returned to the bus with a senior SS officer. When he reached Artur, he stared hard at him, then back at the identity card. Artur decided it would be better if he stood up.

"What are you doing in this part of France?" he said in broken French.

"I'm meeting my aunt who lives near St Nazaire," he replied very slowly, looking him straight in the eyes, even though the officer was several centimetres taller than him. "As you see, I have a return ticket for Friday," Artur explained, again very slowly, thinking it might help.

"Come," the officer ordered, at the same time taking hold of his arm and pulling him towards the front of the bus. To Artur's surprise, most of the male passengers got up from their seats and stood in the aisle, preventing the officer from taking Artur off the bus. He shouted at them, drew his pistol from the holster on his belt and pointed it at the head of one of the passengers standing by his seat.

"I shoot," he said, "if you not sit."

The man didn't move, nor did any of the others. The officer pulled the trigger, but deliberately fired past the man's head, breaking the window, causing splinters of glass to fall on a woman sitting next to it. She screamed as she got to her feet, blood was coming from her face and hands. Artur wanted to move towards her to help, but he was held back by the senior SS man.

"Next time I kill," the officer said, again in poor French.

At that moment, the six men that were close to the three SS men, rushed them, bringing them down in the aisle. However hard they tried to get up or respond, the SS men were pinned down on the floor. Artur pushed his hand into his kitbag, unfastened the false bottom and brought out his pistol.

"If you try to do anything more to anyone else on this bus, I will kill you all," he said in clear German to the SS officer and his two men, as he grabbed the officer's pistol. "Get up, get off this bus and let these people continue their journey without further delay."

Slowly, the three were released by those passengers who were holding them down. They were pushed to the front of the bus where they got off. Artur gave a handkerchief to the injured woman saying that she didn't look too badly injured. The officer ordered the barrier to be lifted, the bus drove past the other men and on towards Lorient. Once the bus was out of sight of the group of men at the roadblock, everyone on board turned to Artur, who was now back in his seat, they smiled and applauded. He gave a little wave as he put his and the officer's pistol into his kitbag. It was a very satisfactory outcome, but he knew he would now be a wanted man, especially by the SS. His description and identity details would be forwarded to other units between Brest and St Nazaire—possibly elsewhere too.

The driver drove the bus up to the bus station in Lorient. The conductor went up to the injured woman, escorted her off the bus and up to the office. Five other people's journeys ended at Lorient, but not before coming up to Artur, shaking his hand and thanking him for saving them from the Germans. The driver got off, went to the ticket office and made his report about the journey from Châteaulin—making special mention of the smashed window. A technical man came to the bus, measured the window, cut a piece of card to the right size and fixed it in position.

Ten minutes later, a new driver led the conductor to the bus. Before he took his seat, he addressed everyone saying that he hoped they would have a less eventful trip to Vannes and on to St Nazaire, to which they all nodded. He told them they would be late getting to Vannes, but it was out of his control. All he could do was to apologise.

As the bus made its way out of Lorient and across the Blavet river, Artur thought about the incident with the SS: the officer in particular. He decided he would get off at Auray or Vannes rather than go all the way to St Nazaire. He was sure the SS officer would send word to his superiors who would arrange for him to be taken off the bus further up the road. The more he thought about it, the more he favoured his idea, especially as he had been given the name of a contact in Auray by Charles; he felt that it would be the right option under the circumstance.

After nearly an hour, they approached Auray. Artur rang the bell. The bus didn't go down to the port area, but swung into a small carpark that was also used by buses. As he walked up the aisle, everyone wished him an enjoyable stay in Auray. The conductor knew Artur had a ticket through to St Nazaire and wondered why he was getting off at Auray.

"It's such a pleasant day," he said, as he put on his beret, "and after all the business with the SS, I need something to eat and drink before continuing my journey."

"I quite understand, monsieur," the conductor said. Examining his watch, he told Artur there would be another bus to St Nazaire at about 4 o'clock, to which Artur thanked him as they shook hands.

The walk down to the port was a little under a mile. He went along the quay and saw a bar on the corner by the road going up to the right.

"Could I have a large black coffee, please, plus a pastry of some sorts?" he asked the young woman who had come out to greet him.

The sun was quite warm for the time of year, so he chose to sit outside—he felt he needed some fresh air after all the excitement in the bus. In next to no time, she arrived at his table. He thanked her with his customary smile, took the bill, placed it under the ashtray and took a sip of the hot coffee. He looked around as he ate his pastry to see a few German soldiers sitting at a table of one of the other nearby cafés, laughing with a young girl. He watched the men chatting up the girl for some minutes, then decided to go inside.

"May I use the toilet, please?" he asked the woman behind the till.

"By all means, monsieur. It's out of the door at the back of the café," as she pointed to further inside. "Here's the key." Artur took the key and found his way to the cubicle in the back yard—a typical French toilet with a hole in the ground and sunken-shaped feet to stand on. On returning inside the café, he asked the woman if she knew a person called François, who lives in rue Saint-René.

"I don't recognise the man's name, but the street you mention is just around the corner from here. Out of the café, turn right and then right again: that is rue Saint-René."

Artur thanked her and returned to his table. He was relieved to see his kitbag was still on the other chair as he had forgotten to take it with him when he went inside. He finished his coffee and pastry, paid the waitress and got ready to leave. He took a last look at the nearby café where the German soldiers had been only to find they had left: he saw them walking arm in arm with the girl. He left the café, turned right then right again: he was in the street he needed. He had memorised the address that Charles had given him and walked up the street as the house numbers increased. He stopped outside the house he needed, knocked on the door and waited, hoping someone was at home. He heard noises inside, he felt hopeful. The door was opened by an attractive young woman.

"Can I help you, monsieur?" she said with a friendly smile.

"Sorry to trouble you, but am I right in thinking that François lives here?"

"Yes, he does, but who shall I say you are?"

"Just say it's Artur, please."

The woman disappeared in through a door to a back room, leaving it ajar behind her. A few minutes later, a man came to the front door.

"There's a bird on your roof." Artur used the agreed opening coded sentence; he waited for the precise response.

"Have no fear, it is friendly," François said with a hint of a smile. Artur was satisfied with the reply.

"My name is Artur Selmer. I was instructed by London to contact you, should I need your assistance."

"You are very welcome here, Artur; please come in. Does anyone know you've come here?" he said, as Artur went inside. The door was then closed behind him and it was locked.

"I asked the woman at the café overlooking the port for directions to rue Saint-René. I didn't mention your house number, but I did ask her if she knew someone called François."

"Artur, you must be much more careful. Not only are there German military and SS men all over the coast from north of Lorient down to St Nazaire and beyond, but there are French informers and moles working for them. The presence and activity of the Germans has increased significantly over the last six months following their interest in developing the ports of Lorient and St Nazaire for their U-boats. Sorry to lecture you as soon as you arrive in my house, but you will be seen as a new man around here: some will wonder about you. We all cannot be too careful. Anyway, come on through to the kitchen."

Artur felt suitably chastised, but was not going to say sorry for his lapse of care; he knew François was right with everything that he said. He followed him into the kitchen, took off his beret, put his kitbag on the floor next to the dresser and was told to sit at the table. A bottle of red wine and three glasses were brought to the table.

"Artur, this is my wife Madelaine," he said. They exchanged greetings as François opened the bottle and poured out the wine. They all touched glasses, but François still looked rather serious.

"You don't have to tell me everything, but how was your journey to Auray?"

"I was brought by fishing boat to the Brittany coast, then bus to Auray from Châteaulin."

"Did you encounter any road blocks on the way?"

Artur told them about the SS men, how they were apprehended by some of the male passengers when the officer wanted to take Artur off the bus. "Here," he said, as he drew his hand from his kitbag, "I managed to take the SS officer's Luger pistol before he was ordered off the bus."

"That could be a very useful acquisition; we don't have many small arms. Let me take a look at it, I'll see if I have any ammunition for it," as Artur handed him the pistol.

"It looks like the standard weapon supplied to the SS; it has the double SS marks on the top side of the grip." François ran the pistol through his hands, extracted the magazine to find that one bullet had been used.

"Do you know when this was fired?"

Artur told him more of what happened on the bus and how he managed to take the pistol from the officer. The magazine was placed back in the grip and the pistol put down on the table.

"Please can you tell me a little about your mission in France?" as he refilled their glasses. "I would just like to know where I might be able to help you."

"I need to get to the port of St Nazaire. As you have already said, the Nazis are wanting to use Lorient and St Nazaire for U-boat bases. From there, they can more easily attack the convoys coming from across the Atlantic. I have been asked to make notes of the construction sites and take photos. I then take them back to London where the powers-that-be will devise a plan on how best to demolish the site or just severely delay the building program."

François rubbed his chin as he thought about the operation.

"Sorry, Artur, I forgot to ask you if you'd had anything to eat recently?" he enquired, as he broke off from what he was considering, looking at his watch.

"Not since this morning, except a pastry this afternoon at the café."

"Madelaine, even if it is only 4:45 p.m., could you please rustle up a little something for Artur? We'll have a proper meal later."

"I would like to mention," said Artur, "that I am expecting to catch a bus to St Nazaire, walk around the dry dock area taking photos."

"You make it sound all too easy, Artur. I can assure you that your task will be far from straightforward. Thousands of men have been drafted for these two building projects. The *Wehrmacht* and the SS are standing guard and keeping a very watchful eye on the area, particularly at St Nazaire. What I suggest is that I take you most of the way on my motor bike. I can also give you the name of a reliable and trustworthy contact in Gron, a few kilometres North West of St Nazaire. In fact, we could go there tomorrow. What do you say?"

Madelaine came over from the far side of the table to place a ham and cheese baguette in front of Artur. He thanked her and smiled as he took his first bite of real food for several hours.

"That's very good of you, François. What I would like to suggest though is that we do go out tomorrow; you can show me where your contact's house is. We'll also see how close we can get to the construction area at the port, as well as where the main guards and sentries are."

Artur finished his baguette in double quick time: he didn't realise how hungry he was. They continued to talk about various aspects of the war for a further forty-five minutes as they finished a second bottle of wine.

"Sorry, Artur, I've forgotten my manners: there is a small toilet next to the front door; let me show you the room you can use. It's a bit small—rather like a box room—but the bed is comfortable."

François led Artur upstairs to a back room that was next to the bathroom. Artur took out his small washbag from his kitbag and went to the bathroom to freshen up. He looked in the mirror at his hair and reckoned he would put more dye on it in the morning; the wound had stopped bleeding. He returned to his room, putting his kitbag under the bed before returning down to the kitchen.

"Have you got everything you need, Artur?"

"Yes, I have. Thank you."

"By the way, Artur, I need to tell you that my real name is Hugo: François is my agent name. That's probably why the woman at the café didn't recognise that name, or associate it with the street name of Saint-René! You had better call me Hugo from now on."

Artur was not going to divulge his real name, especially as all his documents referred to him by his agent name.

After some thirty minutes, Hugo suggested that they should go out, walk around the port, have a drink at a bar he knew well and then have a meal. Madelaine and Artur readily agreed.

Chapter 14
Tuesday, 8 April 1941

Artur woke up with a bit of a head. He remembered some of the previous evening's events, but not everything. He hoped he hadn't said anything that might have blown his cover or referred to his mission. He went to the bathroom, had a good wash and shaved. He put more dye in his hair, at the same time checking that the camera was still in his hair brush, which of course it was. He dressed, went down to the kitchen to see Madelaine and Hugo smiling at him as he entered.

"What seems to be so funny?" he said, as he stared at them both. "Are my flies undone?" as he looked down at his trousers.

"No, it's not that; they're fine. Don't you remember being at that bar after we had eaten? There was a small group playing dance music. You decided to dance the tango with one of the waitresses. You were fantastic, she was really smitten. So much so that she wanted to come back here and spend the night with you. The *pièce de résistance*, however, was when you chose to dance with one of the German soldiers sitting at the table in front of the toilet door," Hugo said, laughing heartily as he did so.

"I don't recall any of that, you must be making it up."

"I most certainly am not, am I Madelaine?" She nodded in agreement and laughed into her hands that were close to her face.

"What you then did—once the Germans had gone—was to mimic Adolf Hitler, at the same time playing German military marching songs on the piano. The place was a riot, everyone was laughing as they followed your actions. Many of them were still holding their sides with laughter as they fell to the ground. The manager said it was the best night's entertainment for many months."

"Oh, my goodness! I don't remember that at all. I have to tell you, however, that there was an occasion in late May last year when I did similar Hitler impersonations and played the piano. It made the same sort of impression on the people in the pub in England, but I hadn't had much to drink that time."

"Never mind, Artur, all the people in the bar enjoyed your performance. I thought I had better mention it now in case we meet some of the people today as we go through the port. Anyway, you obviously slept well so how about some breakfast?"

"A large, strong black coffee first of all, please."

"Coming up," Madelaine replied.

"We've already had ours," Hugo remarked, "so when you've finished yours, I'll go through what we should do today regarding the visit to St Nazaire."

Artur mumbled 'yes' as he bit into his roll, butter and jam. The coffee duly arrived. After he'd taken a second mouthful, he looked at his watch to see it was nearly 9:30 a.m. He couldn't believe it was that late. Within fifteen minutes, Artur had finished and was feeling much more human.

"The way I see it is this," Hugo said, as he spread out a detailed map that contained Vannes and St Nazaire.

"We'll take this road," Hugo pointed it out on the map, "then come into St Nazaire on this very minor road via Herbignac and Saint-André-des-Eaux. Going this way will take us almost directly to the port. Remember, this is only meant to be a recce so we can stop at cafés and bars as close to the port as we can be, if we wish to. I assume you have some change of clothes so that, when you go in for real tomorrow or the day after, you might not be so easily recognised if you are also seen today? Do you understand me, Artur?"

"Of course. As you can see, I'm wearing the same as yesterday, but I have quite different things for tomorrow."

"That's good news. It's after 10 o'clock so we ought to be leaving in about ten minutes, we might then be back in time for a slightly late lunch," Hugo said, as he looked at Madelaine, who smiled.

"My motor bike is in the shed in the back garden. I looked it over earlier this morning before you woke up," he said, with a big grin as Artur put on his beret.

The two men said their goodbyes to Madelaine, went out of the back door to the shed. As Hugo opened the door, Artur saw a bright blue two-seater bike.

"What a fantastic machine, Hugo. It looks so new."

"Thanks, Artur. It's a 500cc Peugeot P515: my pride and joy. I suggest you tuck the bottom of your trousers into your socks. It doesn't look as though it will rain today, so we don't need any waterproof jackets. I forgot to ask you earlier: are you alright with being on a bike?"

"Yes, thanks, I'm fine." Artur wasn't going to tell Hugo about his mission in March 1940 when he and George had used a much smaller bike, escaping from the Germans.

Hugo wheeled his bike out through the gate from the back garden into a sort of alleyway that went down to the port road. Hugo climbed on, started the engine and invited Artur to get on the back. They went slowly down to the port and were soon on the road to Vannes where Hugo put the bike through its paces for about twenty-five minutes. He slowed down so Artur could hear him say that they would be stopping at a café he knew in Muzillac. They went up a side road in the centre of the village, parked the bike outside the café and went inside.

"Monsieur Hugo," said the florid-faced man that came from behind the counter to greet him. "How good to see you after so many weeks."

"This is my friend Artur, from near Boulogne; he's visiting me for a few days."

"Artur, this is André, the mad owner of this establishment," as he prodded André in his oversized belly.

Artur took his hand, but it was a warm, flabby, slightly damp shake; one that he didn't want to hold on to for more than a moment. There was something about André that he didn't like.

"How are things in the Boulogne area, Artur?"

"It has been badly bombed, houses wrecked by artillery fire, it's full of German soldiers. Much like other French ports and seaside places."

"Would you like a coffee, Artur?" Hugo asked. "A large black one, as usual?"

"Yes, please."

André went back behind the counter to make the coffees—Artur watched him closely when he wasn't looking his way. After some minutes, André brought the coffees to the table by the window that Artur had chosen.

Hugo talked to some of the other customers that he seemed to know quite well; Artur enjoyed his drink. Eventually, Hugo came to the table, drank his coffee in one go and stood in front of Artur.

"We ought to be on our way," he said, as he moved towards the door. Artur followed, thanked André as he went out and saw that he was being watched. Artur wanted to ask Hugo about the café owner, but felt it was the wrong time to do so. They got back on the bike, headed for Herbignac after about seven minutes down a narrow road. It was not well made up so they travelled quite slowly; it wasn't very comfortable for Artur on the pillion seat. A few miles on the other side of Herbignac, Hugo stopped at the roadside near a wooden seat.

"I need to look at the map to see where we go from here, Artur," as they got off the bike.

He stood the bike up on its stand, took the map from his pocket and lay it out on the seat.

"We are here," he said, as he pointed to a position on the map. "We need to get to here, coming in on the road from the West that goes around this large marshy area. I am reliably informed that the German hierarchy have stationed thousands of soldiers around the coast to set up the Atlantic Wall, as they call it: this is to prepare for an Allied invasion. So, when we get nearer to St Nazaire, we will undoubtedly get stopped. My aim is for us to get to the railway station where we can reasonably safely leave the bike."

"I've got my papers in my satchel and I'm wearing my beret, so I'm ready," Artur said reassuringly with a smile.

They got back onto the bike, covering the next sixteen kilometres to Saint-André-des-Eaux in under twenty minutes. Hugo slowed down and told Artur that they ought to be at the station in a little over ten minutes. Just after they took the turning to the centre of St Nazaire, they saw a roadblock fifty metres ahead of them.

Hugo slowed the bike down and stopped just in front of one of the soldier's boots: the soldier glared at Hugo. Artur climbed off the back and stood facing three men as Hugo got off and put the bike on its stand.

"Where are you going?" one of them said in German. Both of them pretended not to understand, although Hugo knew for certain that Artur could speak the language well. Both of them shrugged their shoulders with Hugo saying, very slowly in French, that they were visiting a friend in Donges—deliberately giving the wrong place name.

"Papers," the leading soldier demanded, pushing Hugo in the chest with his rifle.

Hugo knew where his papers were, but slowly went through all his pockets before taking something out of the last one; he smiled at Artur. The soldier snatched the papers from his hand only to find that it was a folded map of Paris.

"What is this?" the soldier shouted. "Papers."

Hugo walked slowly over to his bike, opened one of the paniers, pulled out some papers, strolled back to the group of soldiers and handed them to a different man. Artur wanted to laugh at all this time-wasting, but he knew he shouldn't: it could complicate the situation. The papers were handed to the leading soldier who examined the photo. He looked at Hugo and back at the photo several times. He passed the papers to the officer who stood towards the back of the group, which by now comprised of eight men.

"What is the purpose of your visit?" the officer said in understandable French.

Hugo repeated what he had said earlier.

"Do you know that you are about to enter a restricted area around the port?"

"We didn't know about any restrictions." Hugo replied.

Artur thought he would chip in and chance his arm, after he had handed over his papers that had been asked for.

"We are two Frenchmen, this is our country, you are only here for a short time, we expect to be allowed to go through the barrier to see our friend who is sick."

"Where you come from?" the officer asked, looking at Hugo.

"We have come from Redon," Hugo replied, as he looked at Artur giving him a wink: unnoticed by the soldiers.

"Perhaps you could accompany us to our friend in Donges? We will probably come to more roadblocks so you would be able to help us get through more easily."

The officer spoke to the men in German about Hugo's idea. He ordered two of them to fetch the motor bike with sidecar attached and return to the barrier. Artur could hardly believe what he had heard the officer say. Within several minutes, the bike with a sidecar arrived: the man in the sidecar held two rifles: both were powerful Mausers, but one was a sniper's rifle with telescopic sights.

"The driver knows where Donges is: some of his fellow soldiers are billeted there. You will follow him," the officer said to them in reasonable French, as he returned Hugo's and Artur's papers to them. The officer gave them a Nazi salute, clicked his heels and wished their friend a good recovery.

Chapter 15
Tuesday, 8 April 1941

On their way back to Hugo's bike, he whispered to Artur that he had an idea of how they could escape from the German motorbike and go to the station as planned. Artur expressed his concern saying that today's drive was supposed to be a recce, not the real thing. Hugo ignored Artur's concern; anyway, he was the one driving the bike.

The German bike set off, followed by Hugo's. About ten minutes later, Artur saw the sign pointing straight on for the station. The German bike was nearly forty metres ahead of them so, just before it took a left turn, Hugo slowed down to increase the distance between the two bikes. Artur guessed was going to happen; he held on tight as Hugo suddenly opened up the throttle. They were sure the man in the sidecar hadn't seen them, but they knew it wouldn't be long before they would come looking for them.

Hugo slowed the bike down as they neared the station entrance and turned right up a road that went to the Grand Hotel. At the entrance, he asked the commissionaire if he could park his bike around the side of the hotel. He told him he wanted it out of sight as it was very precious to him. He slipped him a ten Franc note for the favour: they smiled at each other. The bike was soon hidden from view behind half a dozen crates.

"According to my friend in Gron, this hotel—and others in St Nazaire—is frequented by many German officers," Hugo said, as they walked back from the side of the hotel. "We will have to be very careful." They turned left down a street that led to the port, past the Hôtel de Ville. There was considerable building activity to their left with some large artillery emplacements on their right already in position pointing out to sea.

Artur asked Hugo to stop for a moment as he dug deep into his right-hand trouser pocket.

"I was given this camera by my boss in London. He told me to take plenty of pictures that could then be analysed by the boffins."

"Wow, I've not seen a camera that small before. Where was it made?"

Artur told him most of what he knew. He put the camera to his eye, pulled out the left side to reveal the lens and viewfinder. He took three photos of the guns to the right, followed by two of the area being built on to his left—perhaps for more artillery guns. He then looked almost straight ahead to a section near the dry dock: there were many people building something vast—probably out of concrete—he took more pictures. He quickly pushed the camera together before returning it to his pocket.

"I thought you were going to do all this tomorrow," Hugo stated, rather firmly.

"That was the plan, but I really couldn't miss this opportunity when we are so close to the port. We might not get the chance tomorrow."

They walked on a little bit further. Artur asked to see the map; they stopped to take a look.

"Instead of coming here tomorrow, would it be possible for you to take me to the other side, to somewhere near Mindin, as he put his finger on the place name?"

Hugo thought for a moment, he carefully studied the map.

"It would mean going towards Nantes, over the bridge at Bouguenais, then west via Paimbœuf. It's quite a long trek, Artur, but not possible today. Are you sure you'll be near enough to the port to get good photos?"

"Maybe. The other consideration, as I look across the estuary from here, is what artillery and how many members of the *Wehrmacht* will be on that side."

Just at that moment, they both heard the sound of a motorbike in a nearby street to their right.

"That must be the men with the sidecar looking for us," Artur said, as he looked in the direction of where the sound was coming from. They both instinctively ran up the next road to their left, towards the railway station. They went past the main postal depot on their right, along a track that they saw would lead them to the many wagons on the main sidings. They slowed to a walking pace, occasionally looking behind them. They stopped for a moment: there was no sound of the motorbike.

"I reckon," Artur said, "they've stopped to ask someone if they had seen us and asked them which way we might have gone. Hopefully, if they weren't pro-German, and we had been seen, they might have put them on to a false trail."

"We can't rely on that, so we had better press on," Hugo responded. As they reached the first of the wagons, Artur noticed a group of German soldiers on the other side of the railway lines. They were about 100 metres further on, marching away from them. The two of them ducked behind a wagon, but were still able to see the platoon of about thirty soldiers under the command of an officer.

"We had better wait here for a while until they get further ahead of us," Artur suggested, as he took charge of the situation. At that moment, they heard the bike again. It was coming up the road on the far side of the sidings heading for the end of the *Bassin de Penhoët*.

"Keep hidden behind the wheel of the wagon. Once they've gone past, we'll turn back towards the road that leads to the Grand Hotel. I'm sure they won't keep their search up for much longer."

"Which way should we go to get back to Vannes and Auray?" Artur asked, as they started to walk back the way they had come.

"We'll have to hope the sidecar men will soon have to return to the officer at the roadblock to tell him they couldn't find us. That means we'll initially need to head for Nantes. I'll have a good look at the map once we get to the bike."

Artur looked at his watch: it was well after midday; they could make out the Grand Hotel at the end of the road—no sign of the bike and sidecar. The same commissionaire was on duty, so they greeted each other as they arrived.

"There were two Germans with a sidecar looking for you soon after you left. I told them I hadn't seen you," he said with a broad grin. Hugo thanked him, gave him a five Franc note and told him to tell them they had returned to Redon, should they turn up again. They collected the bike from the side of the hotel. Hugo examined the map that he took from his packet.

"If we want to avoid that roadblock this side of Herbignac, we'll have to go past the station, out towards Nantes, take the turning to Saint-Joachim and finally go right to Missillac after a further twelve kilometres.

"The road looks alright from the map, so we should be able to go quite fast."

Hugo started up the bike and they settled themselves onto their seats. Once they were well past the station and on the road to Saint-Joachim, Hugo opened up the throttle: it was an exhilarating experience, especially for Artur. They both were thinking that they had been very lucky not meeting any German troop carriers, nor lines of marching soldiers, nor road barriers, but it was a long way back to Auray.

Hugo headed for Missillac knowing that they would meet the road from Nantes to Vannes in less than ten minutes. As they came to the crossroads—just before they turned left—they both looked to the right. To their dismay, they saw a road block about 200 meters down the road.

"Hold very tight, Artur; we need to get out of here very quickly."

Hugo went through the gears to take the bike up to a hundred kilometres an hour in next to no time. Artur hung on tightly to Hugo, occasionally taking a quick glance back to see if anyone was following them. At one stage, he couldn't see too well as they had gone round a slight bend in the road; he waited until they were some distance down the next long piece of straight road before looking again: nothing! The countryside flew past, but Hugo had to slow down as they came to the outskirts of Vannes. He brought the bike to a stop outside a café down a sideroad to their right.

"We must stay clear of the main hotels as they are used for accommodation by senior *Luftwaffe* personnel in the area, as well as crew members, so I've been informed," Hugo advised, as they got off the bike. He wheeled it around the corner: out of sight of any military convoys that might go along the main road.

"Come on, Artur, not far now before we're back at my place, but let me buy you a large black coffee for our efforts today." They felt quite light-headed with being so close to Auray.

Hugo led Artur through the door into the bar only to see four SS men and their officer sitting at a table next to the wall on the right side with beers in front of them. As is usual in France, the two men said 'good day' to everyone there, turned to the woman behind the counter and ordered their coffees. Artur had his back to the Germans as he looked at Hugo: he quietly mouthed to him that he recognised some of them.

As the coffees arrived, Hugo had a good look at the men as he stretched past Artur to get the local newspaper. He mumbled that he didn't recognise them. Hugo scanned the paper, but Artur looked straight ahead, at the spirit and liqueur bottles that were in front of a large mirror. He pushed Hugo further to his left so that he was just able to watch the Germans in the mirror. He didn't want to appear too obvious in case one of them saw him looking at them. After about ten minutes, the officer got up. Artur just about heard him say that they ought to get back to their post and relieve those at the roadblock. They walked to the end of the counter near the door to pay; one of them barged into Hugo as he was drinking. He spilled his coffee onto the counter: Hugo thought it was a deliberate ploy to get him to speak.

"Hey, please be more careful," Artur said, very slowly in French. "My friend is deaf and can't hear very well," he said very slowly with hand gestures over his mouth and then his ears. The officer seemed to understand, but continued to stare at Artur.

"Don't I recognise you?" he said, in very broken French. Artur shook his head, waving his hands in the air, suggesting that he didn't understand what he had said. The officer took a step closer to Artur so that Hugo was now between the soldier and the counter. Hugo had been leaning against the counter, but suddenly he pushed himself away with a great deal of strength. The officer lost his footing and fell to the floor. Everyone in the bar was watching to see what would happen next. Before the other soldiers could react to their officer's plight, most of the men in the bar ran over to grab them and held their arms firmly behind them, whilst two others pinned the officer to the floor.

"I now know who you are: you were the man on the bus going to Lorient," the officer shouted in German, as he turned his head to look at Artur.

"I've paid for the coffees," Hugo said to Artur. "Let's get out of here before these men are set free."

Hugo told the men who were holding the soldiers to keep them in the café for at least five minutes while they got away. The message was understood. They thanked the woman behind the counter for the coffees as they left, quickly went around the corner to the bike. Hugo had told Artur they would go along the narrow back streets so they could get out of Vannes via the road to Baden; that way he hoped they might avoid any more roadblocks.

Luck was on their side as they arrived back at Hugo's garden' gate without further incident. Hugo put the bike in the shed and they went into his house.

"Madelaine, we're back," Hugo shouted.

There was no reply, but he saw a note left on the table saying that she had gone shopping at 3:30 p.m. He looked at his watch telling him that she went out just over half an hour earlier.

"I think after all today's excitement, Artur, I need a drink. Will you join me?"

"An excellent idea; yes, please."

They sat down at the table with a bottle of red. They were both thinking a lot, but not saying much, until Hugo spoke:

"Are you sure you really want to go to the other side of the Loire tomorrow? Don't you think you took enough photos of the port area already today?"

"Maybe, but I won't know until we have another look. My hunch is that the Nazis are not only building a massively secure port for their U-boats, but also installing many protected artillery emplacements to guard the port from sea and air attack.

"From what we saw today, there is quite a lot of evidence, but my guess will be confirmed if we find similar gun defences—either in place or being built—on the other side of the river. Sorry, but we need to take a look. I realise it's a very risky exercise; nobody in London will believe what we have seen without further evidence. They certainly won't devise a plan to attack the port and its defences without more pictures of the construction projects."

"I understand fully what you are saying; I agree to going tomorrow. I would strongly suggest, however, that we leave either early in the morning or late in the afternoon. The latter might well be preferable as the men at the roadblocks could be tired, depending on when they started their watch."

At that moment, Madelaine came in through the back door to see the two men sitting at the table.

"How did you get on today? It would appear that you were not captured or shot!" she said, with a broad smile, as she went over to Hugo and put her arms around his neck.

"We had a few interesting moments that we managed to talk our way out of, didn't we Artur?"

"You could put it like that, yes."

"Grab a glass, Madelaine, and have some wine with us," Hugo suggested, as he took hold of the bottle.

"Good health," they all said.

After a sip of wine, Madelaine said she would unload the shopping so she could get on with preparing the evening meal. Hugo went to get his map from the bike's panier, returned to the kitchen and spread it out on the table. He fetched a piece of paper and a pencil to write some notes about the next day's excursion. They poured over the map for some minutes, wrote down the villages they would go through, avoiding the main roads.

"Are you planning to go out tomorrow, Hugo?" Madelaine asked, as she came over to place cutlery, plates and bread on the table.

"That's what Artur wants to do, yes. Why do you ask?"

"I heard someone saying in the market that there is a very strong likelihood of heavy rain from midday onwards, that's all."

The two men looked at each other. Hugo said to Madelaine that they would make their plan anyway and see what the weather was like after midday. They resumed discussions, wrote down notes and finished the bottle of wine.

"I'm planning for us to have dinner at 6:30 p.m.," Madelaine told them, to which Hugo replied that it was fine. Just before 5:45 p.m., the men concluded their discussions and plans; Artur excused himself as he wished to go to his room: he needed to write notes about the day's findings and the problems they faced.

Over dinner, they talked about the day's activities, their encounters with the SS, the problems at the roadblocks and the narrow escapes. They laughed at most of the awkward situations, but both Hugo and Artur knew it was more of a nervous laugh: they had been lucky, tomorrow might be different. Even though the wine flowed freely, Artur started to feel very tired at about 9 o'clock: the last three days had tested his stamina and his powers of concentration; he knew he had to be feeling at his best the following afternoon.

Chapter 16
Wednesday, 9 April 1941

There were noises that seemed to be coming from outside that woke Artur up. He got out of bed to see what was happening; he drew back the curtain a fraction: it was light outside. He looked at his watch to find it was after 8 o'clock. He looked down to see three German soldiers in the road—quite close to the front door—they were talking to Hugo about something that Artur could not quite hear. Artur tried to get nearer to the window, but he knocked it with his head. He quickly pulled back and let go of the curtain. He hoped the soldiers hadn't seen the curtain move. He waited for a few moments; the conversation started to get rather heated. He moved to the far end of the right-hand curtain where there was enough space for him to see the soldiers without moving the curtain.

"I think you must be mistaken," he heard Hugo say, slowly in French. "There is nobody staying here except my wife and me. How many times do I have to tell you that?"

The soldiers were obviously not convinced as they were getting very agitated.

Artur heard one of the soldiers say—in German—that they would return with someone who spoke French. The three of them clicked their heels, leaving Hugo at the door watching them leave. Without any hesitation, Artur went down stairs to the kitchen in time to see Hugo coming back into the kitchen.

"You missed all the fun, Artur."

"So it appears," he replied. "Do you think they'll come back? If so, when?"

"Don't worry Artur. Even if they insist on searching the house, they won't find you. Sorry if it sounds like I'm talking to a young boy, but go and get washed and dressed. Put all your things in your kitbag, make the bed, double check there is nothing of yours left in the room and make certain it looks as though nobody has been in the room. When you are happy with that, come back to the kitchen with your kitbag and have some breakfast."

Artur said 'aye, aye, captain', saluted Hugo with a smile and went back upstairs. He thought it would be best if he wore his knitted, dark blue, polonecked sweater, the trousers given to him by Delphine, the spotted scarf and the fishing boots. He made the bed, tidied the room, looked under and into everywhere. He was satisfied that the room looked unused.

"All tidy upstairs, Artur?" Hugo asked, as he came into the kitchen where the table was laid for breakfast.

"Before we eat, I need to take you through the emergency procedures you must follow, if or when the soldiers come back. In the hall, there is a door with a curtain covering it; let me show you."

Hugo led Artur into the hallway, drew back the curtain to reveal a door. He showed Arthur that the key was kept on the ledge above the door surround. He opened the door, located the switch inside on the left and put the light on.

"The stairs lead to a cellar that stretches to the back of the house where there is another set of steps that come up inside the shed in which the bike is kept. The door at the top of those steps is always locked, but there is a thick mat on the top step under which is the key.

"If the SS turn up, pick up your kitbag and coat, go to the cellar straight away via the kitchen. Before you go down, remember to lock the door from the inside and take the key with you. When you get to the top of the steps leading up to the shed, there is a key under the mat. Unlock the door, turn off the cellar lights with the switch on the left-hand side of the door. Once inside the shed, lock the door and place the two keys in the tin on the windowsill. Simple!"

"What if the SS try to storm the house once you open the front door?" Artur asked.

"Then we all are in trouble. Usually for this sort of visit, they will ask to look around the house first of all. We'll have time to delay them for a minute or two before agreeing to let them in, which will be enough time for you to get to the kitchen. We will show them into the sitting room so you will be able to leave the kitchen for the cellar. You must do this as quietly as possible, but we will help by 'accidentally' knocking a few chairs over and making as much noise as we dare."

"I can see that you've had to do this before," Artur said. "Was it very recently?"

"Yes, about four weeks ago. Some Free French paratroopers were dropped near the airfield at Meucon, northwest of Vannes. As their mission failed, they needed to escape back to England. Two of them sought refuge here for a couple of days while they drew up their plans on how to reach the coast at Les Sables-d'Olonne. On the second day they were here, five *Wehrmacht* soldiers came to the front door. Their leader insisted on coming in to search the premises. The officer and two others looked everywhere, leaving the other two guarding the house. They found nobody, of course, as the two paras had slipped into the cellar.

"The officer was very angry at not finding anyone; he threatened to have a tank come from the barracks to blow the house apart, but so far he hasn't come back."

"Did the paras get away?" Artur asked.

"We were told that they were picked up by a British sub earlier this month and taken back to England."

"A close encounter for you all. Anyway, let's hope they don't return, but if they do, I now know exactly what to do; thank you."

"Looking out at the weather, Artur, I should be able to take you to St Nazaire this afternoon. Before that, let's sit at the table and have some breakfast."

They all enjoyed their meal, but Hugo's mind was still thinking about the German soldiers and if they might come back to the house.

"Artur, I think it would be sensible if we went through an exercise pretending that the soldiers return to here," Hugo suggested, as Madelaine cleared the table.

"Fine by me."

To Artur's surprise, Hugo suddenly got up, went to the front door, opened it and then closed it. Artur grabbed his kitbag from beside the bookcase in the sitting room and ran into the kitchen, closing the door behind him. He heard a couple of chairs falling over as Hugo talked loudly that the soldiers' visit was most inconvenient. Artur went to the hall, drew back the curtain, found the key and unlocked the cellar door. He did everything he'd been told to do by Hugo and arrived in the shed. Last of all, he locked the shed door, placed the keys in the tin on the windowsill and waited.

"OK, Artur, you can come out now," Hugo said through the shed window after a few minutes.

"You did everything just fine, Artur, except for one vital thing: you forgot to close the curtain before closing the cellar door."

"Oh shit," Artur exclaimed.

"By the way, in the case of a real visit by the soldiers, how long should I stay in the shed? Wouldn't you expect them to go into the back garden and want to see inside the shed?"

"They didn't last time, but we'll have to play that by ear. There's no way we can cover every possible eventuality, Artur."

They went back into the sitting room. Artur looked at his watch: he couldn't believe it was well after midday.

"Madelaine will be preparing a cheese omelette for lunch just before 1 o'clock with some fruit to follow. I'm going out to look over the bike and put some fuel in it from the petrol can. By all means join me if you wish to; otherwise, the map is on the table for you to study."

Artur told Hugo that he would have a look at the map again and familiarise himself with the route. He jotted down a few village names, as well as streets in St Nazaire. Just before 1 o'clock, Madelaine came in with the items for the table so Artur cleared the map and paper away. He was asked to fetch Hugo as she was just about to make the omelettes.

"How are you doing, Hugo?" Artur asked, as he looked into the shed. "Madelaine is ready to serve up lunch."

After a couple of minutes, Hugo stood up at the same time wiping his hands on a cloth.

"Mustn't keep her waiting then," he said, as he followed Artur out of the shed into the kitchen. He washed his hands under the sink tap, saying to Madelaine that he was now ready.

They were quite quiet over lunch, pondering over what might lie ahead in the afternoon. Madelaine knew enough to guess that the trip could be hazardous, but was not in a position to dissuade them from going. She thought she would go and visit a friend, once they had left the house.

"Thank you for the meal, Madelaine," Artur said, as he turned to smile at her.

"It's a bit on the early side, Artur, but I see no reason why we shouldn't make a move, do you?"

"I agree, Hugo."

They cleared away the plates etc, placing them on the draining board in the kitchen. Artur went back to double-check his kitbag, making sure the Luger was beneath the false bottom of the bag and that his own pistol was at the top. He attached his F&S knife to the left side of his belt, put on his jacket and beret, and smiled at Hugo, who was watching him to see what he was doing.

"I'm ready when you are, Hugo."

He smiled as he gave Madelaine a kiss on both cheeks, saying that he appreciated what she had done during his brief visit. She smiled back broadly.

"Don't forget, Madelaine, if the Germans soldiers come back when I'm out, tell them to return tomorrow when I'll gladly show them around."

Hugo embraced Madelaine saying that he would be back later in the evening, probably without Artur.

"Why do you say: probably without Artur?" Madelaine asked, as she withdrew from Hugo's arms.

"The reason is that if he does what he's hoping to do, he will need to go back to England by a different route from the one he used to get here. Alternatively, if he and I have to split up in St Nazaire to escape the SS or the *Wehrmacht,* he will go to a contact I have given him. I, on the other hand, will make haste to come back here to you. That's the arrangement."

Madelaine looked at Hugo, then at Artur, and back again at each of them: both men nodded their heads and smiled.

"Let's be on our way, Artur, time is of the essence."

The men went to the shed from the kitchen back door. Madelaine watched with tears in her eyes; she wondered when she might see Hugo again. He wheeled the bike out just as the sun broke through the light cloud cover: its bright blue colour seemed to shine more than ever. Artur went over to it, brought out his handkerchief and gently rubbed the gleaming petrol tank, at the same time mumbling some encouraging words to it: one of his strange superstitions that he has used on many other occasions. Hugo watched, but said nothing.

Hugo got on the bike, started it up and drove it out of the back gate; Artur followed, closed the gate behind him, stepped over the pillion seat and held on tightly to his friend as they set off down the lane.

They had agreed to take the road to Redon via Vannes, then on another minor road towards Nantes. They had allowed for one and a half hours to reach Redon; by some stroke of good luck, they encountered no roadblocks or delays.

"We've been going for well over an hour and a half, so let's stop here in Redon for a coffee," Hugo said, as he brought the bike to a stop outside the Hôtel de France. He gently leant it against the wall facing the entranceway, he led Artur inside to the bar. He greeted the woman behind the counter with a smile, ordered his white coffee and Artur asked for a large black one. They both looked around at the other people in there to see four SS men sitting at a table towards the back of the bar area. Hugo told the lady that they would sit at the table by the window.

After a while, their coffees arrived with a gratis pastry each. Hugo thanked her then quietly asked her if there were many SS or *Wehrmacht* soldiers in the area. She told him that there had been, but most of them had left some weeks ago for the coast and the Atlantic ports. She mentioned that the ones in today came every other day at this time—they were billeted outside the town on the other side of the river. She was called by one of the customers at the bar, so she left them to enjoy their snack.

"Are you fit?" asked Hugo, as he stood up some ten minutes later.

"I'm ready," Artur replied.

They thanked the lady, said goodbye to the customers and went out to the bike. When Hugo was attending to the bike, Artur had a quick look through the window at the group of Germans inside. To his surprise, he saw them get up: two went to the counter—apparently to pay the woman—the other two walked towards the door.

"Hurry up, Hugo, the soldiers will be coming out at any moment." Artur took his pistol from his kitbag: he released the safety catch

Hugo started the bike. They both got on it as the soldiers came outside.

"Halt! Halt or I'll shoot!" the first one said loudly in German.

Hugo ignored the order, put the bike in gear and accelerated as fast as he could at the soldiers. One of them crouched to take aim at them, but Artur shot him in the arm as the bike sped past. The second soldier went down on his knee to fire at Artur, but, by some good fortune, Hugo heeled the bike over and went around the corner to the left so that the shots went into the wall on the far side. People walking nearby had heard the shooting; some just stopped and stared, whereas others made themselves prostrate on the ground.

Hugo knew they would be pursued very soon so he quickly changed up through the gears as he made for the bridge over the Vilaine river about 300 metres away. Artur hung on to Hugo's jacket for all his worth, occasionally looking behind him. As they reached the far side of the river—just before the twisty section and the straight part of the road to Saint-Nicolas-de Redon—he saw a German military vehicle come into view, but still several hundred metres before the bridge.

"We are being followed," Artur shouted into Hugo's ear.

"OK; hold on tight, Artur."

Hugo took the bike through the twisty part at speed and with great skill. Once at the start of the straighter section of road, he took the bike up to 120 kms per hour; they entered Guémené-Penfao in just over ten minutes. At the Hôtel de Ville, they headed south for Blain. There was no sign of the vehicle, but Artur was sure it would be following them, especially as he had shot one of the soldiers.

Chapter 17
Wednesday, 9 April 1941

As they entered the Forêt du Gâvre about ten minutes later, Hugo slowed right down. Artur knew he was looking for a track leading into the forest on the right-hand side of the road. He saw one, but thought it would be better if he didn't take it: it was too obvious. He slowly went up the second one about 300 metres further on. He took the bike up a short way, swung in to the right and cut the engine. They both got off the bike. Artur reached down into his kitbag and drew out the Luger pistol from beneath its false bottom. He gave his pistol to Hugo and kept the Luger for himself. They both listened.

"I can hear a vehicle," Artur whispered. "It's being driven very quickly."

Artur ran through the trees towards the road with his pistol in his hand; he was followed by Hugo. Artur found a branch that he dragged to the edge of the forest. He told Hugo that he would take the branch into the road and run to the other side. As the vehicle slowed down, he would shoot one soldier with a single shot, Hugo another one with only one shot too. He would signal to Hugo when to fire by raising his left hand.

"I'm going now," Artur said, as he shuffled on to the road, leaving the branch in the way of the approaching vehicle. He reached the other side, stood behind a tree watching the open truck coming along the road about 300 metres away. As expected, it slowed down, the two occupants in the back stood up: one looking half-left, the other half-right. The driver stopped the vehicle knowing that it was likely to be a trap. A few moments later, he got out of the car and crouched by the door. He slowly moved forward—still in a crouched position—to move the branch. Artur raised his left hand: two shots rang out and the soldiers in the back of the vehicle disappeared from view. The driver stood up with his hands in the air looking to his left, then to his right.

"Stand where you are," Artur shouted in German, as he ran into the road, "or I will shoot you too."

Artur slowly moved towards the driver telling Hugo—in French—to stay where he was, but to cover him. He reached the driver who was clearly very young and frightened as he stood rigidly with his hands up watching Artur's every move.

"Are there any more vehicles coming or just yours?" Artur asked, in German, as he looked in the back of the truck. The two soldiers were clearly dead, both with a single head wound beneath the rim of their helmet: they still held their rifles. The driver said his was the only vehicle, but Artur couldn't take any chances. Artur told Hugo to move the branch from the road and the driver to get into the passenger seat, speaking in the appropriate language to each; the vehicle's engine was still running.

"Hugo, get in the truck and drive it slowly up the track towards where our bike is. I will run beside the passenger door with my pistol pointing at the German driver."

"Don't do anything silly," Artur said, "or you will end up like your comrades." The soldier shook his head, then stared at Artur nervously.

Hugo turned off the track to his right, he stopped the vehicle next to the bike. Artur told Hugo to keep an eye on the soldier while he opened the rear door on the driver's side. He felt for a pulse in the first soldier, but there was none. He leant across to the second soldier: no pulse there either.

"Come and help me take your comrades out of the truck," Artur ordered the driver. They laid the two bodies in front of the truck face down, at the same time taking off their jackets and helmets. Artur looked in the rear area where the soldiers had been for any other articles that might have belonged to them: he picked up a pair of spectacles from the floor, as well as several boxes of ammunition for the rifles.

"Hugo, we are going to wear these jackets and helmets so that we look like the soldiers, but before that, we must find a place to leave your bike in Blain."

Artur opened the small boot of the vehicle, hoping to find some rope. He was in luck. He called the driver over and proceeded to tie him up to a nearby tree. He took out his handkerchief and used it as a gag.

"Do you think we should go to Nantes in the truck or continue on the bike?" Artur asked Hugo.

"I think it would be best if we went on my bike; we could always leave the truck up a track further down the road. Forget about the German uniforms as well, Artur. We should break the rifles by hitting them against a tree, throw the ammo into the bushes and get on our way."

"I agree, Hugo. We've spent a lot of time here already."

They did exactly as Hugo had suggested. Artur got in the truck, started it up and backed it out onto the track. He drove to the road, checked for any traffic and turned right, followed by Hugo on the bike. About 400 metres down the road, Artur saw a narrow track and drove up it for about 100 metres. He stopped the vehicle, threw away the keys, ran back down the track and climbed onto the bike.

"Here, take your pistol," Hugo said, "the safety catch is already on. Let's go, Nantes here we come!"

They headed for Blain, then through Faye-de-Bretagne towards Orvault, on the outskirts of Nantes. Artur noticed it had taken a further forty-five minutes: they were behind schedule.

Hugo brought the bike to a halt up a side road in Orvault; he said he needed to look at the map. As he reached into the panier, Artur got off to see what Hugo was planning.

"We'll need to go through the town centre, over two bridges and then take a right to Paimboeuf. The road's a bit narrow, but we should be able to go quite fast, unless we meet any roadblocks. We may be able to get very close to Mindin as I noticed a lot of building going on when we were on the far side yesterday."

"How long will it take, Hugo?"

"Perhaps thirty-five minutes, if we're lucky."

"Let's get going then," Artur said, as he looked at his watch.

They made good progress to Paimboeuf with Artur taking some photos, but they saw a roadblock up ahead of them. They slowed and then stopped when the soldier at the front put up his hand; five other men stood nearby looking very threateningly at Hugo.

"Halt!" said the soldier who had had his hand up.

"Papers!" he ordered, in German.

They handed them over; they were passed to the officer who inspected them.

"Where are you going?" the officer said in very broken French.

"I have recently bought this rather nice bike," Hugo explained in French, "and I wanted to show my friend this side of the Loire."

The officer seemed to smile just a little as he moved forward to examine the bike. He then suddenly stood up straight, took his pistol from the holster and pointed it at Hugo.

"I think you know this is a restricted area and you have come here hoping to spy on what we're doing. Get off your bike," the officer commanded. He and two soldiers led Hugo and Artur at gunpoint to the other side of the road. They were instructed to stand against the wall of a house with their hands up.

"Why should I believe you?" the officer bellowed.

Artur saw a possibility:

"I have not seen my friend for a long time," he said in German, surprising the officer. "I brought my camera to record our meeting. Perhaps you would take a photo of us, please?"

Artur slowly lowered his right arm towards his trouser pocket. The officer, however, thought he was reaching for a gun, so ordered him to stop. He walked quickly to Artur, put his hand in Artur's pocket and brought out the tiny camera.

"There you are," said Artur, "I'm not lying."

The officer examined the camera with a great deal of interest, saying that he had never seen anything like it before.

"Give it here," Artur said, "I'll show you how it works."

He lowered his arms, snatched the camera from the officer—who was now standing a few feet in front of him—slid the left side out and took a picture of him with all the men in the background. "There you are, it's as easy as that," he said, and handed it to the officer.

"Take one of us, but we want our arms down by our sides."

The officer nodded in agreement. Hugo brought down his arms and moved towards Artur, putting his arm around his shoulder; they both smiled at the officer as he took a picture. The officer handed the camera back. Artur thanked him, put the camera back in his pocket and gave him a Nazi salute. The officer responded and clicked his heels together as he said 'Heil Hitler'.

The officer seemed to have no further interest in what they might be doing in the area near Mindin, so they were led back across the road to their bike. He told them to be on their way, but to look out for more roadblocks as they travelled nearer to Mindin—if they were going that far.

"To make our life easier when we reach the roadblocks, would it be possible for you to write a note to say that you have given us clearance here at Paimboeuf?"

"That's a very unusual request."

The officer told one of the soldiers to give him a sheet of paper and pencil. He wrote out the note, signed and dated it, handed it to Artur.

"I'm so sorry, but I can't quite read your name, sir; please could you write it in capitals for me?"

After the officer had done as requested, Artur read it, put it in his jacket pocket, nodded his head and climbed on to the bike's pillion. Hugo started the engine with the soldiers staring as they went slowly down the road that went around Paimboeuf to Mindin.

A little way down the road—out of sight of the soldiers at the roadblock—Hugo stopped the bike and turned to Artur, who was smiling like an idiot at him.

"I can't believe what we have just managed to do, Artur. One moment we were against the wall waiting to be shot, the next you were taking a picture of the officer and his men. It's almost unreal. I don't understand why he let you do it? And then, allow us to continue to Mindin with permission."

"Hugo, I don't understand it either, but we need to get on our way. If I see a gun emplacement or one being built, or anything else to do with the Nazis, you won't need to stop as I will take a photo. Just don't go fast, as I will not be holding on to your jacket."

They continued on their way at a leisurely pace with Artur taking the occasional photo. After a few kilometres, they came to another roadblock. They stopped in front of two soldiers, with many more behind them; there was also a large truck on the other side of the road. Artur put his camera away in his pocket; he didn't like the look of this group: they each had a rifle or a pistol, that they were pointing at them. This time it was the officer that stepped forward:

"Papers!" he ordered in German.

Having got off the bike, both Hugo and Artur slowly fumbled through their pockets, eventually producing them for the officer to examine. He looked at the names on a list that had been passed to him by one of the soldiers, then at the papers, and next at the two men.

"Why are you here? What is the purpose of your visit to this side of the river?" he asked in German. As before, Hugo said—slowly in French—that he was out with his friend who had come from Boulogne; they were out on his recently acquired bike.

Artur thought it might help if he showed him the paper that had been signed at the previous roadblock. He took it out of his pocket and handed it to him. The officer looked at it and smiled at Artur.

"What is this? I know this officer; he is young and is junior to me, it means nothing."

Artur snatched the paper back, put it back into his pocket and glared at the German.

"We have done everything we can to get clearance to continue," he said in very poor German. "We have every right to be here."

The officer looked angrily at Artur and hit him in the face with his fist.

"You do not try to be clever with me, Herr Selmer." He ordered the two soldiers nearest to him to take hold of Artur and lead him to the truck. Artur struggled, but couldn't break their grip. Hugo was unclear what to do for the best as he saw Artur being led away, but as all the soldiers were focussed on Artur, they had their back to him. In an instant, he leapt on his bike, started it up and drove away at high speed around the corner before anyone could shoot at him.

"Stop him," the officer shouted at the ones not involved in handling Artur. All of them knew it was a hopeless case chasing the man on the bike, but they took a shot anyway.

One of the men was ordered to fetch rope from the back of the truck. Artur didn't struggle as they tied his hands behind him; he was more concerned that they might empty his kitbag that was still over his shoulder and find the two pistols. Once they had tied Artur, they led him to the truck and pushed him into the back next to one of the soldiers. The officer got in next to the driver whereas the rest were told to stay at the roadblock.

"Drive us to Nantes," the officer barked at the driver. "We will take him back to our military headquarters for questioning." Artur understood all that was being said, of course, but the Germans were totally unaware.

Chapter 18
Wednesday, 9 April 1941

Artur noticed that they were going back to Nantes by the same route that he and Hugo had taken nearly an hour earlier. He thought hard about how he was going to get out of the situation when he realised the rope holding his hands was not very tight. He carefully twisted his hands and gently pulled first one hand free then the other, but he still kept them behind him. There were vehicles in front of the truck that were not going very fast; he could see the officer was getting rather impatient. All of a sudden, just as they turned sharp left towards the first bridge, Artur opened the door and pushed himself out of the vehicle as hard as he could. He rolled over and over, holding on to his kitbag: his beret came off. He stopped himself by putting out his right arm, but he grazed his hand on the road's surface. He got up onto his knees to see the army vehicle in between two cars and having no opportunity of turning back until it got to the other end of the bridge.

Artur quickly looked about him; he immediately made the decision to go back across the road as he reckoned the officer's first thought would be to go up the road that Arthur had rolled towards. Vehicles slowed as Artur ran across the road—at the same time picking up his beret—and trotted along a path by the trees for about 100 metres to a bridge. He turned right, noticed it was like a box-girder bridge with a single railway line and a wide footpath going across the Loire. He felt this was a real opportunity to shake off his pursuers, so long as they had used up time going the wrong way.

The light was beginning to fade as Artur reached the footpath on the bridge. He glanced to his right to look for the army vehicle: he couldn't see it. He breathed a sigh of relief as he ran at a steady pace over the river; he knew, however, that they wouldn't give up their search for him, even if it was getting dark. He followed the footpath until it joined another road. He could see the main road about 150 metres ahead of him. If his sense of direction was right, he believed it must be the one that came from the main bridge that the truck would have come over before turning round.

Artur reached the main road where he hoped to catch a bus into the centre of the town—he knew he needed to find a hotel for the night. He crossed the road to the bus stop; he was sure a bus would come soon as there were a few people waiting. The woman he spoke to said there should be a bus in about seven minutes, but it would depend on whether it had been delayed at a roadblock or not.

Daylight had almost gone when the bus arrived. Artur had kept a keen eye on traffic passing by, but no sign of the German truck. He asked the conductor about small hotels in the town centre, but as the bus was due to terminate at the railway station, he recommended the station hotel. Artur thought it a good choice, particularly as he had to work out where he should go next.

The bus duly arrived at the railway station bus terminal; the conductor pointed out the hotel to Artur. He thanked him and set off for the hotel that was only a short distance away.

"I would like a room for the night," Artur asked the female receptionist in French.

The young woman smiled at Artur before looking at her booking sheet.

"We have quite a few vacancies, sir. Would you like to be on the ground floor or the first? May I see your papers please?"

Artur said he would prefer the first floor; he handed over his papers. While she was transcribing information to the booking sheet, Artur looked through the window into the bar to see who was there. Not surprisingly, he saw seven German soldiers sitting at two tables not far inside the bar. The bar area was quite large with other non-military people seated at other tables.

"There you are, sir," said the young woman, as she handed back his documents and a key. "I've given you room nineteen at the far end of the first floor. The stairs are just to your right. Will you be wanting a meal tonight, because the restaurant closes at 8 o'clock?"

Artur took money from his satchel to pay for his room and collected his papers. He asked her which room she might have given him on the ground floor; she looked at the sheet and told him room two. He looked at his watch, thanked the woman with a rather nervous smile, telling her that he would like to eat at 7:45 p.m. He picked up his kitbag, but decided to look around outside before going to his room. On getting outside, he turned to his left. After about thirty metres, he saw two German trucks that presumably belonged to the soldiers in the bar; nobody was guarding them. He looked inside the front windows, but the keys were not there: probably taken by the drivers. *Shall I slash a tyre of each vehicle?* he thought to himself. He looked back at the hotel's entrance as he took his F&S knife from its sheath on his belt. *On second thoughts:* he said to himself, *no, it would probably draw their attention to the station hotel.*

Artur went back to the reception area and upstairs to his room. He put his kitbag and beret on the bed, picked up a towel and some soap, and walked back along the corridor to the bathroom. As he washed himself thoroughly and cleaned the graze on his hand, he wondered how Hugo had got on: did he manage to get home? It was at that point that he made the decision to go back via Hugo, thence to one of the Brittany ports. Back in his room, he felt suitably freshened, put on his only change of clothing and went down to the restaurant as the clock in the reception area showed 7:50 p.m.

"Good evening, sir. Table for one, is it?" the waiter said.

"Yes, please; the table over by the window."

The menu was somewhat short of options, but he knew he should eat what he could in case tomorrow turned out to be another difficult one.

After he had finished his meal—together with one small beer—he returned to the reception area: he noticed it was closed and unmanned. All the room keys hung from hooks on a rectangular wooden board. He looked down the register that was on the counter to see who was staying that night: only ten rooms had names against them and the room he could have had on the ground floor was vacant. He leant over the counter, took the key for room number two and went upstairs.

Artur had had some sort of premonition that the hotel would be 'visited' by the *Wehrmacht* or the SS during the night, so he was going to have some fun with them, if they did come looking for him. He pulled back the bedcover, the sheet and the blanket. He placed the bolster lengthways in the bed, untidily remade the bed and placed the rolled-up towel on the pillow—at a quick glance, it looked like someone was in the bed. He put all his belongings into his kitbag, locked the door and went downstairs. He went through a door to the right of the reception counter, he opened the door to room number two and went inside, closing the door behind him. *This is where I shall spend the night,* he said to himself with a slight smirk on his face. He saw that the window looked out to the hotel's carpark, he checked that it would open—should he need to escape—and closed the curtains.

Artur didn't have any pyjamas so he decided to sleep in his underwear. Before getting ready for bed, he took the key for room number two back to reception and hung it in its right place on the board. Once back in the room, he put the latch on the door, he took his pistol from the kitbag, placed it under the pillow and stripped down to his pants and vest. He placed the rest of his clothes on the chair, with his boots underneath it. He got into bed and was asleep almost as soon as his head hit the pillow.

Artur was suddenly woken by a man shouting loudly in German and banging on a door—presumably the hotel's front door. He immediately became alert: he took his pistol from under the pillow, jumped out of bed, quickly put the light on and off so he could see where the chair was with his clothes and got dressed as quietly as he could. He put his pistol into his jacket pocket. The commotion continued, but there was now another person speaking very calmly in French—Artur thought it might be one of the night staff.

"I order you to open this door," shouted the German soldier. "I need to examine the register to see who is staying at this hotel."

The other person replied that it was the middle of the night and that the hotel's guests would not be pleased to be woken up. It seemed to Artur that both the people talking were not able to understand the other's language; it was turning into an impasse, but before too long he expected the German to lose patience and force his way inside.

"We give you twenty seconds to open this door or we will break it down."

Artur realised that the situation was about to get very nasty. He was fairly certain the Germans were looking for him, especially after having escaped from a German military truck late in the afternoon. He slung his kitbag over his neck so that it hung from his right shoulder on to his left side.

His eyes had become accustomed to the small amount of light in the room so he could see enough to walk to the window. He carefully opened the middle of the curtain to see what was outside. He looked out onto an almost empty carpark that was at the side of the hotel.

Just at that moment, there was a tremendous crash followed by the sound of several pairs of military boots running into the reception area. The officer told the Frenchman to give him the register. Artur imagined him running his finger down the list until he saw 'A Selmer' and then looking at the board for the key to room nineteen which wasn't there, making him assume it had to be occupied. He then heard the officer ordering the men upstairs to the first floor and running along the corridor.

Artur drew the window's curtains; a little light came in so he could see his watch showing 3:30 a.m. He looked all the way along the carpark, but couldn't see any army vehicles: *they must be at the front entrance*, he said to himself. He opened the windows, climbed on to the window sill and lowered himself gently on to the ground. He drew the curtains together, closed the windows as best he could and listened. He could just hear voices from the end of the building: the officer was asking the night staff man where Herr Selmer was as he wasn't in his room. The man didn't seem to understand as he mumbled something in French that Artur couldn't quite make out.

Artur walked carefully towards the front of the hotel with his pistol in his hand, looked around the corner to see two German army vehicles parked outside the entrance. He wasn't certain, but he didn't think there was anybody in either of them. He reached the first: nobody! He slowly went to the next: again, no one! He went around the back to the driver's door and looked inside: the keys were in the ignition—this was his chance, he thought.

He took off his kitbag, threw it onto the passenger seat, jumped inside and started the truck. He drove away from the hotel, past the bus station to the centre of the town. As there was a curfew, there was no traffic about. He didn't think he would be stopped as he was in a German vehicle. He saw a sign to Orvault, a place he remembered coming through with Hugo the previous afternoon, so he turned right. The gauge showed there was over half a tank of fuel, but Artur didn't think he'd be going all the way to Hugo's in the truck; after all, it wouldn't go down well if he parked it outside his house.

He kept a steady speed once he was through Orvault for nearly half an hour, all the time checking his rear-view mirror for any following vehicles. Just before he reached Redon, he took a left down a narrow road which he knew would eventually take him to the coastal road to Vannes. He crossed the Vilaine river twice within a kilometre and, after fifteen minutes, he went over the main road to Vannes.

From the sheer concentration of the drive, as well as the nervous energy he had expended, he suddenly felt tired. He drove down a narrow track and found himself near the side of the river. It was nearly 5 o'clock; he needed some sleep before it started to get light. He brought the truck to a standstill and turned off the lights and the ignition. He looked at the back seats to see an army greatcoat behind the passenger seat; he brought it over the front seats, wrapped himself in it and fell asleep with his hand on his pistol.

Chapter 19
Thursday, 10 April 1941

The sun shining in his eyes awoke Artur. He quickly realised it was being reflected from the rear-view mirror. He sat up to look around him, but the windows were steamed up. He got out of the greatcoat, opened the truck's door, stepped outside and had a good stretch as he took in the scene. He got back inside the vehicle, turned it round and reversed back towards the river: just in case he needed to make a quick getaway.

It was the first time that he had had time to look properly inside the truck to see if there was anything he could use: like a map, for instance. The glove compartment contained folders about the technical side of the truck plus its registration documents, two luger pistols, identity cards of three of the soldiers, two pairs of sunglasses, some pieces of blank paper, two pencils, an envelope with a woman's name and address in Germany, and a few unidentifiable items.

He got out to look in the pocket behind the driver's seat. He found a map, but it was no ordinary map. It was dated 1st April 1941 and was understandably typed in German, marked Confidential, SECRET. It had been hand-drawn giving names of the places along the coastal roads between La Rochelle and Brest. It showed details of the positions of each roadblock: how many men were to be at each, the name of the officer in charge of each barrier, the times of when they should be manned; it said it was valid for a month. Artur could not believe what he was looking at; the officer whose truck he was in was obviously a very senior man, a man who was trusted and respected by his seniors in the *Wehrmacht*.

Artur was suddenly aware that he might well be in very great danger. As soon as the officer realises that he has been duped at the hotel, he will put as many men as possible on the roads searching for Herr Selmer—according to his watch, that could be over four hours ago. Artur knew he had to make a plan: one that included getting rid of the truck. The map showed him there would be a roadblock at La Roche Bernard from 8 o'clock, so he couldn't go back to the road to Vannes—not the way he came—it was already 8:30 a.m. There was another roadblock east of Vannes and another just west of Vannes; he didn't remember there were that many when he came through with Hugo.

Time was marching on, so he got back into the driver's seat with the map and started up the truck. He drove west for about five kilometres hoping to find a bridge crossing the Vilaine river. Just before Camoël, a road went to the right with a sign showing 'to the ferry', but no bridge. He stopped the truck as he wondered what the ferryman might do or say when he saw it was a German registered truck. He felt he didn't have any alternative so he took a chance and drove to the ferry embarkation point. As he got out of the vehicle, he saw that the ferry was on his side of the river with only one car on it.

"Good morning, sir," Artur said, in French, to the man who looked to be in charge. "What time are you due to leave for the other side as I would like to book a single journey, please?"

The man looked at the truck and back at Artur.

"What are you doing with a German military vehicle? You're not German, are you?"

Artur thought he would be honest with his answer as it would be quite implausible to the man.

"I've just stolen it," Artur replied.

The man rocked back and forth as he laughed, saying equally outrageously, that his father was Hitler's brother! Artur knew the man wouldn't question him any further so he handed him his papers, apologising for not having any proper documents for the vehicle, even though they were inside the tuck. He asked Artur for money for the one-way trip, gave him a receipt and ushered him on board with a huge smile. He didn't wait for any more vehicles—the maximum was seven standard-sized cars anyway. He went over to the right-hand side of the ferry and turned the large handle to bring up the loading ramp. Once done, he waved at the driver who then proceeded to move the ferry away from the quay to the other side of the river.

"So, what are you going to do with the truck when you get to the other side?" the man said to Artur. "Where have you come from? Won't the Bosch be out looking for their missing truck?"

"It's a bit of a long and complicated story, but I managed to escape from Nantes in the middle of last night. The truck is used by a senior *Wehrmacht* officer, so you are right, they'll be searching everywhere for it, and me!" Artur said, with a smile. "I eventually need to get to Auray, but I want to leave the truck somewhere and then I'll risk catching the bus to Auray."

"My name is Pierre. This ferry is privately run by me and my brother, Franck, so we operate it when we choose. Perhaps we could help you."

Artur shook Pierre's hand and told him his name.

"I happen to know where the roadblocks are on the Nantes to Vannes road as I found a map in the truck: look," he said, as he brought it out of his pocket to show Pierre.

"That's quite amazing, Artur," Pierre said, as he studied the hand-drawn map. "My brother and I have lived in Arzal all our lives, we know all the side roads between here and the Brest peninsula. I will talk to my brother to tell him that I want to take you to Auray."

"That's very good of you, Pierre, but not only is it a long way, but you have the ferry service to operate. Where do you suggest we leave the military truck anyway?"

Franck called out to Pierre that they would be on the far side of the river very shortly, he should be ready to lower the ramp at the end of the ferry in four minutes. Pierre responded with a wave and told Artur to walk with him so he could tell him of his plan.

"You will drive me to my house, I will collect my car and you are to follow me. We take the small roads to Billiers where I have a cousin who has a farm. He will not argue with us about putting the truck in one of his barns. I will drive you to Auray. Most of the officers that are at the roadblocks between Nantes and Vannes know me and they trust me. You will be in the boot and they never ask to look inside—as long as my papers are in order and I can give them fresh vegetables every now and again."

Artur was just about to say something when Pierre went to attend to the lowering of the ramp, as the ferry had arrived at its destination. He went back to the truck, waited for the vehicle at the front to drive away, then drove the truck off the ferry and parked to the side of the roadway. He saw in the rear-view mirror that Pierre was talking to Franck for a few minutes, then he walked off the ferry and got into the passenger seat of the truck.

"This all sounds too easy, Pierre. Why can't I see a flaw in the plan you are suggesting?"

"We, in this part of Brittany, have had to put up with the Germans since June 1940, when the French Government decided to sign the armistice. We have lives to live and small businesses to run, some of which make life a bit easier for us and the Germans while they're here. If we don't comply, we either get shot, or they send us to work in the armament factories in Germany or they enlist us in the army. In general, we do what they want and remain reasonably friendly, but we will always be ready to help people like you when they get into trouble."

"But you have no idea who I am, where I'm from or what I'm doing here."

"Look, Artur, I might not be the brightest man around, but your French doesn't come from around here—probably nearer to Calais. You might not even be French, for all I know. But if you arrive at my ferry terminal in a German military truck, you must be involved in something of real interest, something that's anti-German for sure. Am I right or wrong?"

"As I have already said, I managed to escape the *Wehrmacht*. That means they must have had a very good reason to want to catch me in the first place."

Artur was uncertain how much he should tell Pierre, but he really did need to take up his offer of getting rid of the truck and being taken to Auray.

"Look, Artur, I definitely think you're doing something to help the war effort against the Germans: that's enough for me. Let's get going and head for my house."

Pierre directed Artur to his house in Arzal. On their arrival, Pierre's wife saw the German military vehicle heading for the house so she went straight for the firearm cabinet. Pierre guessed she would do that so he told Artur to stop the truck just off the road. He got out and ran to his house just as his wife came out of the front door with a rifle pointing at him.

"Don't shoot, Natalie, I will explain everything," he shouted. He saw her lower the rifle as he ran up to her. He quickly explained about the German truck and who the man was that was driving it. He told her that he needed to take the car, that he would be back later in the day to give her a fuller explanation, but in the meantime to take great care. He brushed past her as he went to fetch the keys and gave her a kiss on his way out. He went over to the open barn, drove the car away from the house and stopped next to the truck. He told Artur to follow him to his cousin's farm, this side of Billiers, about fifteen kilometres away: they would be using the minor roads.

Pierre returned to his car, drove to the centre of Arzal with Artur following, then took the road for Bourgerelle. After about a further ten minutes, Pierre turned right down a long track. The two vehicles drew up outside a farmhouse, but nobody seemed to be around. Both men got out of their vehicles with Pierre walking to one of the barns from which cows were making noises. He went inside to see his cousin's wife feeding the animals.

"Hello Gabrielle. Is Jean-Claude here or is he in the fields?"

"How nice to see you, Pierre. Is everything alright? We don't often see you unless you need something," she said with a smile. "Jean-Claude should be in one of the other barns. Go and have a look."

Pierre wasn't going to tell her what he needed so he wandered away to the opposite barn calling out for Jean-Claude. No answer from the first barn, but he heard his voice coming from the second one. He went inside to see him underneath one of his tractors with his ten-year-old son looking on.

"I need a favour from you, Jean," said Pierre, shortening his name, as he usually did.

Jean-Claude wriggled out from under the tractor, came over to Pierre and shook him with his very greasy hand.

"Thanks for that Jean," he replied, wiping his hand on Jean-Claude's already dirty shirt. They both laughed and slapped each other on the back as they walked out of the barn.

"My goodness, Pierre, where on earth did you get that truck?"

"It's a long story, but it was 'acquired' by this man," he replied, as Artur walked towards the two men.

"Rather than go into lots of details now, Jean, I need your help to get rid of it," he said, as he introduced Jean-Claude to Artur. "Could we park it in a barn you are not using for a few hours while I take Artur to Auray? Then, in the night, we drive it to Tréguen and leave it in the woods nearby. What do you think?"

"I agree for you to leave it in that empty barn over there," he said, as he pointed to the far end of the of the yard. "The barn can be kept locked until such time as we decide where to take it."

"So, you don't want to do the job tonight then?"

"No, I don't. I think it would be better if we left it for a few days. People will have seen the truck on your journey here; some will question what it's doing in their neighbourhood and a few others will tell the German authorities that they had seen it."

"You are probably right, Jean. In view of that, would you mind if we put it in the barn now?"

Jean-Claude agreed and went to the house to get the barn's keys. Artur went back to the vehicle, drove it to the barn, waiting for Jean-Claude to return. He went through the glove box and took out some items that might be of use. He got out of the vehicle and had a look in the small boot to find there were four semi-automatic rifles, ammunition, army jackets and helmets. He closed the lid as Jean-Claude opened the barn doors for Artur to drive in.

"You had better take a look at the things in the boot, Jean-Claude," Artur suggested, as he opened the lid again. "I'm not sure if these will be of use to you, but it's important you should know they're in here in case you want to discard them somewhere separate from the truck."

"Leave it all with me, Artur. We'll make a decision about all that at another time."

Artur took the keys out of the ignition, locked the vehicle and walked out of the barn. He suddenly remembered that he'd left his kitbag in the passenger seat well, so he rushed back inside, retrieved it and took the greatcoat from the back seat; he went back outside the barn.

"Are you sure you've not left anything else of importance in there, Artur?" Jean-Claude said with a smile. Artur said he was sure, as he wiped his brow.

"Have you got time for a glass of wine, Pierre, or do you have to rush off?"

Pierre looked at Artur, who was within earshot of Jean-Claude's suggestion; they both nodded and smiled. They followed Jean-Claude through the front door to the large farmhouse kitchen at the back of the building.

"I take it you'll have red, Artur?" he was asked, to which he said 'yes please'.

They all spent another thirty-five minutes talking about the farm, the family, the war, until Artur looked at his watch when Pierre was looking at him: it was 10 o'clock.

"I thank you for the wine, Jean, and for housing the truck, but Artur and I really do need to be on our way. We are bound to be stopped at more than one roadblock, even before we reach Vannes."

Artur handed the truck's keys to Jean-Claude, thanked him for all he was doing and followed Pierre out to his car.

"When do you want me in the boot?"

"You had better go in there now as there are not many kilometres before we reach the main road."

Artur didn't argue; he was pleased he had brought the army greatcoat from the truck when he went back for his kitbag. They all said their farewells, Artur wrapped the greatcoat around himself and squeezed into the boot; the lid was then closed. He had been told by Pierre that he would have to drive a few kilometres to the main road to Vannes. Shortly after that point, the map showed a roadblock at one of the roads that went right to Muzillac. As he reached the main road, he could see the manned barrier about a kilometre ahead of him: this would be the first challenge for him.

"Papers," the soldier said, as Pierre came to a stop and wound down the window. He got out of the car leaving the door open and walked a dozen steps away, at the same time taking his papers from his jacket pocket. Two soldiers followed him as he approached two more men, including an officer.

"How are you today?" he said in broken German. "Have you had many drivers give you problems today?"

The men smiled at his attempt at their language as the officer examined his papers.

"Why do you ask?" the officer enquired.

"I heard someone had escaped with a military vehicle of yours in Nantes last night; have you found it yet?"

"How do you know that?" the officer said, as he looked at Pierre.

"It was on the local radio this morning. The news broadcaster was asking for any information on the vehicle's whereabouts to be sent to the Mairie in Nantes. I was going to send a message, but now I've seen you, I can tell you and save myself a phone call. If you have a local map, I can show you where and when I saw it."

The officer sent one of his men to the truck telling him to go quickly to fetch the map from the glove box. In a short time, the man returned and handed it to the officer. Pierre noticed straight away that it was practically identical to the one Artur had shown him.

"I have come from Béganne, a small village west of Redon; I saw it by the river here," he said, as he pointed to the map. "You can't miss it; it's definitely just like yours over there. I was over that way about forty minutes ago. You should send communication to the officer at the roadblock near La Roche Bernard and also to the Nantes Mairie. You might get an award."

The officer thanked Pierre, handed back his papers and saluted him with a smile.

"Let this man proceed," he said, as he ordered the barrier to be raised. Artur could hardly stop himself from laughing out loud at Pierre's story as the car moved forward. Within a short time, Artur sensed the car turning left.

Chapter 20

Thursday, 10 April 1941

"We're on our way to Ambon," Pierre said excitedly. "I'll let you out of the boot in a moment, Artur."

The car came to a halt, Pierre got out and opened the boot. Artur crawled out, took off the greatcoat and put it in the boot.

"I wasn't aware that you spoke German," Artur said, as he stretched himself.

"It's not very good German, but it can be useful on occasions to get myself out of tricky situations. Let's be on our way, Artur, we've got to travel about sixty kilometres until we reach Auray, so we don't want to hang about."

Before too long, they went through Ambon and were on the way to Theix via Surzur through rather flat countryside. Pierre mentioned that they might encounter at least one roadblock in or near Vannes, so he wasn't sure how they would get on. He did suggest, however, that they take the minor road to the north of Vannes and enter Auray from Mériadec, north of the main road. Artur didn't disagree, as he looked at the German officer's map.

"I don't understand why we haven't encountered a road block in Vannes, when it clearly shows one on the map," Pierre remarked some twenty-five minutes later as they drove out of Vannes.

"Maybe they've been sent to look for the missing truck as per your information," Artur replied with a smile.

The rest of the journey to the north of Auray was uneventful; they both sighed with relief.

"Where do you want me to take you, Artur?"

"Drop me at the bus station and I'll walk down to the port. Can I buy you a coffee or a glass of wine before you head back to Arzal? There's a waiting room at the end of the bus station parking area that has a café in it."

"That's a very good idea: a white coffee for me, Artur; I could do with going to the toilet anyway."

Pierre parked the car near the café; he dashed into the toilet while Artur ordered the coffees inside. As he was just about to collect the coffees and take them to a table by the window, he heard the sound of vehicles being driven quickly towards the bus station. To his surprise, he saw three German army trucks similar to the type he had 'acquired'. They didn't stop, but went down the slope to the port. He looked towards the toilet block to see Pierre turn his back and go back inside out of view. Once they had gone, he walked purposefully to the café and came in through the door. Artur and Pierre looked at each other, but said nothing as they took a sip of their coffees.

"Look after my coffee, Pierre, it's my turn." He picked up his kitbag and went to the toilet block. Within a few minutes he returned having changed his clothing—he now looked a little like a fisherman: roll-neck sweater, spotted neck scarf, ankle-length boots.

"Where did you get those clothes? Why do you have to wear them, Artur?"

"Pierre, you haven't seen my identity papers, have you? I need to be a bit like the German soldiers expect me to be; I am supposed to be a fisherman from near Boulogne. I'm sure the men in those trucks will be looking for me, I can't take any chances."

They finished their coffee without any further questions from Pierre. He did think Artur was being a bit paranoid, but he didn't know enough about him and what he was doing in France. They wandered out of the café to continue their conversation.

"Look, Pierre, I cannot thank you enough for what you've done and how you've helped me. I think you should leave as soon as you can before one or more of those trucks comes back up here. They might not have noticed your car when they passed the bus station, but if they don't find what they're looking for down in the port—that is to say, me—you can bet they'll come back up here again soon and start searching. There are nosey folk about, as you know, some will be German informers."

Pierre nodded; he knew Artur was right, but before he was to leave, he had to ask him one more question:

"I am sure you are not really French, Artur, so am I right in saying that you must therefore be an Englishman who speaks perfect French and behaves like one of us?"

"Pierre, as I said a moment ago, leave now. My life is already in danger, don't make it more difficult for yourself by hanging around here any longer with me. Run man, run; get back to Arzal, or the ferry, as soon as you can. Don't forget to get rid of that German army greatcoat that's in your car, they might kill you if they find it in your possession: no questions will be asked."

Artur started to walk away, but turned around to see Pierre walking rather disconcertedly to his car. He knew he had warned Pierre of the possible consequences of staying at the café any longer; he was pleased he had taken the warnings seriously.

He walked down the slope to the port, but he still felt vulnerable. What if Hugo isn't at home? What does he do if neither Hugo nor Madelaine is in their house? He told himself to get a grip of the situation and not worry unduly till he gets to the house and knows they're not there. Just as he was about to turn right away from the port up the slight slope, he saw the German trucks coming very fast from the old bridge. He quickly slipped into the café just in time to see them drive past. He looked around the bar as he moved to the counter and, to his relief, there were no German soldiers in there this time.

"Would you like a coffee, monsieur?" the young woman asked.

"A large black one please, and a large brandy too," he replied. "I'll be over there by the back of bar," he said, as he pointed to an empty table that was in the corner.

"I'll bring them over to you, monsieur."

Artur greeted people as he walked to the table, hung his kitbag over the back of the chair and sat down. In a short space of time, his drinks arrived. He took a note from his satchel and paid the waitress straight away. She smiled at him as he thanked her for the service. He wanted to drink the brandy down in one, but he thought better of it. He poured a small amount into the coffee instead.

He was just about to take a third mouthful of the laced coffee when he saw two German soldiers stop outside the café. After a few moments, they looked inside. Artur had noticed and had already gone to the toilet taking his kitbag and the coffee which now had all the brandy in it. He bolted the door, put his kitbag over his shoulder and finished the warm drink. He knew it was cheap stuff, but it didn't matter when mixed with the coffee.

"Is anybody in there?" a Frenchman said, as he banged on the door and tried to open it.

Artur was trying to work out how he was going to escape from the soldiers who, he assumed, must now be at a table—maybe his one.

"Give me a few minutes," Artur replied, but the man just grunted and seemed to go back inside the café.

Artur unlocked the door and hoped nobody would come into the toilet area as he crept out. He put the coffee cup on the wash basin, turned right through a door into the garden area. He looked around to see a gate that went to an alleyway on the right. *That's the one that goes past Hugo's back gate*, he said excitedly to himself.

He went out of the café's back garden and turned left. Within about sixty metres, he was outside Hugo's back gate. He tried to open it, but it was locked. The fence was too high for him to look over. There was a gap by the latch that he put his eye to and he saw the back door from the kitchen was open. *At least it looks as though they must be in*, he said, as his spirits were raised.

"Hugo, it's me, Artur," he shouted, then waited as he looked up and down the lane. After several minutes, he walked purposefully up the alleyway as it went around to the left; he hoped it would soon intercept the road running along the front of all the houses: it did. He carefully looked left down to the port area. He didn't see any German army vehicles or soldiers so he walked down to Hugo's front door. He used the knocker and waited. The door was opened by a young woman that he didn't recognise, but seemed to look a bit like Hugo.

"Please could you tell me if Hugo or Madelaine are at home?"

"Who shall I say is looking for them?"

"My name is Artur, I stayed here with them a few days ago."

The woman left the door ajar as she disappeared from the hallway into the lounge. Artur heard voices, but couldn't work out what was being said. He then heard someone running towards the door.

"Artur, you are safe. We have been very worried about you; we thought you might have been taken to the SS centre and interrogated," Hugo said, with relief in his voice. "Come in, please."

Artur was almost dragged into the house by the arm as he closed the door and locked it behind him. He was led into the lounge-diner.

"Artur, this is my sister, Mélanie, who met you at the door; she has come to stay for the weekend."

Artur greeted her properly and embraced Madelaine.

"This causes for a celebration," Hugo said, as he went into the kitchen to fetch a bottle of wine and some glasses. On his return, he placed the glasses on the table; he opened the bottle, but he couldn't stop smiling and looking at Artur. He handed the glasses out, raising his to congratulate Artur on his escape and return to Auray.

"You must have an amazing story to tell," Hugo said, hoping Artur would tell them everything.

"Hugo, I'm very pleased to be here with you all, I thank you for your generosity, but I need to tell you that I'm a wanted man. I managed to escape from the clutches of the German soldiers in Nantes, not only after injuring one of them, but also for steeling one of their trucks. The soldiers in Nantes and Vannes don't know I'm in Auray—not at the moment, anyway—but once they find out, there'll search everywhere in the port area."

Silence came over them as they thought through what Artur had just said.

"I need to tell you, Artur, that after we left for Nantes on the bike, several German soldiers and an officer came to this house. They wanted to search the place, but Madelaine managed to persuade them it was a waste of time. They reluctantly went away, but it wouldn't surprise me if they returned. Now that you are here, have you had a chance to think through your next move?"

"I need to get back to the Brittany coast. You may recall that I had a lift to Châteaulin and then took a bus to Auray. Have you got a map of the Brittany area, Hugo, I'll show you the port that will give me the best chance of getting back to England?"

Hugo went to the hallway, pulled a few things out of a drawer in the hall cupboard and came back to the table.

"This should be what you want, Artur," Hugo said as he opened the map out for everyone to see.

Artur ran his finger along the line from Auray to Quimper, to Brest and the coast above.

"That's the place: Portsall," he exclaimed. "I need to get there as I know a few people: I stayed the night in that place before I was taken by car to Châteaulin."

"It's a long way, Artur. It must be over 180 kilometres, and that's without taking the minor roads. You ought not to go via Lorient as there are many German military personnel overseeing some huge building projects to house their U-boats. There will be a number of roadblocks in that area too."

"I could go from another port on the Brittany coast, but as I know my way around in Portsall, it's my best choice. As for roadblocks, take a look at this," he said, as he took out a piece of paper, unfolded it and placed it on top of the map.

"This came from the German truck that I borrowed," Artur said with a smile. "It shows all the roadblocks from Nantes to Brest for the month of April, as well as those from Brest to St Malo. See here, the words at the top translate into TOP SECRET. It also gives the name of the officer in charge of each roadblock."

"That's quite an amazing find, Artur. Do you think they'll make changes to the number and location of each roadblock now they know one of their trucks is missing?"

"No, I don't think so. One of the other key pieces of information is that it says the barriers will be manned from 8 o'clock in the morning till 6 o'clock in the evening. It's possible there is another similar rota for the night time, but I didn't find one."

"So, Artur, you have presumably come here hoping I could take you some— or all—of the way to the coast?

"If I do agree to that, I recommend we leave on Friday evening, with the hope of arriving on Saturday evening, but I need to give it some careful thought first. What I will need to do is look at the route that will take us away from the main road and go inland a bit."

"Hugo, surely there must be a bus from somewhere like Châteaulin to here," as Artur pointed to a coastal port, "but I suppose it might only operate from Monday to Friday?"

"I'll check it all out, Artur; we'll talk further about it later," he said, as he poured out more wine. "You stay here and relax; I'm just going up to the bus station to find out times of buses to Brest and beyond. Madelaine will make you something to eat as I'm sure you must be quite hungry."

Madelaine went into the kitchen with Mélanie, Hugo went out to the shed in the back garden to get his motorbike and Artur sat at the table examining the maps. He didn't fancy going via Lorient, especially with the likelihood of all the security around there. He thought it might be lighter at the weekend, but then there probably won't be as many buses to the coast.

Madelaine brought him a cheese baguette that Mélanie had made plus another opened bottle of wine. He didn't realise how hungry he was until he tucked in: almost more cheese than bread too! He poured some more wine.

"Anyone else going to join me?" he said, as he turned towards the kitchen. They said they would be in soon; just doing some tidying up. Artur returned his attention to the map as he took another bight at the baguette. He didn't hold out much hope of the buses running north from Brest at the weekend so he thought his best hope was to leave Auray on Friday. He pondered over it all for some minutes, then he heard Hugo's bike coming into the back garden. He went into the kitchen to look through the window.

"I've got some good news and some bad," Hugo said to Artur as he entered the kitchen. He changed out of his kit, washed his hands and walked Artur back to the table. He poured more wine into his glass; he smiled at Artur.

"So, what's the good news, Hugo?"

"There's a bus service from Brest that goes north to here," as he points on the map, "then to Ploudalmézeau, along this road here, then ends up in St Pol. A funny route, I have to say, but that's it."

"What's the bad news?"

"The service only operates on Mondays and Thursdays, leaving Brest's main bus station at 10 o'clock."

"That's not really bad news, Hugo, but what about services to Brest from Quimper for instance? Do you think they operate daily except Sundays, perhaps? My main concern is Lorient and the surrounding areas."

"I understand that, Artur; it's for that reason that I will be willing to take you to somewhere like Quimper. Once you are there, you will be better on your own to get north of Brest. I could do that tomorrow morning if you so wish?"

"I think the sooner the better, Hugo, but we must avoid the main road to Quimper."

"Fine, so that's agreed then. We'll leave at 6:30 a.m. so that we are ahead of when the barriers are supposed to be manned."

Chapter 21
Friday, 11 April 1941

Artur woke up to hear someone walking around upstairs: presumably it was Hugo as Artur's watch showed it was 6 o'clock. He had had to sleep on the sofa that night as Mélanie was using the spare room. He looked through the curtains of the front window to see it wasn't raining, but it was starting to get light.

"Ah, good; I see you are up already, Artur," Hugo stated as he came into the room. "It probably wasn't the most comfortable of nights for you, but it was the best we could offer you."

"I've had many worse places to sleep, Hugo, so I did get several hours of good rest. May I go and use the bathroom, I need to get rid of some of that wine we had yesterday," he joked. Hugo told him it was free so he went lightly upstairs so as not to disturb the ladies. Within ten minutes, he was back down in the kitchen where Hugo had made some coffee.

"I take it you'll have some fresh coffee, Artur?" to which he replied that he would. In less than ten minutes, the two men were outside in the garden. Artur checked that he had everything in his kitbag and his satchel, especially his French papers and his pistol.

"I'm ready when you are, Artur," he said as he wheeled the bike out of the shed. Hugo sat astride the bike as he started it while Artur went to the gate to let him out. Once in the lane with the gate locked, Artur took his place on the pillion; they set off towards the port.

They had decided the evening before that, even though they would be leaving well before the barriers would be manned around Lorient, they would take the minor roads inland, just to be on the safe side. They would go via Baud and Gourin with a stop at Huelgoat for coffee; it would take about two hours, if they were lucky.

They had an arranged signal between the two men, especially if Artur needed to stop. He tugged Hugo's jacket twice as they went through Gourin and up the hill. Hugo pulled over to the side of the road; Artur got off.

"I need to stretch a leg, Hugo, and have a pee."

He went to some rocks to relieve himself. He looked at the countryside as it stretched out to the north below him.

"Sorry, Artur, I should have stopped earlier, but I thought we should press on while the going's good. It's only about another forty minutes to Huelgoat where we can stop a bit longer and have a coffee."

Artur didn't reply; he climbed back on the pillion seat as Hugo started the bike. The next part of their journey to Huelgoat passed quickly. They entered the old town and parked the bike outside a café overlooking the lake, next to a hotel.

"This will do for us, Artur. Let's go inside to see what they can offer us." Artur removed his beret, chose a table near the window where he placed his kitbag and joined Hugo at the counter.

"Good morning, gentlemen, what can I get you today?" the young woman asked with a smile.

Artur ordered a large black coffee, Hugo asked for a large white and they each had one of the baguettes from the display cabinet.

"This is a very nice spot," Artur remarked. "Do many people come here these days?"

"Business is not good, sir. The locals only come in when they know the German military will not be around."

"Do they come on particular days or do they just turn up when they feel like it?" Artur continued.

"They tend to come on Mondays, Wednesdays and Fridays at about 10 o'clock, after they've finished the first session at the barriers on the road to Châteaulin."

"But that's a good twelve kilometres south of here, isn't it?" Hugo mentioned, as she took the coffees to their table.

"Something like that, yes, but they like the old village and the view over the lake," she replied, as she returned to bring them the baguettes.

"Sorry to ask you another question, but do they often arrive early or are they quite punctual?"

"At the end of the week—such as Fridays—they do tend to get to the village early, especially if the weather is fine like today. There often are a couple of trucks together with two motorcycles with sidecars; that makes about ten soldiers."

"OK, thanks for that," Hugo said, as they sat down.

"We had better keep a careful watch out for them, Artur, and try to leave here before 9:45 a.m.; at least they'll be coming from the south and we'll be going north."

They tried to relax as they worked through their food and coffee; it wasn't easy, especially for Artur. He wondered how the news of a missing truck had been sent out to all the roadblocks' officers? Would the incidents in Nantes and St Nazaire have been received this far away? They debated the possibility endlessly. The only real conclusion they came to was that they should assume the news was sent out and received as soon as they realised the truck had gone missing.

Artur went to the counter to pay as Hugo went to the toilet.

"Thank you very much," Artur said to the young woman with his customary smile. She wished them a safe onward journey, but without any semblance of a smile.

Hugo came out to Artur, who was standing looking back towards the old village; he thought he heard the sound of heavy vehicles coming from the other side of the village. Before placing his kitbag over his shoulder, he put his hand down to the bottom of it and brought out his pistol; he checked it and put it in his right-hand jacket pocket. They set out from the café, but Artur strained himself to look around as the noise became louder. He saw a German truck come from the centre of the village towards the café, closely followed by a bike with a sidecar, a second vehicle and another motorbike.

"We might have some company, Hugo," as Artur put his mouth close to Hugo's ear.

"Go around the lake, back into the village and come past the café to see if they've all gone in."

Hugo did as Artur suggested; within ten minutes, they were going through the village before the hotel and the café. He slowed the bike down so they could have a good look through the window as they went by; the trucks and the bikes were parked further up the road.

"You're not going to steal another truck are you, Artur?"

"Stop for a moment past the last truck, Hugo."

Artur got off the bike and looked inside the truck's cab: no keys in the ignition. He tried the passenger's door handle: it was unlocked. He opened the door, he felt inside the glove compartment and withdrew two pistols, a few papers, a map of Brittany and a type-written note. It had yesterday's date at the top, it was marked URGENT. He quickly scanned the text that described how a truck was stolen from the station hotel in Nantes. In the next to last paragraph, it mentioned ARTUR SELMER in capitals as being someone the military commander of the area wants found. Artur put the pistols in his kitbag and the map plus the note in his inside jacket pocket. He closed the door carefully and went to the bike.

"Hugo, I have found a note issued by a senior German officer in the area with my name on it; I'm a wanted man. You now have to make a decision: do you want to hand me over to the men in the café or are you prepared to risk everything and take me to the coast? Please think over these options very carefully."

"Look Artur, I have been here for you ever since you called at my house a few days ago. I'm not going to stop now and I'm certainly not about to hand you over to the *Wehrmacht*. I'm here to help you."

"Sorry, Hugo, I didn't really mean to say it quite like that; I'm extremely grateful for everything you've done. As I have said, I need to get to the coast where, hopefully, I can find my way back to England in one piece. I have been wondering if I should do something to these vehicles before we set off; what do you think?"

"I strongly suggest that we leave straight away. They're not likely to come after us unless the woman in the café tells them about us."

Artur agreed they should leave, but before doing so, he took out the camera and photographed the note and the hand-drawn map of the roadblocks. Hugo started up the bike, Artur jumped on the back and they headed for the road that would take them over the *Monts d'Arrée*. At the top of the pass, they stopped to look at the scenery.

"That view is quite spectacular, don't you think, Artur? Not much habitation at this altitude, only bracken and heather seem to survive."

"I agree, but now it's my turn to say that we should be on our way. You did say when we were in the café that you would take me to Portsall, for which I'm really grateful, but I just have a feeling in my water that it will not be plain sailing from here; don't ask me why."

They set off down the other side of the range heading for Landivisiau which was at the intersection of the road from Morlaix to Brest. Hugo brought the bike to a halt at the crossroads, almost in the centre of the village. Artur got off the bike, put his hand in his jacket pocket and brought out the hand-drawn map showing the positions of the roadblocks: one on the northwest side of Brest, another just outside Morlaix. As they needed to go left for a few kilometres, he stared in that direction down the road. He had had a premonition that there would be a manned barrier close by, even if it wasn't on the map.

"Am I seeing things, Hugo, or is there a roadblock down there?" Artur enquired, as he nudged Hugo in the chest and pointed.

Hugo strained to find what Artur thought he could see, but without success.

"Just before we came to the intersection, there was a small road off to the left, it looked as if it would go parallel to this one. Let's go slowly down it and see if we get nearer to the barrier."

Hugo agreed, he turned the bike round and they followed the small back road for about a kilometre. Artur told him to stop, he got off the bike and carefully walked up the left-hand side of the lane to the right. As he went nearer to the main road, he started to hear voices: they were discussing what they might do at the weekend: in German. He walked a bit further, but suddenly froze in a shop doorway when he heard them talk about one of their trucks being stolen down near Nantes—it still hadn't been found. He saw a vehicle go along the larger road to the left, the driver was told to stop and present his papers in quite good French. After a moment or two, they must have been handed back as one of the soldiers appeared to show him a picture or a drawing.

"Have you seen this motorbike on your travels?" the soldier asked. He said he hadn't, but he was then asked where he'd come from. He replied that his journey had started in Morlaix: he said he was on his way to visit his aunt in Châteaulin. He also said that he visited her every two weeks on a Friday in the afternoon. The soldier told him to pass. Artur turned and went back to where Hugo was.

"As I suspected, there is a manned barrier to the left on the main road," Artur said. "I heard them talking about their missing truck; they also appear to be showing drivers a picture of a motorbike, asking if they'd seen it. It must be your bike, Hugo."

"So, that barrier is not on your map, Artur?"

"No, it's not. The German area commanders must have set up more barriers in order to try and catch us. Let's continue along the back lane and see where it brings us." They did as Artur suggested. They crossed a minor road before taking a turning to the right at the next small road. Hugo went slowly towards the main road for a few metres where they got off the bike; Hugo leant it against the wall of a house. Keeping close to the houses, they came to the corner with Artur in front. He looked right and then left: there were no barriers in sight.

"The road we want is straight opposite and there are houses on both sides. Let's get on the bike and go across. In fact, I'll walk across to the other side and you come with the bike."

They did as Artur suggested; they met about twenty metres up the road. Artur took the map of Brittany from his jacket pocket and laid it on the bike's seat.

"If we take this road, we will go very close to this airfield here," Artur said as he pointed to a place north of where they were.

"We don't really have any alternative route, if we're trying to keep to the secondary roads," Hugo replied.

They discussed various options for several minutes, but kept coming back to the route they first considered.

"We ought to get a move on, Artur. By my reckoning, we still have over an hour before we reach Portsall, assuming we don't get any more delays! We'll stop in Lesneven at the railway station; there should be a café for us to get a much-needed coffee."

Chapter 22
Friday, 11 April 1941

They set off feeling the worst might be behind them, but they hoped there weren't any military barriers on the road near the airfield. They were in luck. They arrived without any difficulties in Lesneven and easily found the station. A strange little building with a restaurant on one side of the entrance area and a bar on the other.

"According to the map, it is only a branch line going from Roskoff to Brest, but I expect the German *Wehrmacht* use it for ferrying troops to and from the Brest area quite regularly; we had better take care," Hugo commented. He walked the bike through a gate in a picket fence to the right of the station building, putting it behind a large bush that concealed it well enough. They went into the bar. Hugo ordered their usual coffees, Artur started to talk to the attractive young woman behind the counter:

"Do many trains come through here?" he asked, in his best French.

She looked up at the clock behind her, turned back to face Artur saying there was one due from Roskoff in about eleven minutes. "I'm reliably informed that it will be a longer train than usual with mostly German soldiers on it."

Artur took the coffees to the table near the window where Hugo was standing.

"Do you hear what I hear, Hugo?" he asked as he paused drinking his coffee.

Hugo went out into the hallway to the front door and opened it, followed by Artur.

"You've got good hearing as well as excellent eyesight, Artur!" he joked. "What on earth is that noise?"

"It sounds like some German heavy half-track personnel carriers coming to the station to collect the soldiers from the train that's due very soon."

"How do you know that?" Hugo enquired.

Artur explained his recollection of seeing similar types of vehicles a year ago when he was in Germany; a sound and sight he would never forget. Just as he finished telling Hugo, two armoured half-track troop carriers came into view. Hugo closed the door; they went back into the bar where they both peered through the window to see six Henschel personnel trucks following the two armoured vehicles.

"Good Heavens!" Hugo exclaimed at the sight of all the vehicles. "How many soldiers are they coming to pick up?"

"Probably as many as 120," Artur replied, "as each Henschel truck can take about eighteen men, depending on how much kit each soldier is equipped with."

Artur walked over to the counter and drew the attention of the young woman.

"You are not expected to give a drink to all the men coming off the train, are you?" he said with a smile.

"Certainly not," she replied, "but the officers in charge will come for a coffee while they wait for the train. Usually there is one officer for each truck."

Artur thought he had to be honest with the woman as he explained their situation:

"My friend and I are on the run from the *Wehrmacht* so we have a slight problem with all these soldiers arriving. We would like you to do us a favour, please. From the shape of the building, there should be an upstairs, yes?" She nodded. "Would it be possible for us to hide up there until the vehicles have left?" She looked over to the young girl who was cleaning the tables in preparation for the German officers' arrival; she called for her to come to the counter. Artur heard her say that she needed to go upstairs for a few minutes so she would be left in charge.

"Come with me, please," the woman said. Artur told Hugo to bring the coffees and to follow him. They went to the first floor to a large storage room. It had two windows: one overlooking the railway line and another looking out to the front where they could see some of the trucks. Artur saw four chairs and a table on its side, as well as some large boxes, all on bare boards.

"You can stay here, gentlemen, but I must now go down to help the officers in case they come in early. Follow me down to the door and lock it before returning up here. I'll knock two times then again two times to tell you it's clear for you to come back to the bar." Artur did as she asked and thanked her for her help.

"What do we do with the bike?" Hugo asked rather anxiously, as Artur came back in the room.

"There's nothing we can do now," Artur replied, "except hope for the best that nobody sees it."

They heard the bar door being opened followed by a number of heavy-booted soldiers walking in from the booking hall, talking and laughing together. One of them ordered eight white coffees in very broken French.

"We must keep away from the front window, Hugo, and not make any noise walking around: I suggest we take our shoes off. Artur took his off first and gently laid them under the now upturned table. Hugo took his first boot off very carefully, but he dropped his other one on the floor. The talking in the bar was stopped by someone ordering them to be quiet. Hugo and Artur sat motionless, the silence from the bar continued for what seemed like an age.

"Who is upstairs? A soldier barked, probably at the young woman. Artur and Hugo could quite easily hear the soldier speaking.

"Oh, that's my mother," she replied. "I told her to go upstairs as she has a young dog that doesn't like men in uniform. I knew you would be coming so I didn't want it to be a nuisance to you men. The noise you heard was probably the dog knocking something over," as she smiled sweetly at the officer.

After a few minutes, the men's conversation continued. They heard the soldiers go from the bar to the hallway and out to the station platform. One of the soldiers said that the train should be arriving in less than five minutes. Artur moved carefully to the back window, but he couldn't see the soldiers as there was a sloping roof over the central part of the platform. As he knew he wouldn't be seen by the men below, he got very close to the window. He saw in the distance smoke from the engine that was pulling a number of carriages, coming around a slight curve towards the station.

Artur saw the train come to a halt. Even with the engine and tender beyond the far end of the platform, one of the carriages and the guards van were not in the station, so men had to jump down from the open doors onto the gravel. Men poured out of the train; most were carrying large heavy-looking kitbags and a rifle. He removed his camera from his pocket and took about four pictures of the activity. The majority were wearing the familiar tin helmets, whereas the few officers present were in caps. Someone ordered them all to fall into ranks of three on the platform and to face the way that the train had come from. After some moments of the men shuffling into position, they were ordered to march around the side of the station to the waiting vehicles.

"Did you see how they all dutifully goose-stepped to the front of the station, Hugo? Some of them hardly looked old enough to be out of nappies, let alone be in the *Wehrmacht*!"

Artur and Hugo sat on the chairs in the middle of the room; they dare not be seen at the window when the men were being ordered to get into the trucks. It took over fifteen minutes to get them all in before the engines were started and they drove off with a great roar towards the village. Once the last truck went out of view, they heard two loud wraps on the door at the bottom of the stairs, followed by two more a few moments later: that was the 'all clear' signal given by the woman in the bar.

"It looks as though we might have been very lucky, Hugo; let's go down to the bar and prepare to leave."

Artur picked up his kitbag. They left the room and unlocked the door at the bottom of the stairs.

"Thank goodness you allowed us to be upstairs," Artur said to the woman, as they entered the bar. "We could have been in a lot of trouble otherwise. Thank you so much, but we really must now be on our way."

"Won't you have a drink before you go?"

"I'm afraid we don't really have enough time, especially after being upstairs for so long."

They smiled at the woman as all three of them went out of the main entrance. Hugo was very relieved to find his bike exactly where he had left it. He brought it to the entrance, sat on it and started it first time. The two men thanked the woman for her help as Artur got on to the pillion seat. They wished her well for the rest of the war and set off along the road going west. She had told them to take the road to the Mairie, then look for the sign for Plouvien.

After twenty minutes, they were in the village of Plouvien. They stopped by the church to have a look at the map. Artur suggested they should take the road to Tréglonou which would allow them to be in Portsall within thirty minutes.

"There's a wonderful little café run by a lady called Madame Claudette" Artur said. "It will be my pleasure to buy you a coffee before you set off for Auray to return to your lovely wife."

"Let's go!" Hugo retorted, as they both got back on the bike. Artur was especially in good spirits as he felt he was now on the penultimate leg of his journey back to England.

Before too long, they were speeding through the countryside and entering Portsall. Artur directed Hugo to the main harbour area and pointed out the café of Madame Claudette. Once they were off the bike, Hugo put it on its stand to the side of the café. The weather was quite warm, even with the breeze coming from the sea. They went inside to find half a dozen fishermen enjoying a drink. Artur acknowledged everyone in the customary way as he entered and went to the counter.

"Good afternoon, Claudette, could I have one large white coffee and one large black one please. Also, two large brandies?" Artur asked, as he smiled at her.

"Don't I recognise you, monsieur?" she said

"Yes, you are correct. I was here last Sunday; I was with Jean-Luc, but my friend here was not," he said, pointing to Hugo and introducing him. He deliberately didn't mention that he saw her soon after he had just arrived on Jean-Luc's fishing boat from England: there were people around that he didn't recognise.

"We'll be outside, Claudette, if you could bring the drinks to us." She nodded in agreement as she was making their coffees.

"Here you are, gentlemen," she said, as she placed everything on a table that the men were standing at.

"Please, I need to speak to you privately," she said to Artur. She gently took his arm and led him to one side.

"I need to tell you that one of our fishing boats was captured by a German motorboat on Tuesday night. The fisherman was taking two Polish aircraft pilots back to England. The three men have been taken to the *Luftwaffe* airfield north of Landivisiau where they will have been flown to an interrogation centre in Germany. We are all worried that the fisherman will be shot, and the two pilots taken to a prisoner of war camp."

"How did it happen, Claudette?"

"The weather was terrible that night and, by all accounts, they were a long way off course!"

"Was the fisherman Jacques or Jean-Luc? Have the other fishermen stopped taking men to England after that unfortunate incident?"

"No, it was someone quite new; the others will continue to take men back to England. In fact, a boat is scheduled to leave with two English pilots on Saturday evening. The weather forecast is set fair for the next few days so it should go ahead as planned. Sorry, I must get back inside, but I thought you ought to know."

Artur thanked her for the update and walked back to Hugo.

"It looked as if she was telling you some bad news, Artur." He quietly explained to Hugo what had happened as they drank their coffee and brandy.

"I won't be a moment, Hugo, I need to ask her about something."

"Claudette, can you tell me who the fisherman is that's going on Sunday night?" he said in a whisper.

"I'll come and tell you in a few minutes, once I've finished doing a few things." Artur nodded and went back outside.

"What time do you think you need to leave here, Hugo?"

"I shall go back the way we came here, so probably about 3 o'clock. All being well, it should take me less than four hours."

"You'll want something to eat before you go, so when Claudette comes out, I'll ask her what she has to offer us."

Before they knew it, Claudette was standing beside them. She whispered to Artur that it was Jean-Luc who was leaving on Sunday. "He'll be down at his boat in the harbour around 4:30 p.m., should you want to speak to him. I'll get you two fish pies," she said with a smile, "and bring them to you in about six minutes," and left them.

"I think I could do with a drink of wine; will you join me, Hugo?"

Hugo smiled in agreement, so Artur went inside. Within a few minutes, he returned with a bottle of red and two glasses. He brought two chairs to the table, so they sat down after Artur had poured the wine.

"I drink to your health, Hugo. Have a safe and uneventful trip back to your home," he said as they raised their glasses. "You have been an exceptional person who has helped me enormously and taken many risks; thank you."

As there were other people outside the café, they both were in very careful agent mode when they talked: they didn't mention any names of towns or villages, nor what Artur had been tasked to do. They didn't know who any of the other people at the café were, or if any of them might be German informers.

After some minutes, their food was brought out by Claudette; they didn't realise how hungry they were so conversation was at a minimum. They finished the bottle of wine, but refrained from having a coffee. After the meal, Hugo went inside to use the toilet. On his return, Artur stood up and embraced him. Artur put his kitbag over his shoulder and walked with him to his bike; he noticed it was already 3:10 p.m.

"My kind regards to Madelaine and Mélanie. Please take care," as he gave Hugo the piece of paper on which the roadblocks were marked. "You might find this useful."

Hugo jumped on his bike, started it up and drove off without looking back. Artur watched him till he was out of sight. *I don't know what I would have done without that man*, he mumbled to himself.

Chapter 23
Friday, 11 April 1941

Artur walked up to the café, waved to Claudette and strolled down to the harbour. He knew he would be a little bit early to see Jean-Luc, but he thought he would recognise his boat. As he walked along the quay, he saw the tide was coming in. At first, he couldn't see Jean-Luc's boat, but then he saw it next to a similar sized boat; they were both still on their sides. As he looked at it, he recalled the trip to Portsall from the middle of the Channel. He couldn't believe so much had happened in less than a week.

The weather was only a little blustery, so, as he had some time before Jean-Luc would be at his boat, he followed the road to the promontory. He looked out to sea as he sat on the wall. He pulled the small camera out from his trouser pocket, turned towards the village and took a few pictures. He then noticed a man walking along the quay from the café. *That looks like Jean-Luc,* he said to himself. He put away the camera and walked quickly towards the figure in the distance.

"Jean-Luc," he shouted, before he got very near to him. The man stopped, looked at Artur and waved. As Artur got closer, he could see he was smiling at him.

"Artur, how nice to see you. Claudette told me you were here. How was your trip?"

"It's good to see you too, Jean-Luc," he replied as they shook hands. "I hear you are hoping to leave on Saturday evening for England with some airmen; do you have space for me?"

"Of course, Artur; it will be a pleasure, but as I only have two crew, you will have to help."

"I will do whatever you need me to do, Jean-Luc; thank you. It looks as though the tide is on the turn so we will be leaving tomorrow as the tide is just going out, is that correct? What time will that be?"

"We'll be leaving just after 10 o'clock so all of us will meet at Claudette's at 8:30 p.m. The café will appear to be closed, but she'll let us in through the back door."

"Understood," Artur replied.

"Do you know if Madame Delphine has anyone staying at her house?" Artur enquired.

"Not that I am aware of. The pilots are staying with the chap that took you to Châteaulin. For security reasons, they've kept themselves indoors. We tend to keep moving pilots from one place to another after a few days, again for security reasons, until they can be shipped to England by boat. The capture of the boat on Tuesday night by the *Kriegsmarine* has made everyone very nervous, as you can imagine. We are sure someone in the village is friendly with one or two of the German soldiers who then informed them of the trip. We have an idea who it is, but we can't take the law into our own hands until we know for certain."

"I suppose it's inevitable that someone leaked the plan to a German soldier; probably in return for a favour? Life is getting tough in France—particularly in the countryside—with food shortages, irregular supplies of petrol and very little money. Women fraternising with the Nazis must be quite tempting, especially if their husbands or sons have been taken away to Germany."

"As we say in this part of France: *c'est la guerre,*" Jean-Luc stated.

"Just while we've been standing here and talking, the tide has come in quite a lot. It won't be long before your boat will be floating properly again. If you don't mind, I'm going to see if Delphine can let me stay at her place tonight. Do you want me to help you in any way tomorrow to prepare your boat for the trip?"

"That is a good suggestion, Artur. Perhaps you could find your way down here at about 9:30 a.m.? I would rather like to move the boat and moor it this side of the last pier; it will then stay in the water even when the tide goes out."

"Fine, Jean-Luc; I'll see you here 9:30 a.m."

Artur shook his hand and walked purposefully off to Delphine's house in rue de l'église, passing Claudette's café on the way. As he came to her house, he saw her working in the front garden. He called to her, she got up off her knees to see who it was.

"Artur, how nice to see you," as she came to the small gate near to where he was standing on the pavement.

"I heard from Gabriel that he had taken you to Châteaulin. He also told me about the German soldier finding the box containing the kitten in the boot of the car! It always seems so amazing how naïve and gullible the soldiers are. I assume you have come to me because you're looking for a room to stay in for a night or two?"

"Well, yes, I am; I suppose it is a bit obvious really. Is it possible, Delphine?"

"Of course, Artur," she said as she opened the gate for him. "Please excuse my gardening clothes, but it's important to grow everything I can these days. I spend what time I can tending to the vegetable patches; I have even built a chicken run in my small back garden for eggs."

Delphine went in front of Artur as she walked around the side of her house to the back door. She took off her boots and gloves, she led Artur through the small utility room into the kitchen.

"I'm pleased you have come here for accommodation, especially after the terrible incident of last Tuesday night. Those two Polish airmen had been staying here for two nights before they left for England. The weather forecast was not good for that night, but the skipper of the boat, Henri, was a very experienced sailor, even if he hadn't been living in Portsall for many weeks. The centre of the weather front was supposed to have been passing where he was to be several hours later. Obviously, the wind must have freshened so that he ended up in the eye of the storm; he was blown off course."

"It must have been a terrible shock for everyone in the village. Was there any suggestion that the officers in the German boat had had prior knowledge of Henri's crossing that night?"

"It does seem that way, but nobody really knows. On the night of each mission, the boat's crew—plus the men returning to England—have been meeting at Claudette's: nobody else is present. Anyway, perhaps you would like to take your kitbag upstairs and freshen up, you are in the same room as before."

Artur did as was suggested; after about fifteen minutes, he went back downstairs to the lounge where Delphine was standing, looking out of the window.

"Are you alright, Delphine? You seem to be rather preoccupied?"

"It's been reported from some of the other fishing ports nearby," she said, as she turned to face Artur, "that there has been an increasing presence of German soldiers in Brittany. They have been carrying out house to house searches, asking questions, occasionally taking people away to interrogation centres, never to be seen again. I'm getting worried that they'll soon come to Portsall."

"Would you rather I didn't stay here?"

"No, please stay; it helps me to stop thinking about what might happen if German soldiers come here and do what they are doing elsewhere. I am nervous because I have been giving shelter to those brave pilots who will risk their lives to inflict even more damage on the Nazi regime."

Artur understood Delphine's words and her sentiment. He wanted to take her in his arms and try to console her, but he thought it best not to.

"Have you family elsewhere in France?" he asked.

"Yes, I do. My grandparents have fled from Paris; my parents were in Dijon, but—according to my sister—they were captured; nobody knows where they are or even if they are still alive.

"Anyway, Artur, whatever is happening elsewhere, I will continue to do my best for you during your stay in Portsall. I have only a few bottles of red wine left so let me get one. We can drink to better times ahead."

Within a few minutes, she returned with the wine, two glasses and some bread and local cheese.

"This cheese is from the Finistère region: I think you will like the texture as it seems to melt in the mouth," she explained, as she opened the bottle of wine and poured out two glasses. "First take a piece of cheese then swill the wine around in your mouth before you swallow it."

Artur followed Delphine's suggestion; he was so pleasantly surprised by the flavour.

"Can you just taste the seaweed?"

"Is that what the flavour is? I have never had anything like it before; it's fantastic."

They chatted, drank and ate cheese for over forty minutes. Delphine then excused herself as she wanted to prepare supper. Artur turned to look out of the window and, to his surprise, he saw a man he didn't recognise standing in the street staring at the house. He quickly turned away and walked out of his view. After a few minutes, he went back to the window, but the man was gone. He got close to the window to look up and down the street, but he was not to be seen. *I hope that's not a bad omen,* he said to himself. He was brought back to the present when Delphine called him to come and lay the table in the kitchen for supper.

"Now that you've finished laying the table, Artur, please be seated so I can dish up the meal."

"It smells delicious," he said, as he sat down.

Delphine portioned out the fish that was served with potatoes and green vegetables.

"Help yourself to the sauce; it's a favourite recipe of mine that my mother gave me, so I hope you like it."

"It would be rude of me not to!" he remarked.

The meal was over in an hour. Artur asked if he could look at her garden, to which she agreed as she was going to clear up.

Artur went out to the back garden and wandered around for a while. He mainly wanted to go to the front to see if the man had come back. He knew he wouldn't have, but he wanted to check anyway. After some minutes, Delphine came to tell him to come in as she had made some coffee: it was also starting to get dark.

They talked and laughed as they relaxed in the lounge: drinking their coffee and consuming quite a lot of local Calvados.

"I hope you will excuse me, Delphine," as he looked at his watch, "but I have a long couple of days ahead so I ought to get some sleep."

"I quite understand, Artur," she replied, as they stood up at the same time. "I'm very pleased you came to stay with me again; you have really cheered me up." He kissed her on the cheeks, thanked her for a wonderful evening and went upstairs. Within twenty minutes he was in bed and fast asleep.

The following morning, Artur woke up to the sound of movement from the kitchen. He saw it was after 8 o'clock, he remembered he was to meet Jean-Luc at his boat at 9:30 a.m. Within fifteen minutes, he was down in the kitchen: Delphine had just taken the baguettes out of the oven.

"Good morning, Artur. Did you sleep well? I was about to wake you when I heard you go to the bathroom. Please take a seat while I pour out the coffee."

"I slept very well; must have been the Calvados!"

They talked amicably over breakfast. He told her what time he was due to meet Jean-Luc at his boat as he would have to leave very soon with it to be moored at the far end of the quay.

"Can I help with any of the chores before I go, Delphine?"

"No, thank you; I can manage. It's important you meet Jean-Luc on time."

She walked him to the front door as he collected his kitbag from the hallway. He asked if she would like to meet him at Claudette's café at about 12:30 p.m. to which she said she would like that.

Artur walked briskly past the café; he could see Jean-Luc in the distance standing by the quay. They wished each other 'good morning' when Artur arrived.

"I know you are familiar with my boat from last Sunday, but I need the two of us to check the boat out very thoroughly: this time we will be going all the way to Newlyn, not meeting anyone in the middle of La Manche."

Jean-Luc led the way down the gangway on to the boat. He told Artur that he wanted him to be his number 2; there would only be two other crew members, and one of them was rather inexperienced. They went down to the saloon, Artur put his kitbag on one of the benches; Jean-Luc brought out the charts that would be needed from a drawer and placed them on the table. He reminded Artur of the small islands just out of the estuary, the lighthouse at Île Vierge.

"I need you to be in charge of everything to do with the engine, to assist with the raising and lowering of the sails, to watch out for mines, to update the log on every hour. All being well, we should be in Newlyn about 8 o'clock on Sunday morning. In half an hour, I hope you can join me in taking the boat out beyond the estuary so as to check everything, but not under sail."

Artur took his kitbag to the forward cabin and changed into his other set of clothes: the ones that made him look more like a French fisherman. He went up to the aft deck, raised the hatch and lowered himself into the engine compartment. He checked everything out: topped up the oil from the can that had been handed to him and cleaned the plugs.

"Is everything in order, Artur?"

"All is shipshape, captain."

Jean-Luc started the engine. After a while, he checked the dials to find that they all showed the right reading. He told Artur to release the ropes from the quay. As the boat moved slowly away from the quay, Artur brought in all the fenders and stowed them in the forward hatch as he was instructed.

The water was calm as they motored out of the estuary, but was noticeably more choppy as they went further out. After about twenty minutes of putting the boat through its paces, Jean-Luc turned the boat to head back to the harbour Artur put the fenders out and jumped on to the quay with the bow rope which he attached to the capstan. Jean-Luc threw him the aft rope so he could pull the boat in when the engine had been turned off. Artur went back on to the boat, updated the log that he had taken from a drawer and went back on deck.

"I'll fill up with fuel just before we leave," Jean-Luc remarked. "Is there anything you wish to report or ask about, Artur?" He thought all was fine.

"If you wish to go, I'll get the headings plotted and generally potter about on board. By the way, I have heard that only one of the pilots will be coming with us, so it will be a very select band. Not sure what's happened to the other man, but we will no doubt hear more when we meet at 8:30 p.m. tonight at Claudette's."

Artur collected his kitbag and wandered off to the café. As he drew near to it, he saw Delphine coming from the other direction. He stopped to take out the camera from his trouser pocket: he took pictures of the boat and the village of Portsall.

"I wasn't sure if you would be joining me, Delphine, but I'm pleased you have," as they met outside the café.

They greeted Claudette as they went inside.

"Do you want coffee or wine, Delphine?"

"Some wine would be nice, thank you."

A bottle and glasses were brought to the table at the back where they were sitting, as well as a small lunch menu.

They spent over an hour, drinking, eating, talking and laughing. Artur then asked if he could go back to her house as he thought it would be sensible to get some sleep before the trip. She agreed to his suggestion so he settled the bill; they walked back to the house. Artur went straight upstairs, took off his shoes, jacket and trousers and slipped under the bed clothes; he was asleep in no time.

The next thing he knew was the sound of the bedroom door opening. Delphine could easily see Artur was well over to one side of the bed. She carefully lifted the blanket and sheet as she lowered herself on to the bed, at the same time pulling the bedclothes over her body. She gently slid towards his back and moved her right hand down to the front of his underpants. He was warm and still, but she guessed he was not asleep anymore. She slipped her hand inside his pants to find his member was already starting to swell. She gently rubbed it as Artur brought his right hand around searching for the part that went between her thighs.

They teased each other for some minutes until Artur rolled onto his back bringing Delphine on top of him. He lifted himself up so that together they could remove his pants while she still held firmly to his enlarged arousal with her right hand. He pushed her nickers down to below her knees and used his foot to take them off her feet.

Artur was suddenly fully awake; it had all been a dream. *Shame!* he thought to himself and smiled. He was hot as he lay on his back, nobody else was in his bed, but he did have an erection. He looked at his watch: it was 7 o'clock. He got out of bed and looked out of the window: it was cloudy with a slight breeze. He tipped everything out of his kitbag, picked up his few washing materials and went to the bathroom. He returned to his room within fifteen minutes. He checked the three pistols, put two of them under the false bottom section of the kitbag. He placed everything else back inside, wrapped his own pistol in his shirt before placing it at the top.

"I heard you get up," Delphine said as she knocked on his door. "Would you like a coffee, Artur?"

He replied that he would like that very much. He finished getting dressed, made the bed, put his satchel over his shoulder, put on his jacket and went down stairs with his kitbag into the kitchen.

'Good evening' they said to each other.

"I've made an omelette so please take a seat; help yourself to coffee and bread."

Artur did as he was told. He mentioned his dream to her, but not in any detail.

"That's very strange," she said with a smile. "I was tempted to come into your room, but I knew you needed a rest before the trip!" They both laughed.

Chapter 24
Saturday, 12 April 1941

Artur embraced Delphine as he left the house; he thanked her for her kind hospitality and wished her well. He strode off to Claudette's café where he was to meet the others at 8:30 p.m. He went to the back of the building and knocked on the door. Jean-Luc welcomed him and let him inside. He introduced him to Lieutenant Rodney Johnson and was told just to refer to him as Rod. Artur recognised the two crew members from a week ago; he realised it was Jean-Luc's son, Loic, that wasn't joining them this time.

"I've prepared some coffee for you all," Claudette mentioned; "please also help yourself to the homemade biscuits that are on the table."

The conversation was rather subdued, especially after the events of the previous Tuesday night. In a way, they couldn't wait to get to the boat and be underway, but they had to leave when the tide was starting to go out.

"Your attention, gentlemen, please," Jean-Luc asked as he brought their conversations to a close.

"We will be leaving for the boat very soon, but before we do, I would just like to say a few things: our mission is to return Artur and Rod back to England, to the port of Newlyn; the local weather office is forecasting a moderate wind from the south east over La Manche with significant cloud, but no storms. After about two hours, we will hope to continue under sail for as many hours as we can; I have appointed Artur as my number 2; we will be doing this trip in one hop, that's to say there will be no transfer of personnel to another boat in mid-Channel; we expect to be in the port of Newlyn around 8 o'clock on Sunday morning. Do you have any questions?"

There were none so he recommended they used the facilities and walked off to the boat. They all thanked Claudette as she saw them out through the back door. As in all these sorts of trips, she just said 'au revoir'; it was considered a bad omen if anyone wished them 'good luck'.

When they reached the boat, Jean-Luc—as skipper—went on first, he then invited the others to join him on board. Rod and Artur had been told to put any of their personal things in one of the cupboards in the cabin. If anyone should need a rest, they should lie out on one of the benches in the cabin.

At 9:30 p.m. precisely, with the engine ticking over quietly and the minimum of lights on, Artur and one of the crew were ordered to cast off the ropes from the quay's capstans. The other crew member brought in the fenders and stowed them in the forward hold. They were now underway. Even though the captain knew his way out of the port, Artur was told to use the bright light to help him navigate through the semi-submerged rocks and small islands for just under an hour.

The ship's log had been completed by the captain just before they had left the mooring, so it was Artur's duty to complete it at 10:30 p.m. and at hourly intervals from there on, but not to mention Rod's or Artur's names being on board.

The sea got rougher as they motored further away from the French coast. The skipper gave the order to the crew and Artur for all three sails to be raised as he brought the boat about and into the wind. After several minutes, the sails were up, the boat was brought about for the wind to catch the sails, the engine was cut. The boat picked up speed and the only noise was the sea breaking against the bow and the wind catching the sails. They seemed to be making good headway, but Artur—with his excellent eyesight—was given the task of keeping a sharp lookout for any other craft, especially to the starboard side, now that the Germans occupied the Channel Islands.

After over an hour's sailing, the captain asked Artur to take control at the helm as he needed to rest for a while. Artur was comfortable being in charge so long as there wasn't a change in wind direction or if he spotted lights from a ship or another vessel. He remembered how Jean-Luc's boat seemed to travel through the water more quickly than Jacques', so it wasn't surprising to Artur that it would take two or three hours less time to cross La Manche.

For the past two hours, one of the crew had been leaning over the bow with a bright light watching for mines. Should he spot one, he was told to push it to one side with the quant pole as there wasn't enough time to tell the man at the helm to alter direction. He had already done this once, he hoped he wouldn't see another as it was a very nerve-racking responsibility. In the last half hour, the waves had become larger and, as each one broke over the bow, the crewman held on to the anchor chain with one hand, the torch in the other and the quant pole to his side. He didn't feel he was being very effective, but as they went further away from the French coast, the chances of there being mines would reduce significantly.

At around 3 o'clock, Artur found it more difficult to keep the correct heading as the wind had veered more into a southerly direction. He blew the whistle twice to draw Jean-Luc's attention—as instructed by the skipper. In next to no time, he appeared from the cabin and was next to Artur.

"We need to tack," Artur shouted. "You take control and I'll prepare the crew." As he went forward on the starboard side to the man on the bow deck, the boat went over and down the other side of a very large wave, throwing Artur off balance forward of the jib mast. He just managed to grab hold of the jib sheet, holding on with all his strength to prevent himself from being thrown overboard. *Christ, that was a lucky escape*, he said to himself, as he steadied his position. He shouted to the bow man that they were about to tack which fortunately he heard. Artur held on as the boat was brought round, the sails quickly and noisily shot over to the port side.

"I saw you had a narrow escape," Jean-Luc said, as Artur appeared at his side. "Thought we were about to have a man-over-board situation."

Artur said nothing in response, but resumed his duty of looking out for ships, fully aware that the skipper was right. They were making good progress despite some areas of rough sea that the boat seemed to ride over with ease. The moon appeared from behind the clouded sky, but, unexpectedly, there was no sign of any vessel in sight.

After a further hour, the skipper ordered for another tack that Artur conveyed to the rest of the crew. During most of their time at sea, Rod had remained on deck, near to whoever was at the helm. Not knowing much French, he had said very little; he knew when he and the boat were in good hands; he felt his safety was assured.

A while later, Artur looked over to the east as he was aware of the sky lightening with dawn starting to break. He looked back over the bow of the boat to see a faint view of Cornwall. He knew that they had been most fortunate in coming this far without encountering any enemy vessels.

"You no doubt see what I see, Jean-Luc?" Artur said to the captain.

"I do indeed, Artur. I think for once we have been blessed with a relatively uneventful trip to the English coast. By my reckoning, we ought to be in Newlyn by 8 o'clock; that is to say, in just over two hours."

The order to lower the sails was given at 6:40 a.m. so they turned into the wind, brought in the sails and continued the rest of the way on engine power. It started to drizzle as they entered Newlyn harbour: a few people had gathered on the quay to greet their arrival. Jean-Luc brought the boat around so it was facing out to sea, the fenders were put out and they moored her on the port side. The crew carried out the final checks of the deck area while Artur collected his kitbag from the cabin.

Jean-Luc filled in the last entry of the log book in the cabin, picked up his small bag and locked the cabin door. Once they were all on the quay, Artur took a photo of the group. Tony had arrived on the quay so he was duly introduced to Rod.

"Where do you have to go from here, Rod?" Artur asked.

"Now that I'm safely back on English soil, I need to phone my squadron leader and make my way back to my base at RAF Ibsley, near Ringwood, in southern Hampshire. As I told you on the boat, I'm a Spitfire pilot, but my plane was badly hit by enemy anti-aircraft fire when I was over Brittany just over a week ago; I had to bail out. My squadron leader had given each pilot a short list of harbours on the French coast where fishermen were willing to take us back to England, should we need to. Portsall was one such place and it was nearest to where I was."

"Tony will probably be able to give you some change for the phone. Penzance station is about a mile up the road and there's a phone box outside—it usually works."

"If either of you need to get back to London," Tony said, "I would strongly suggest you change in Exeter and avoid Bristol. The city of Bristol has had an absolute hammering from the Luftwaffe since November: bombing the harbour and the Bristol Aeroplane factory at Filton. Even though they weren't always on target, the surrounding areas have been badly damaged with over 1,300 people killed and the same number badly injured.

"I have already made enquiries in anticipation of your return to Newlyn, Artur: there's a train leaving for Exeter at 10:05 a.m. It gets there in time to catch one to London. As today is Sunday, there are only a few trains to Exeter, the others being in the afternoon."

"Tony, you are obviously unaware that Rod needs to get back to his base near Ringwood, so how could he do that?"

"I suggest you both go to Exeter; Rod then takes a train to Southampton, whereas you get one for London. The ticket office will give you train times for both journeys."

Rod and Artur felt they had more than enough information to get to their respective destinations. They shook Jean-Luc's hand, thanking him warmly for getting them safely back to England. They said goodbye to the crew and walked with Tony to Penzance railway station. Tony gave some change to Rod for his phone call while Artur and Tony went to the ticket office with Artur paying for Rod's and his first-class fares to Southampton and London respectively.

"My squadron leader can't believe that I survived the mission," Rod said with a smile, as he reached the other two at the booking counter. "Sadly, only two aircraft out of the squadron of sixteen returned to base."

Artur looked at the station clock to see it was coming up to 9:50 a.m.; he thought it was a good time to walk to the platform. They thanked Tony for all his help and wished him well.

They presented their identity papers and tickets at the barrier and wandered up the platform to the first-class carriage. They found the correct compartment that, so far, was only occupied by one other person.

At exactly the right time, they heard the engine's whistle and the train jerkily started to move forward with great puffs of smoke. With another person in their compartment, they couldn't talk much about their respective missions, so they used the opportunity to catch up on some sleep.

They were awoken from their slumber by the ticket inspector.

"Tickets please," he said.

"Where've you come back from then?" he asked Rod, who was in his flying gear and jacket.

"I lost my plane over Brittany," Rod replied, "so I'm now on my way back to my base," knowing that he shouldn't divulge much else.

"Very careless of you, if I may say so, sir. Well, if you go out again, you give the Nazis hell; after all they've made a real mess of my station at Penzance and an even greater mess of Bristol. They need to be taught a right old lesson they do."

"I'll see what I can do next time," Rod said with a smile.

The inspector left and they laughed at his words.

"Shall we find the buffet car, Rod? I could do with a drink, couldn't you too? May not be much to shout about, but let's go anyway."

They found the buffet car, ordered a couple of large black coffees and two strange looking biscuits each and sat at a table.

"So, Rod, are you a married man, perhaps with children?"

"Certainly not on both counts. I did have a relationship with a Danish girl who wanted to get married and have children. Children are not for me so we parted."

Artur asked most of the questions that Rod seemed to answer quite willingly. After about forty minutes, they returned to their seats for another nap. They were aware of the speaker system telling everyone that Plymouth would be the next stop in six minutes.

"About another hour to Exeter, Rod," Artur said, with his eyes half opened as they entered the station, but Rod said nothing—he was dead to the world.

Chapter 25
Sunday, 13 April 1941

On hearing the train's tannoy system struggling to make itself understood, Rod prepared to leave the train at Exeter: he had about forty minutes to wait for the train to Southampton. He thanked Artur for paying for his ticket and said that he would pay him back somehow, one day. As the train stopped, he shook Artur's hand; it was only then that he realised Rod had lost the last two fingers on his right hand. Eventually, the whistle went and the train pulled away; Artur leaned out of the window to wave farewell to a lucky pilot.

The journey to Paddington was uneventful: no conversation with the other man in the compartment. Artur was pleased to be back in London; he would call his boss in the morning. He realised that the mission had taken a lot out of him, but he hoped the pictures on the camera would be of value to the Service and the War Cabinet.

When Artur got back to his flat, he told himself that he was now no longer in agent mode. He checked with the two people in the sitting room if he could have a much-needed bath. He asked if anyone had phoned for him, but he knew it could only have been Charles—nobody else had his number. He unpacked his kitbag, sorted out the things he needed to wash and put the rest away. Before he had his bath, he sat at his desk and wrote the rest of his report for Charles. With everything that had happened, he couldn't really believe that he had only been away for just over a week.

He had a good night's sleep, a light breakfast and phoned Charles just after 9:15 a.m.

"I really didn't think you would be back so soon," said Charles. "You must have some interesting stories to tell. Can you come to my office at 2:30 p.m. so you can take me through your mission?" Andrew agreed. He went back to the kitchen to make himself a large coffee, after which, he went back to his room to thoroughly go through his report again, ensuring nothing was missed out.

He put on his suit jacket after he'd put the camera, his report and some other papers into his briefcase. It looked quite chilly outside from his bedroom window so he took a scarf from the wardrobe and left for the pub near his flat as it was after midday. He had a pint of beer with a rather disappointing sandwich and walked purposefully to Charles's office in St James. He rapped the brass knocker and was let inside by Miss Jones with a big grin.

"Nice to see you again, Mr Williams. I trust you are well? Please sign in, Mr Carlton-Browne is expecting you."

As on some previous occasions, he strode up the stairs two at a time, knocked on Charles's door and went in.

"Hello, Andrew; welcome back to England." They shook hands as Andrew put his report on the desk. Rather unusually, two chairs had been placed on either side of the window with a small table between them; Charles pointed to one of them, Artur sat down.

"You're looking well, Andrew. I take it all went to plan? Sorry, a silly question as it seldom does!" Charles said with a chuckle.

Andrew handed the camera to Charles. He reached inside his briefcase to bring out the F&S knife, but Charles told him to keep it. He went through his mission in outline only as the details were in his report.

"Well, I never did! What a story. Do you think the German truck has been taken from the barn yet? Fancy coming back to England with the pilot, Rodney."

They continued to discuss the mission and the people Artur encountered for nearly an hour. Charles then changed the subject:

"I didn't know how long you would be away, I thought it would be longer. Now that you are back, however, I need to talk to you about Fraulein Marta Schwartzman: the person with whom you went to Munich in November 1939, and the *Abwehr* contact in Koblenz mentioned by Herr Heinrich Knipp when you were in Camp 020.

"The Service has tried unsuccessfully to locate her through their normal channels so C and I have been thinking that we should send you to Koblenz, once you had returned from France. Our plan is to drop you by parachute into German occupied France where you will make your way to Koblenz. Obviously, you will have to undergo further training so I need to make a phone call while you are here to find out when the next parachute course starts."

Charles went to his desk, picked up the handset of the red phone and dialled a number. He talked for several minutes before ending the call.

"Parachute training courses for recruits hoping to become members of a parachute regiment are every three weeks: one starts on Saturday 19th April, the next on Saturday 9th May, both at Manchester's Ringway airport. I have spoken to the officer in charge about giving you a place on 9th May; he has reluctantly agreed and hopes you will be as fit as his young trainees.

"In the meantime, and to live up to my promises, I suggest you go up to Scotland to attend a sort of refresher course of physical training, unarmed combat and field craft."

"But I did all of that stuff soon after I joined the Service," Andrew explained.

"I realise that, but it was a long time ago. Just remember, you are going to be sent into German occupied France followed by enemy territory, we therefore want you to be in the best possible condition and state of preparedness for a very dangerous assignment.

"I need to make one more call to find out if they will take you and when you can start."

Charles had remained behind his desk during this exchange; he picked up the red phone again and dialled a number. Andrew tried not to listen to only one side of the conversation, but rather wait until Charles had eventually finished. During the call, Charles was making copious notes; the call seemed to go on for over ten minutes.

"Right," Charles said, as he put the phone down.

"I either have a very persuasive manner or there really is something they can do to help. They are running courses for SOE trainees at Arisaig in Inverness-shire. The chap in charge understands your needs and is prepared to slot you in, even though you are part of the SIS. They have as many as six separate courses of five people running at one time, so you can attend the ones that are most appropriate. For instance: extensive physical training starts on Saturday 19th April for a week, followed by a three-day unarmed combat course—he called it silent killing—starting on Monday 28th. Five days of field craft and raid tactics from Friday 2nd May; you will then be finished on Wednesday 6th. You can either return to London or go straight to Manchester Ringway for parachute training that begins on Saturday 9th May.

"How long do you expect the parachute course to go on for?"

"I am told it usually lasts twelve days. As you might expect, the weather in Manchester might delay things for jumps from planes! You ought to be back at your flat by 23rd May. Do you have any questions, Andrew?"

"How do you recommend I get to Arisaig?"

"There's a sleeper train service from Euston to Fort William most weekdays at about 9:15 p.m. Come back to my office on Wednesday morning at 10 o'clock when I will give you all the necessary joining instructions, papers, money and a list of things you will need for the trip."

Andrew left Charles's office only to find he had been there for nearly two hours. He decided he would go to Euston station to find out about the sleeper trains; he had enough money with him so he could pay for it while he was there. The taxi took him to the main entrance; he joined the short queue in the booking office. Charles was almost right: the train would leave at 9:30 p.m., but he had to be there at least fifteen minutes beforehand. He paid for his ticket and went back to his flat.

The following day, in view of comments made by various people, Andrew thought he should try to start getting fit again. He walked in Hyde Park for two hours in the morning and a further two hours in the afternoon in St James' Park. It didn't stop him having a couple of beers and a meal at a restaurant near his flat in the evening. The following morning, he walked to Charles's office as the weather was dry even if it was rather cold.

"Good morning, Miss Jones," Andrew said, as he entered the reception hall. He was greeted with a smile, completed all the usual administrative things and went into Charles's office where they shook hands and exchanged the normal pleasantries. Charles handed Andrew a bulging A4 envelope and recommended he studied the contents thoroughly before arriving in Fort William. They talked for over two hours about the courses and, even though Andrew still viewed the courses in Scotland as being unnecessary, Charles managed to persuade him otherwise.

"By the way, I spoke to the man in charge at Arisaig and as there will be others arriving at Fort William at the time you arrive, he will arrange transport to Arisaig.

"Anyway, as I shall not be seeing you for a few weeks, I think you deserve a good meal before you go—bearing in mind war rationing."

Charles took him to the O&C Club in Pall Mall where they had what Andrew thought was a rather average meal, but the beer and wine were most enjoyable.

Andrew turned down the offer of a taxi so he walked back to his flat. He made a coffee in the kitchen and retired to his room to look through all the papers that his boss had given him. There was a separate smaller envelope containing a sizeable number of one-pound and five-pound notes. All the reading material made him feel a bit drowsy—or was it the wine—so he lay on his bed and fell fast asleep. The next thing he knew was to suddenly wake up to find it was after midnight. He immediately got properly changed for bed and went back to sleep.

The following day was still cold for the time of year, but dry so he once again walked for two hours in the morning and the afternoon. On the Friday morning, Andrew sorted out the clothes he would take with him including his French polo-necked sweater—he knew it would be much colder in north Scotland. He took another two-hour walk in the afternoon before packing his suitcase to leave the flat by taxi for Euston.

Andrew arrived in good time for the train which left on time; the buffet car was open from 10 o'clock so he had a meal then went back to his cabin. The movement of the train helped him to sleep until nearly 6:30 a.m., at which point he went through all the paperwork in the envelope again. He had time for some breakfast before arriving at Fort William at 9:30 a.m. Outside the station there was a man standing in front of a bus; he had a small board with the word 'seaside' written on it: Charles had told him to look out for the coded word so he and three other men boarded the coach.

The journey to Arisaig took over one and a half hours, but with the weather being fine, the trip seemed less because of the views of the countryside around. On their arrival at the house, they were greeted by two strange-looking older men wearing thick horn-rimmed spectacles; not quite what Andrew was expecting. The four from the bus were sent to a hut in the grounds, told to change into the kit on their beds and be at the flag pole in fifteen minutes. Over the next three days, they were severely put through their paces: cross-country running for three hours at a time following set routes with a map and a compass over the vast area of moorland that had been requisitioned from the landowner. They were wakened on the fifth morning before dawn when their limbs were starting to say 'stop'. None of them wanted to be the first to show any weakness as they put on the heavily laden backpacks for an assault up a nearby mountain. The last exercise was crawling on their bellies over marshy moorland for four hours to a hut where an examiner was stationed: they all had passed the tests.

At the end of the week-long training sessions, Andrew felt he had never been fitter—he was ready for anything—Saturday was a rest day. He thought the next three days of unarmed combat and weapons training were relatively easy, although it did involve some new techniques. They were also introduced to the Colt .45 and .38 pistols—as well as some German automatic rifles—and were told to take two shots from the hip rather than the more usual way of taking aim: it was known as the Double Tap system. The final exercises involved a life-sized figure on a winch suddenly coming at the trainee at speed that had to be shot at.

Thursday 1st May was another day off, but was mostly spent listening to the instructors discussing what was expected of them from the field craft exercises and what they would entail. The first assignment was a day and night exercise involving the capture of a hidden enemy group. They were given two map references: one of them was the real location, the other a false one; they had two compasses and maps covering the vast Arisaig estate.

They set off at 8 o'clock on the 2nd in heavy rain carrying all they needed in backpacks. The majority of the terrain was boggy or covered in heather, with the occasional gorse bush and a few wooded areas for cover. They each had a pistol loaded with blanks and an F&S knife. Andrew fell into the role of leader and they completed the assignment without any injuries and executed a surprise attack on the hideout.

The second task was similar to the first, but Andrew was told to work separately from the other three—mainly to find out if one of them was leadership material. Andrew achieved the objective two hours before the group, as one of them had tripped and sprained his ankle.

On the last day, they each operated individually, but had to support one or more of the others if they were captured by the 'enemy' or were threatened with 'enemy' arms fire. This all went well until one man got too close to the 'enemy': he fired his pistol at the left side of his head and rendered him deaf for several days.

The courses for Andrew finished on Wednesday 7th May, whereas the others went on to further training at Arisaig. The instructors debriefed Andrew early the following morning. They were impressed by his leadership skills, his self-reliance, his natural ability to work with the others in the group, to think quickly on his feet and make snap decisions. They believed that all the members of his group will have learned much from his overall skills. Their report would be sent to his boss in the next few days. Andrew thanked them for allowing him to attend the courses and prepared himself to leave for Manchester on the following morning's train.

Chapter 26
Friday, 9 May 1941

Andrew's train to Manchester arrived just after 5:30 p.m. He took a taxi to Ringway Aerodrome where he asked to be taken to one of the officers in charge of the parachute training courses. On entering the hut concerned, he saluted the officer behind the desk at the same time giving him his name and telling him that he had arrived for the course that would start on Saturday.

"Good to see you Williams," the officer said as he welcomed Andrew. "You are just about in time to attend the pre-training briefing that will be held in the large hangar over there," he said, as he pointed out the large building from the window.

"Your sleeping quarters are in Hut 3, so get over there sharpish and be in the hangar at 7 o'clock." They saluted each other after Andrew had signed in and went to find his hut. He found a bed with his name on it, unpacked his clothes into the small wardrobe with drawers beneath and checked that his pistol and F&S knife were still in the small false bottom section of his suitcase. He placed the towel that was on his bed over the rail on the outside of the wardrobe. He was now ready to meet the others in the hangar to hear what the next twelve days would entail.

"Good evening gentlemen and ladies, welcome to Ringway," the RAF officer said to the group of some forty people. "The course you are about to embark on is an extensive programme of various routines that will turn you into a competent parachutist. I need to point out that not all of you will pass, but it is our intention to help you be successful so that you can play an invaluable role in the newly formed parachute regiments. A small number of you are here to be trained for other wartime activities All the instructors are RAF personnel and you will be shown how to pack the parachutes by specially trained members of the WRAF."

The officer went on to mention that the carefully constructed course would take them through all aspects: how to land on the ground without breaking an ankle; to jump from a barrage balloon at 800 feet; how to leave an aircraft such as a Whitley bomber at day and night; lastly how to conceal the chute after a safe landing. He then went through a number of administrative issues before wishing them a successful course and dismissing them.

The following morning, everyone was properly kitted out and formed into groups when they entered the hangar. The next few days were spent perfecting a proper landing after falling from a moving trapeze attached to ropes some six feet above a rush matting surface. It was stressed over and over the importance of keeping knees and feet together.

On Tuesday 13th, before being sent out on an assault course, the senior officer in charge told them in the hangar about the terrible bombing that the *Luftwaffe* had inflicted on London over the two previous days and nights. Most of the bridges west of Tower Bridge and businesses south of the river had been the main targets. It was devastating to hear of the Nazi atrocities, but it made everyone even more determined to complete the course and inflict damage on the Germans in their own way.

They were dismissed and sent out on an assault course that seemed to hold greater poignancy as well as to develop their physical strength and stamina. Andrew was pleased that he had completed the courses in Scotland a few days earlier as he felt very fit; he actually enjoyed the course and did better than most of the younger recruits.

The next day was spent in the packing rooms where the silk parachutes were initially laid out on long tables. The WRAFs demonstrated how the chutes should be folded and packed watched very intensely by Andrew, who kept his eye on one of the attractive girls in particular. He thought he recognised her, then suddenly he realised it was Chloe. She glanced up, looked him in the eyes:

"Hello, Andrew," she said with a big smile; "fancy seeing you here."

"My goodness, how good to see you, Chloe!" he responded, as she looked down at what she was doing.

"I'll speak to you later, Andrew."

Andrew watched as the chute was folded in a particular way and placed inside the pack. Each recruit was then told to repeat the exercise of folding and packing a parachute. Those were never actually used, but unpacked and refolded by the WRAF experts in case they were not properly folded.

They finished at around 3:30 p.m. and were told to take the rest of the afternoon off. Andrew found Chloe and they couldn't believe it was nearly two years since they had last met, when he was working at the bank's Manchester office for a few weeks in July 1939. They talked amicably for some while, then she told him a dance had been organised for a week on Friday at the end of the course, if he was interested.

"Will it be as good as the Unicorn dance hall that we went to?"

"Probably not," she said, "but it should be fun."

They agreed to join the others at the dance, but she explained that she had to leave to train some of the other WRAFs in the art of packing a parachute.

The next day, the recruits were back in the hangar, this time to practice with the parachute harness on. The first exercise involved hanging from a swinging slide about five feet in the air that was unexpectedly released by the instructor. Andrew enjoyed the next exercise better: jumping from a platform in full gear about fifty feet from the ground with the speed of descent controlled by an electrical device. This was repeated several times at slowly increasing speeds and it took up the whole day.

The next two days involved parachuting from a barrage balloon. In the hangar, each trainee took his parachute pack that came through a covered hole from the packing room, so the issuer had no idea who received the chute and vice versa.

Once they were fully kitted out, Andrew and three others walked out to where the barrage balloon was held fast. They climbed into a square cradle that hung from the balloon which was then winched by a motor up to nearly 900 feet; Andrew was the first to jump. The instructor sat behind the men. On the command 'GO', Andrew pushed himself through the aperture in the bottom of the cradle. He felt himself plummeting towards the ground when he was suddenly swept upwards as the silk canopy of the parachute opened. He was hugely exhilarated by the experience as he floated earthwards to make a perfect landing. He twisted the release button at the front to slip out of the harness, he rolled the parachute up into a tight ball as he looked around him—he almost felt in agent mode. His second drop from the balloon the next day was just as exciting.

On Monday, the next day, Andrew looked forward to parachuting from a moving aircraft: after all, that is what he had come for. The first group of twelve, including Andrew, were on the first flight of the old Whitley bomber, together with an instructor. They took off for Tatton Park at 10:15 a.m. after a long briefing by the instructor. They sat either side of the fuselage as the bomber taxied down the runway, the engines roaring as the whole plane shuddered and vibrated. Once off the ground, the noise changed to a loud whistling as the air passed by. In front of the first two men was a large hole cut in the underside of the fuselage through which the parachutists would fall.

As soon as the plane had reached the dropping zone, a green light came on. Each trainee was attached to a line in the roof which would automatically open the parachute after so many seconds. The instructor called out the numbers from one to twelve of those jumping: Andrew was number one.

"Go, number one," the instructor shouted above the noise of the plane.

Andrew did exactly as he had been told: he shouted his number as he pushed himself forward through the hole allowing the pack with his folded parachute to clear the edge of the aperture. He thought he was falling like a stone—out of control—when suddenly he felt a jolt and looked up to see the parachute open, he saw three others above him. He quickly averted his gaze to the ground to see the round, concentric white circles that he was to land inside. He pulled on the strings to alter direction and landed just inside the outer ring.

"Well done, number one," an instructor hollered through a loud hailer, as Andrew rolled up his chute looking for somewhere to hide it. "No need to hide it this time," the instructor said.

Andrew ran away from the dropping area before the others landed: one was almost in the centre ring, but most of the others had been taken by the breeze over forty yards away. Nobody suffered any sprains or broken ankles, just a bit of bruising.

The next day it rained only the way it can around Manchester, so they carried out further parachute training in the hangar. On Wednesday, the last day of parachuting in daylight, Andrew was number six as they entered the plane. This time everyone had all their kit on: an F&S knife plus a short-handled spade placed down their left gaiter for burying the parachute.

They reached the dropping zone. The first four jumped out perfectly, but the fifth man failed to push himself forward enough so he knocked his face badly on the opposite side and cracked his forehead. Andrew followed him out before the instructor shouted his number as he wanted to land as close as possible to him to give him help. Unfortunately, the man was almost unconscious and wasn't able to control his descent or his landing; Andrew followed him down anyway, landing almost next to him. He disconnected his harness, took off his pack and rolled up his chute as the man rolled around holding his ankle. Andrew called over the instructor on the ground who blew his whistle to alert the ambulance.

"Very good work, Williams. He will be fine once he's been patched up by the medics," the instructor said.

At the end of the day's session with the instructors, Andrew was commended for his quick thinking for one of his group who is now on the mend. They were then told that the night time jump would be from the balloon. This disappointed Andrew as he knew he needed to have experienced at least one jump from a plane at night to prepare himself for his next Service mission.

"I know it's a bit of a tall order, sir, but would it be possible for me to be dropped from a plane tomorrow night instead of the balloon?" Andrew asked the senior instructor. "I am sure you are aware that I'm not training to be in a parachute regiment, but at the request of the SIS?"

"Williams, I have signed the Official Secrets Act and I'm fully aware of why you are here. Your request is a very valid one; you have had excellent reports from all the instructors as well as members of your group. I will have to talk to the commanding officer to get his approval. I will let you know tomorrow morning."

"Thank you, sir, I'm sure my boss will be pleased to know that I've completed one."

The following morning after breakfast, the commanding officer asked Andrew to join him in his office.

"Williams, my senior instructor has passed me your request for a night jump from a plane rather the balloon. To help me make the correct decision, I have spoken to many people, but especially the pilot, air traffic control and your boss in London. Based on your considerable progress on this course, as well as what your next mission might entail, we have agreed to allow your request to go ahead. You will need to be fully kitted out in the training hangar at 9:30 p.m. In the meantime, you are to continue with the course with your group and have one more drop from the balloon."

"Thank you, sir, I very much appreciate the decision. Rest assured, I will complete the exercise to the best of my ability."

"You are dismissed, Williams; good luck!"

Andrew tried not to smile to himself as he left the office to join his group in the training hangar, but he was very pleased to be having what he considered was a proper night drop.

During the day, all the groups completed a further jump from the balloon, but this time the men exited the cradle one after the other very quickly. The only problem was that three men from the group before Andrew's all landed on top of each other with one of them breaking a leg

Andrew joined everyone for supper in the NAAFI, but, even though he had said nothing, it had leaked out that he was being allowed to complete a jump that night from a plane: they wondered why only him, but he said nothing when asked.

After a rest for an hour on his bed in the hut, Andrew got himself ready in his kit. He entered the training hangar just before the appointed time and saluted the senior instructor who checked all his kit very thoroughly: that his parachute harness was correctly secured and that he had remembered his small spade in his gaiter. He went through the pre-flight briefing telling him that the drop zone would again be Tatton Park. He was told there would be four goose lamps set in a square and that he was expected to land inside it. He would be flying in the same Whitley bomber as before for a take-off time of 10:15 p.m.

"One of the main reasons we're allowing this night jump," said the instructor, "is that we believe you have more than adequately shown us that you are as ready for it as you can be. I will be on the plane with you, but I will not be jumping," he said with a slight smile.

They walked to the plane, climbed up the ladder with Andrew in number one's position and the instructor two places further back.

"Now, Williams, remember all that you have been taught," he shouted, as the pilot started to taxi the plane to the end of the runway, after clearance had been given by the traffic controller to proceed.

Andrew's excitement was tinged with apprehension as the plane rattled down the runway and was eventually airborne. The instructor said very little during the short flight to Tatton Park except to warn Andrew that the drop zone was quite close to the mere.

After not many minutes, the green light came on and the instructor shouted 'Go'. Andrew immediately leant forward and propelled himself out of the aperture in the bottom of the fuselage. He thought he had been falling for a long time when suddenly the parachute opened. He immediately looked around for the lamps to find that the wind had taken him quite a distance from them. In the short time he had available, he skilfully manoeuvred the chute's lines to take him towards the square of lights. He slightly underestimated the distance to the ground and landed rather heavily before rolling sideways and releasing the harness. An instructor on the ground ran up to Andrew to congratulate him just as he was gathering up the parachute.

"Well done, Williams, you landed just inside the square."

"Thank you, sir. It's so very different at night, especially trying to judge one's distance to the ground."

The instructor led Andrew to a nearby truck and they were taken back to the hangar at the aerodrome where the commanding officer welcomed them with a hot 'toddy'.

Chapter 27
Friday, 23 May 1941

The weather had turned very wet when Andrew woke. He was pleased it hadn't been like that when he did his jump: he thought it probably would have been cancelled. Further training was being held inside the hangar in the morning with individual assessments in the afternoon. Now that the course was practically over, he couldn't take his mind off Chloe and being with her at the dance.

"Your next, Williams," one of the junior officers said to Andrew as the trainees waited for their final appraisal. He knocked and entered the office, saluted the men present and was told to sit on the chair to the side of the desk.

"How do you think you got on, Williams?" the senior instructor asked as he glanced at Andrew.

"I believe I got more confident as the course went on. Obviously, I am pleased to have done last night's jump."

"We don't rank recruits at the end of the training, but we would put you in the top three out of the thirty-six that passed. You showed considerable aptitude, leadership skills and determination, all with good humour at the appropriate time. You are more of an individual than a team player, but you helped men in your group when they needed it most. The course has shown some of your strong points, but we don't want you to get big-headed as the real test will come when you are dropped in enemy territory with very different terrain from Tatton Park. We have no doubt that you will do everything asked of you to the best of your ability. It's been a pleasure having you on the course and your boss will receive a full report during next week. You are dismissed; enjoy the entertainment tonight."

"Thank you, sir, for your kind words; for all the encouragement and guidance given to me and the whole group by your instructors and staff. I look forward to seeing you in the NAAFI later on."

Andrew stood up, shook hands with the commanding officer and his team, saluted them and left the room. He felt on cloud nine, he could now focus on enjoying the evening with the other group members and with Chloe, of course.

The notice outside the NAAFI said that the bar would be open from 6:30 p.m. with a buffet supper and dance band starting at 7:30 p.m. Andrew was pleased to see that dress for the evening was mufti as he had no formal attire or uniform with him. He noticed it was only 4 o'clock so he went back to his hut to rest for an hour or so before getting changed.

Andrew arrived at the NAAFI door just after 6:30 p.m., walked over to the bar and started talking to some of the men in the group. He looked around for Chloe, but she wasn't there, although some of the other chute packers were. He bought a pint for himself as well as two of the men in his group when he noticed one of the packer women come in and look at him. She walked quickly over to Andrew and told him that unfortunately Chloe has had to go to her parents' house as her father has been taken ill. She handed Andrew a piece of paper on which was written her apology and her home phone number. Andrew was disappointed, but thanked her for telling him.

The evening went well, the band was good and Andrew danced with one or two of the packing ladies, but he couldn't help thinking about how much better it might have been if Chloe had been there. He decided not to stay to the very end.

The following morning after breakfast, he joined some of the recruits outside the hangar to wait for the bus to take them to Manchester railway station. The station commander was there to say cheerio, as were most of the instructors; *a bit like the end of term at school*, Andrew said to himself.

He booked himself a first-class ticket to London for the train that would leave at 11:30 a.m. It left on time and he had some lunch in the buffet car at about 1 o'clock. It was very cold for the time of year with rain in the air as he hailed a taxi to take him back to his flat. As he got nearer, it wasn't difficult to notice how badly places were damaged by the bombing raids, especially around the area of Victoria Street. He thought the flat had had a lucky escape.

He unpacked everything, sat down at his desk and completed his report for the last three days of the course. At about 9:30 p.m., he suddenly felt very tired so he retired to bed: he had one of the best night's sleep for many weeks.

On Sunday, Andrew wandered along the embankment towards Westminster, where he saw the damage to the Houses of Parliament and Westminster

Cathedral, as well as fires still smouldering on the south side of the river. When he returned to the flat just after midday, one of his flatmates described the night raids and how much damage had been inflicted. They were lucky, but thousands had not been.

On Monday morning, Andrew phoned his boss only to find that he wouldn't be in till after lunch. He asked the secretary to tell him that he would be at the office by 3 o'clock. He duly arrived on time, signed in, went upstairs and knocked as he entered.

"Andrew, very good to see you," Charles said.

"Sorry I wasn't in this morning, but I had a meeting with C and the Foreign Secretary. All very interesting, but enough of that till later. I looked at my diary before you arrived and noticed you haven't been here since 14th April. You may have noticed how much of London has been affected by the German Blitz. Thousands of people have died with many more homeless.

"My conversation with Mr Eden this morning suggests that Hitler is going to turn his attention on Russia and away from the bombing raids on England. We will see if indeed this is the case over the next few weeks.

"I hear from various sources that you did well on your courses, but did you enjoy them?"

"I learnt a lot, Charles, and I can't wait to put it all into practice."

"That's very good to hear as over the last months, the resistance in France has been gaining momentum. The SOE have started providing bombs, weapons, false papers, money and radios. De Gaulle's preference is for agents to be French nationals living in France or England. The SIS, however, regard the choice of agent very differently—take you, as a good example—you have more than proved your worth.

"What we have in mind for your next mission is for you to find your way into the *Abwehr*. To the best of our knowledge, Fraulein Marta Schwartzman— alias Maggie Pierce—is still operating out of Koblenz. We want you to go to Koblenz to use her to persuade her seniors that you want to operate as an agent for the *Abwehr*; this request comes direct from the Cabinet. Do you think you could do that?"

"I'm flattered, but, as you well know, I will give it my best shot; how do I get there?"

"The RAF have been persuaded to use a few of their planes over the last few months to drop agents inside enemy territory in France. They have set up two squadrons—known as Special Duty Squadrons—of Whitley bombers and Westland Lysanders based in Tangmere and Newmarket; they tend to operate when there's a full moon: particularly the Lysanders, as they have limited instruments with pilots relying on visual references.

"Now that you have completed all that training, we can start planning to get you to Koblenz. It will be quite a complicated route, but we have contacts in a number of places who will be able to help you. The suggestion is that you will be flown in a Whitley bomber, similar to the one you trained on at Ringway."

"Will I be the only person doing a jump?" Andrew asked. "Will I be dropped in German occupied France or inside Germany?"

"Our thinking so far is that you should be dropped in NE France where there are a few resistance groups. In order to gain their full cooperation, we will be dropping rifles, grenades, ammunition and so on in canisters, similar in dimension to the ones you saw at Ringway."

"What name will I be travelling under?"

"You will be Artur Selmer: as you have been for the majority of your missions. Your papers will show you to be the Danish fisherman that you pretended to be when you were in Camp 020. The plan so far is for you to leave Newmarket airfield on Saturday 31st at 10:30 p.m. You should arrange to get there by mid-afternoon, in time for a full briefing by the pilot and the navigator."

"Where do I collect my kit, my papers and money? What extras should I take with me?"

"All your parachute kit will be given to you by the ground crew at Newmarket. Come to my office on Thursday morning at 10 o'clock to collect money and your papers. You only need to take casual clothes and perhaps wear your fisherman's clothing. By the way, those photos you took of the massive construction work in Lorient and St Nazaire were fantastic. They are being carefully studied so the senior staff officers of the RAF and the War Office can come up with a plan to bomb them."

Andrew left Charles's office after nearly three hours of discussions covering various topics. He had offered to buy Andrew a drink, but he declined as he wanted to be on his own. He needed some time to think over how he will be running his life from Sunday onwards. He wondered if he would be interrogated by the Gestapo before being accepted into the *Abwehr*. He walked past Buckingham Palace to see the rebuilding work, then down Palace Road where there was appalling destruction from the bombing. He found a pub that was open.

"Good evening," Andrew said to the barman. "A pint of your best please."

He took it from the bar to the table near the window where there were two chairs. It tasted good; it was what he needed. He wondered where he would be dropped and what sort of people would be helping him on his arrival. He finished his pint and ordered a second one plus a cheese roll. He couldn't help himself thinking that he might be dropped near some places that he passed through with Gerhart, just over two years ago. But he thought it wasn't worth wondering too much until he's given the information on Thursday, or it might not be till he's at the aerodrome on Saturday. He finished his roll and drink after forty-five minutes and walked back to his flat in the light rain.

Up in his room at around 8 o'clock, he sorted out his clothes for the next mission. He had no idea how long he would be away for, but he would only be taking his kitbag and his satchel which helped to limit his selection. He laid things out on the bed, together with his pistol and the F&S knife; he didn't think it was wise to take the Luger with the SS markings on it. After much soul searching, he became comfortable that he had made the right choices so he put all other things away in the wardrobe. He now needed a coffee so he went down to the kitchen and chatted to one of his flatmates for well over half an hour.

The following morning was cold for the time of year with the occasional light drizzle, but Andrew needed to get out of the flat for some air. He was more anxious about the next mission than he had been for any of his previous ones—he didn't really know why—probably because he was going back into Germany for the first time in over a year, this time on his own. Walking around the nearby parks helped him think things through, on the way seeing bombed buildings with people searching through the rubble for something of importance—or a missing person—without fear of masonry falling on them. He saw a pub was open: he needed a drink.

Late that afternoon, he got back to his flat. He looked through the notes he'd written when on the courses, as well as the printed handouts from the instructors. He went over in his mind the procedures he should follow when parachuting from the Whitley. He knew it all, but this was for reassurance. Before he knew it, it was time for some sleep. The following day, he repeated what he had done the previous day.

On Thursday, Andrew walked to Charles's office arriving at 10 o'clock. He received a warm welcome from Miss Jones, signed in and went upstairs.

"Come in," Charles said, after Andrew had knocked and gone straight in to find C was also in the room.

"How are you, Andrew? Have you been able to occupy yourself these past two days, or has it been a bit of a drag? You remember my boss, don't you?"

"Yes, of course," he said, as he shook C's hand. They then all sat on the chairs provided.

"I'm fine, thank you;" he wasn't going to say anything more.

"All is in place for your flight out of Newmarket on Saturday evening," Charles said.

"C wanted to be here today as he has a few words he'd like to say to you on this very important mission."

"Thank you, Charles. The view of the Foreign Secretary and the War Cabinet is that we have nobody who has infiltrated the *Abwehr*. We do have some of theirs who are now working for us, but it is not the same as having someone like you on the inside. What you have to realise is that they might smell a rat, so to speak, and not believe your intentions are serious. As a result, they might imprison you for being a spy or possibly shoot you. As a last resort, if Fraulein Schwartzman does not play ball, she might have to be annihilated by whatever means you consider is appropriate.

"We have sent coded messages to our contacts in the French Resistance and there will be a reception committee near the dropping zone. Until you get into Germany proper, they will be responsible for your safety and for getting you to Koblenz: probably via Luxemburg. Assuming you are successful in becoming an *Abwehr* agent, you should be able to get to Vichy controlled France as you will have been given German papers. You will then be needed back in England with whatever information you can get hold of: names of German agents, military research projects and so on."

"Excuse me, sir," Charles said, as he interrupted C to say something relevant to Andrew:

"Our chaps have produced a map of Luxemburg and western German, including Koblenz—it's on silk so you can screw it up into a small ball and easily conceal it: perhaps keep it in the hairbrush, where you kept the small camera." He passed it to Andrew, who was dumbfounded by its quality.

"In the papers we give you," C continued, "you will have coded names of the resistance people you will meet in the dropping zone. When you mention them, they will know you are for real and not part of the enemy. Your code name will be Stingray, so you ask them what you are known by for identification purposes, just in case you land in the wrong area and are met by either German sympathisers or the Gestapo in disguise.

"Some of the resistance groups in NE France have access to radios or Morse transmitters so you have been given a call sign and a book for encoding any transmissions back to England. Lastly, if you are captured for interrogation with torture, or you find yourself in a life-threatening situation, or your identity has been compromised, you have a small box with an L-pill inside. This is a suicide pill containing cyanide which, when bitten and consumed, will achieve death within seconds."

Silence came over all three men before Andrew suggested that perhaps he should take it before he is even dropped in enemy territory. They all laughed rather nervously at the joke.

"So, there you have it, Andrew," Charles remarked. "I am reliably informed that C has arranged for his driver to collect you from your flat at 10:30 a.m. on Saturday and take you to Newmarket aerodrome." C nodded in agreement.

They continued to discuss Andrew's role, as well as the way he should deal with Fraulein Schwartzman in Koblenz, for a further forty minutes. Charles ended the meeting by telling Andrew that he could call him any time before Friday evening, should he have any questions; he handed him the envelope with all his papers. They all stood up, shook hands and thanked Andrew for his endeavours.

Chapter 28
Saturday, 31 May 1941

Heavy rain pounding on the window woke Andrew just before 6 o'clock. He hoped it wouldn't last into the evening, but he was pleased to be taken by C's driver to Newmarket rather than going by train and taxi.

All his clothes were on the desk and the chair as he had spent most of the previous day selecting what he should take and what he would be wearing over and over again. Once he had been to the bathroom to have a bath and shave, he dressed in his fisherman's clothes and packed the rest in his kitbag. All his papers and money were in his satchel; he looked around his room to check that everything was in order and that he had forgotten nothing. After a light breakfast and a large black coffee, he was as ready as he could be.

C's driver, Don, knocked on the flat's door at precisely 10:30 a.m.

"Good morning, Mr Williams." he said, as Andrew opened the door to him. "Your driver at your service," he said, smiling as he took Andrew's kitbag.

"I would like to sit in the front passenger seat, Don, if I may."

The door was opened for him and before too long they were on their way, passing some of the worst bombed areas of east and north London. Conversation was easy between the two men, helping to pass the time of the journey. Andrew was pleased to see that the rain had stopped with patches of blue sky appearing from time to time.

"Do you want to stop somewhere for a pint, Don?" Andrew asked. "We're not far from a place called Therfield," he continued. "I know a pub called the Fox and Duck that has good beer; we might even get a sandwich."

Don looked at Andrew, grinned at him and agreed it would be a good idea. After some minutes, he pulled into the carpark that was quite full. They took their time over a pint and a ham sandwich before setting off for Newmarket aerodrome which they came to after an hour. They were stopped at the entrance by the guard, they gave their names and showed them their identity papers—plus a letter from C. The guard wrote their details on his visitors' document; he pointed out the building that they should head for. He saluted them as the barrier was raised.

"That looks like the Whitley bomber that I shall be flying in tonight," Andrew remarked, as he pointed over to a hangar. They drove to the office complex. Andrew got out of the car and went inside the bigger of the two huts. An RAF officer was behind the desk with a few others studying a large map on the wall.

"Good afternoon, sir," Andrew said, as he saluted the officer. "My name is Andrew Williams; I believe you are expecting me?"

"Ah, Williams; good to see you old chap. My name is James Talbot, I'm the officer in charge of this aerodrome. Some of the men over there are looking at the route to be taken for tonight's flight. Davis, White, can I introduce you to Andrew Williams, your passenger for tonight." The two men came over to shake Andrew's hand; they greeted each other, they all smiled. Andrew was surprised how young they both looked: *they're barely out of nappies*, he thought to himself.

"I suggest the three of you go to the other hut and have a chat about the mission," the officer said. They left the larger building, but before going to the smaller one, Andrew went to the car, took his kitbag from the back, thanked Don for bringing him safely to the aerodrome and waited to see him head out of the exit gate.

Andrew followed the two men into the hut and they were engrossed in discussions about the assignment for over two hours: Andrew did most of the listening. The drop zone was a field a lot further east than on previous occasions: a little west of Metz near a village of Gravelotte. They had received a forecast of the dropping area at dawn that morning which looked favourable, but they would wait for an update at 2000hrs before confirming the departure time of 2200hrs.

The meeting finished at 6:30 p.m., so Andrew went back to talk to the senior officer who then took him to the large hangar to collect his kit and parachute. He told Andrew to return at 2130hrs for his final fitting before departure.

When he entered the NAAFI, he saw many people in flying gear; others just in uniform were probably ground staff. He bought a pint and wandered over to the two crew he had been introduced to earlier.

"Good to see you, Andrew. Our first names are Colin Davis and I'm Bill White, usually known as Chalky. Missions we've been on before have required a crew of five, but we will only be four to keep the weight down. I'm the pilot, Colin's the second in command. The chaps over there," as he pointed to the other end of the bar, "are Jim Faulkner, the navigator and Freddy Cardew, the gunner. As we won't be dropping any bombs, we will be leaving our bomber behind."

"Pleased to meet you all. I feel very privileged to have you helping me get to my destination," Andrew remarked as he touched their silver tankards with his pint glass. They talked and joked between themselves and others in the bar for well over an hour and a half before Andrew excused himself: he wanted to walk around the aerodrome while it was still light and get some air; the time seemed to be passing rather slowly.

He'd sat down on a bench at the far side of the airfield for a good half an hour. There were clouds around, but he didn't think it would prevent them from taking off; it just depended on what it was like near Metz. He looked at his watch: it was 9:15 p.m. He didn't want to be late so he set off for the hangar. When he reached it, the crew were already there talking to the aerodrome commander.

"Ah, Williams, we were just talking about you," the commander said with a smile.

"All complimentary, I hope, sir?" as he put down his kitbag.

"We've got all your gear here," he continued, "so we would like to help you put it on."

Andrew put on the gear, was helped into the harness with the parachute, went over to his kitbag where he extracted the small shovel to put down his gaiter. He took out the F&S knife and slotted it through his trouser belt.

"How do I look, gentlemen?"

"Looks fine, Andrew. Can you remember how you release the harness and the parachute after you've landed?" Chalky asked.

Andrew demonstrated exactly what he had been taught when he was at Ringway.

"What will be our flight time to the dropping zone?" Andrew asked the navigator.

"We hope it will be less than three hours, but it depends on what we could encounter: anti-aircraft fire, enemy night fighters, change in weather for instance," Jim replied.

"Well, gentlemen, I suggest you all move out to the plane. The ground crew have done all their tasks and are awaiting your arrival," the commander said.

"By the way," he said, "Andrew's boss phoned a couple of hours ago wanting to know your take-off time and estimated time over the dropping zone so he could alert the reception committee that will be putting out the goose lamps; I gave him the details."

They all walked to the plane where Chalky completed the pre-flight checks before being the last person up the ladder and into the fuselage. Once the gunner was in place and the others in their places, the second pilot started the engines and studied the dials; he was happy with what he saw, so he indicated to the ground crew for the chocks to be taken from the front of the wheels. Permission was granted by the tower to taxi to the end of the runway. The senior pilot had now taken over as the engines were brought up to full power. After a few seconds the brake was released and they started down the runway and put on maximum flaps. Andrew's belt held him to the seat in the fuselage as the plane rattled its way down the runway. The next thing he knew, they were airborne. He had been given headphones so he could listen in on the pilots' and the navigator's conversations.

They flew low over the sea and into Belgium airspace after which they climbed to 8,000 feet. Searchlights lit up the sky trying to pick out the plane, but the pilot zigzagged to avoid the anti-aircraft fire.

"Fifteen minutes to the drop zone," Andrew heard Jim tell the pilots. He felt the aircraft start to descend to the agreed height of 800 feet. The second pilot came into the fuselage, attached the harness to the runner in the roof, slid away the cover from the hole in the floor of the fuselage and checked that all was in order. Andrew had attached his kitbag to one of the canisters so as not to get it snagged when he jumped and when the parachute opened. Jim brought the five canisters with the arms and other munitions towards the hole, attaching them to the bar above their heads.

"Two minutes to go," Andrew heard the pilot say.

"Canisters away." Jim pushed them out and saw all their chutes open. Andrew took off his headphones and handed them to Jim.

"Go, Andrew, go!"

He fell out of the plane and saw the lamps in a line along the field ahead of him. Suddenly, with great relief, he was pulled upwards as the chute opened. He directed the chute as best he could towards the line of lamps, but the breeze coming from the south took him past them in the direction of a road. Fortunately, there was enough moonlight allowing him to judge the distance to the ground, just in time for him to execute a perfect landing. He quickly unhitched the harness, pulled the chute to him at the same time folding it all up. He saw he was next to a ditch so he dug deep into it with his shovel, buried the chute as well he could, took off his gear and covered everything over with earth. He looked around to see four people extinguishing the lamps and collecting the canisters. He ran over to help them take the things to the small thicket on the west side of the field.

"Please tell me what name you know me by," Andrew said in French, as he picked up his kitbag.

"You are Stingray. We four are known as the DOME resistance organisation or cell: Dominic, Olivier, Marcel and Emile. For the moment we will speak French."

"You all are known to me. My Service name is Artur Selmer," he said as he shook their hands.

"We must be quick, follow us to the wood as the chutes might have been seen coming to ground."

They dragged the canisters to the wood where there was a track with a truck waiting. Artur unhitched his kitbag from one of the canisters. They threw back the tarpaulin, placed the canisters on the boards and covered them up again. All five of them squeezed inside the truck's cabin.

"You were dropped near Jeandelize, there is a safe house in the town of Briey about twenty kilometres north of here," Dominic said. "As you probably know, there is a curfew until 6 o'clock so we must stay here or in the truck for the next two hours."

They said little to each other; two dozed off, but Artur stayed fully awake, looking at the men, wondering who they really were. Charles had told him that quite a few of the resistance members were communists, but very committed to the freedom of France.

Just after 6 o'clock, Dominic started the engine. He told Artur and Olivier to get in the back under the tarpaulin so that there were only three in the cabin, just like it always was when they travelled together: it then wouldn't raise any suspicions with the military or the Gestapo. Dominic fastened down the cover, returned to the driver's seat and set off. They joined the road, turned left heading for Briey. It wasn't long before they came to the village where the truck stopped.

Dominic opened part of the tarpaulin to let Artur and Olivier out. Artur put on his beret and stood in the road with his kitbag stretching his limbs after a rather bumpy ride.

"We're in Rue Pasteur, Artur. If you go up the alleyway to the side of this house," Dominic pointed to their right; "knock twice on number six and ask for mademoiselle Madelaine. She will give you safe accommodation until you are contacted early tomorrow morning by someone called Heidi; she will be the one to accompany you to Koblenz."

"Thank you for making all the arrangements, Dominic. I hope you find the contents of the canisters of some use to your cause. Will I see you again?"

"It is unlikely, Artur," he said, as they shook hands.

Artur didn't wait for the truck to leave, but did as he was told and knocked twice on number six.

"Are you Madelaine?" Artur enquired.

"What is your name, please?"

"I am 'Stingray'," as he mentioned his code name.

"You are welcome, monsieur. Please come in."

Artur stepped up and went inside to a small hallway; Madelaine locked the door behind him.

"Please go through to the kitchen and I will get you some coffee."

Artur stepped down into a long room with a range on the left side, with a door opposite that presumably went out to a yard. He turned as he reached the centre of the room to see a very attractive woman, probably in her mid-twenties. She fussed over the coffee pot on the stove, then brought it to the table.

"Please take a seat," she said as she poured out the dark brown liquid into a mug.

"My real name is Artur Selmer, please call me Artur," he said, as he smiled at her in his usual charming manner.

"Please may I have black with no sugar or milk."

Madelaine came back to the table and nearly fell into Artur's arms as she tripped over his kitbag.

"I'm so sorry, I should have put it under the table," he said, as he lifted her gently into a standing position. She just smiled as she took her seat.

"How long do you expect to be here, Artur?"

"Until sometime tomorrow."

"You are aware, are you not, that Alsace and Lorraine have been taken by the Bosch—as has Luxembourg—and will become part of the German Reich. We are not really allowed to speak French as we are supposed to only speak German; even the schools are teaching German.

"You ought to know that I shall be going to church for the 9:30 a.m. service very soon so I'll show you to your room."

Artur finished his coffee and followed Madelaine up a stone staircase into a small bedroom that looked out over the back garden. He placed his kitbag on the bed. She then pointed out the bathroom and told him that there were two entrances to it: one from the landing outside his room, the other from her bedroom at the far end of the landing.

"Make sure you lock the door into my room when you wish to use it, otherwise we might find ourselves in there at the same time," she said with a smile. Andrew thought he wouldn't mind that.

"I must go now, Artur. Make yourself some breakfast and I'll be back at about 11 o'clock, but don't go out of the house and don't answer the door to anyone."

"I understand, Madelaine; thank you."

Artur decided he would have a rest while Madelaine was out; he felt exhausted from having no sleep: the excitement of the flight, the anxiety of finding his welcoming group after the parachute jump, the trip to the safe house.

Chapter 29
Sunday, 1 June 1941

Artur was suddenly aware of someone coming into his room; he had no idea where he was, immediately jumping out of bed, reaching for his pistol in his kitbag, he stared at the open door.

"Artur, it's alright, you're safe. It's me, it's Madelaine. You probably had a bad dream and you are a bit disorientated after your flight."

Artur stared at the voice as he slowly put the gun down. She came to him and embraced him to try and make him feel better. They stood there in each other's arms for some minutes; she could feel his heart returning to a more normal beat.

"You need something to eat, Artur," as she released him from her arms. "I noticed you hadn't had anything yet when I went to the kitchen. Follow me downstairs in a few minutes and I'll get you something." He thought she had a soft, gentle, caring voice as he returned to some sort of normality. He heard her going downstairs so he went to the bathroom to freshen up.

"Please sit over there, Artur," she said as he came into the kitchen. He helped himself to fresh bread and jam and sat at the table while she organised some coffee. He noticed the clock on the wall showed it to be well after midday.

"I put my head down almost as soon as you went to church; I obviously needed a rest. Do you have any plans for the rest of the day, Madelaine?"

"Not really, especially as you ought to remain inside my house; you would be quickly noticed as a non-local if you went out and maybe thought of as a German with your slightly Aryan features. You have some bread and I'll get something a bit more substantial in a few minutes," she said, as she passed him his coffee. He reminded her that he preferred it black with no sugar.

"I've made you something that I hope you will like, Artur," she mentioned, as she put the plate of hot food in front of him about twenty minutes later.

"What is it?" he asked, as he took in the aroma.

"As you know, produce is scarce in this country, but I have a friendly farmer who brings me the occasional rabbit: it's rabbit pie cooked in a red wine sauce with potatoes."

"It smells delicious; thank you."

Artur and Madelaine ate together without much conversation, but she had only a small portion compared with his.

"What happens tomorrow, Madelaine?" he asked as he wiped his plate clean with the last of the bread.

"We have to be up by 6:30 a.m.; to have finished breakfast by 7 o'clock. You will be collected at that time by one of the resistance people who will take you to Koblenz. You will pass into Luxemburg then to the capital and on the road to Koblenz. It has been estimated that the journey will be over three hours, but it will very much depend on how many road blocks and diversions you encounter. Please do remember that the French language is forbidden in Luxemburg, just as it is in Alsace and Lorraine. I assume you speak fluent German, Artur?"

"Yes, I do, although it is recognisable as someone who comes from Munich."

"That could be an advantage to you."

Madelaine got up from the table and cleared away the crockery and glasses. She washed everything up and came back to the table.

"I have to go out, Artur. My parents live this side of Metz so I need to go and see them. They are frightened for me and all my four older siblings. They are not in good health; they particularly worry about my two older brothers who have been conscripted into the *Wehrmacht*."

"How will you get there, Madelaine?"

"My sister will take me; she will arrive here at 2 o'clock and bring me back before the start of the curfew. You will have to stay here on your own. Make sure the back and front doors are locked, keep away from the front windows so that you are not seen by anyone passing by. Do not answer the door if somebody should knock asking for me; say nothing to anybody. Help yourself to any food you might want."

Madelaine went upstairs to change and came back down ten minutes later in very ordinary clothes. She checked that she had her identity cards in her handbag. She told Artur to lock the door after she left and to put the key on the ledge above the doorframe; she had her own key to get back in, but she would knock three times before entering so he knew it would be her.

Artur heard a car draw up outside at precisely 2 o'clock. Madelaine said 'goodbye' and went to the front door. He did as he was told and put the key on the ledge after locking it. He went back to the kitchen where he would be out of sight of anyone passing the front window. It was a large room with a table, four chairs and a dark-coloured desk under the window that overlooked the untidy back garden. There were no photos of her family anywhere so he opened the drawers of the desk one by one. Lots of papers in the first, a file with photos of some people in the second, maps of the Alsace and Lorraine region in the third with a pistol underneath: it didn't surprise him. He took out one of the maps, laid it on the table so he could study it and saw it covered Luxemburg and eastwards into Germany, including Koblenz.

That must be over 150 kilometres from here to Koblenz, he said to himself. After half an hour studying the map, he went upstairs to her room. A double bed with a crucifix over her dressing table. A photo of an older couple on the bedside table: *probably her parents,* he thought. No jewellery in sight, so he looked in the centre drawer of the dressing table. He found envelopes with letters inside; he took one out to find—very surprisingly—that it was written in a very passionate manner by a German officer. He noticed the date was in December 1940. He looked through the other six letters and they all were of earlier dates in November of the same year from the same man.

What's happened in the intervening months? He asked himself. *Why a German officer?* He put everything back as it was, and went to his room. He was now very concerned about Madelaine, he wondered where her allegiances really lay. *Can she be trusted,* he mumbled, *especially after I leave for Koblenz?* He checked his kitbag for his weapons and they were still there. It didn't appear that she had searched his belongings, but she might have been very clever.

He lay on his bed, he must have dropped off as he heard the three knocks on the door, then the front door opened.

"I'm back," he could hear her say, as she closed the door behind her. He heard a car drive away.

"I'm coming down in a moment, Madelaine."

As he reached the kitchen, she was already starting to prepare the evening meal.

"How were your parents?" he asked her.

"A bit worse than last time I visited them a week ago," she replied, as she continued preparations.

"Sorry, not much for tonight, Artur; I'm rather short of any luxury items, just a simple salad."

She got on with supper in silence, but Artur wanted to ask her more questions. After twenty minutes, the table was laid and she asked Artur to open a bottle of red wine that she produced from the larder by the back door.

"So, what did you get up to while I was out?"

"I looked around to try and find a map of the area; I must confess that I looked in the drawers of your desk where I found one," he said, at the same time looking at her to watch for any reaction to what he had done: there was none.

"Have you looked after any other agents who have used your place as a safe house?"

"There was one man who was here in February. He was helping to set up a resistance cell based in Metz; he was only here for two nights."

"What about Germans, particularly when they overran Alsace and Lorraine? Did the *Wehrmacht* not visit every house in the village?"

"Not every house, but they did hand out leaflets informing us all that French and our own language were outlawed; they were no longer to be used: only German."

Artur thought he couldn't pursue his questioning any further in case she became suspicious of what he had found in her dressing table drawer.

Madelaine laid the table, put out the food and asked Artur to take his place. She seemed to be very preoccupied during the meal, saying very little, even though he tried to engage her in talking about her parents.

"Do you know the person coming tomorrow to collect me?"

"No, I don't; it could be one of a number of people and never the same one twice. Don't worry, Artur, you will be in good hands."

Once everything was cleared away, she made two coffees; they were going to sit in the lounge, but it was still light outside. She never drew the curtains until 9:30 p.m.; routine was all important in the village, as well as for the *Wehrmacht* or the SS patrolling the streets, but also for the locals.

As Madelaine sipped her coffee, she looked at Artur, she placed her hand on his.

"Artur, I need to tell you that I am very frightened. I may not show it, but inside I'm very anxious. Lorraine—with our capital city of Metz—was annexed into the German Reich last November. Even before that date, the German soldiers were here. I was befriended by an officer, but if any locals find out, I would be considered a traitor to France: I could be paraded in the streets with my hair shaved, ostracised by the community for fraternising with the enemy, perhaps executed. On the other hand, I willingly help the allies by offering my home as a safe house. If the Germans found out, I could be sent to a concentration camp, or maybe shot. These are the secrets that I have to keep to myself. Do you have any secrets, Artur?"

"No, I don't," he replied.

"Everyone has secrets, Artur; go on tell me some of them."

"If I told you, Madelaine, they wouldn't be secret anymore, would they?"

"So, you do have some. What about the women in your life, for instance?" she enquired, as she got up to close the curtains.

Artur was starting to feel uncomfortable with this questioning, but he didn't want to show any annoyance. He decided to just smile at her which brought a smile back from her. He looked at his watch, as he saw it was after 9:30 p.m., he excused himself saying he ought to get some sleep, in preparation for what tomorrow might bring. She said she would wake him in time for some breakfast at 6:15 a.m., for which he thanked her.

Up in his room, Artur checked everything in his kitbag very carefully once he'd finished in the bathroom. He decided to sleep just in his pants and vest. He fell asleep quickly, but after some while, he was aware of his door opening. He pretended not to notice only to feel Madelaine sliding into his bed. She was shaking as she put her arms around his torso.

"I'm very frightened, I need this to try and relax," she said, softly in his ear.

He tried to lie still as she moved her right hand down inside his pants, but it was not possible. His member stiffened quickly as she massaged it. She murmured something and rolled him over onto his back. She had no clothes on so she was easily able to put her legs astride him. He held her head gently, kissed her for a minute, then moved his hands over her breasts. With her right hand, she pushed his phallus inside her, at the same time moving downwards to take more of him. She rocked backwards and forwards, each time giving a soft groan. After some minutes, she raised herself up on her hands; he sensed Madelaine was smiling as she climaxed before he did. She lowered herself gently onto Artur; they lay still for some while: he was sure she had fallen asleep.

Chapter 30
Monday, 2 June 1941

Artur woke up to find he was alone in bed; he had not been aware of Madelaine leaving him. He looked at his watch: it was 6 o'clock. As he went to the bathroom, he heard some movement down in the kitchen. On his return to his room, he dressed, repacked his kitbag with his pistol near the top. He checked that the silk map and the L-pill were in his hairbrush. He went down to the kitchen.

"Good morning," Madelaine said. "I trust you slept well, Artur?"

"Very soundly, thank you," he replied, as he smiled at her; she seemed more relaxed this morning. He asked him to sit at the table, help himself to bread and jam while she finished making the coffee.

"I know I asked you this yesterday, but do you know who will be collecting me?"

"No, I don't, but whoever it is will only know you as 'Stingray'; you don't mention your real name."

Artur knew that, but he said nothing more. When he had finished breakfast, he went to the toilet to make himself more comfortable for the journey. At precisely 7 o'clock, there was a knock on the front door. Madelaine answered it.

"I have come to collect 'Stingray'," a man's voice said with some authority, in German. "I will be outside waiting for him."

Madelaine went to the kitchen and told Artur to put on the balaclava that the man had given her. Artur was a bit surprised, but did as he was told. He embraced Madelaine, thanked her for letting him stay and walked to the door without looking back at her.

"Get in the passenger seat," the man said in German. "From now on, we all must speak German."

As he went around to the passenger door of the truck, he saw there was a woman seated in the middle, also with a balaclava on. She smiled as he got in; he immediately recognised who it was from her eyes: he couldn't believe it, but he knew it was Monique. He was well aware that he should say nothing, even if he wanted to. He closed the door at the same time as the driver got in. Artur briefly put his hand on Monique's without looking at her: he gave it a squeeze. Each other's recognition was complete.

The driver drove up the narrow street, turned right, then to the left after about 150 metres.

"It's a long journey," the driver said; "we are bound to encounter road blocks as we enter Luxemburg and, more especially, as we get near the border with Germany proper. This vehicle is registered in Germany and has German number plates. I hope you have all the necessary papers? By the way, this woman's name is Heidi Schmidt."

Artur knew he had his papers, but he touched his satchel under his jacket for his own reassurance. After about fifteen minutes, when in open countryside, the driver stopped the truck.

"We are supposed to be working for a building company. Under the tarpaulin are our tools, as well as a bag with dark blue overalls; we all must put them on. I have come this way several times in the last few weeks to check the route out, once I heard you were coming. The man we had in the seat that you're in looked a lot like you, 'Stingray', we should be alright. We dropped him off at the end of the street where you were staying. Here," the driver said, "use his papers just to be on the safe side."

Artur looked at the papers to see that he had been given the name of Klaus Leitner. He and Monique had still said nothing as they put on their overalls, but they did look at each other from time to time: they both smiled.

"What are you doing here?" Artur whispered, when the driver was out of earshot. "I assume Heidi is your agent name?"

"About three months after de Gaulle's broadcasts from London, a few people got together to form a resistance cell north of Dijon. One of the leaders lived in Pesmes; he asked if I wanted to join the group, so I did. I was given the name Heidi, so that's what you must use."

"I didn't know you spoke German?"

"I've never needed to when you were around," she replied with a wink.

Artur couldn't help thinking about the times he had met Monique, particularly when he and Gerhart stayed with her at her house in Pesmes in April 1940, when they were escaping from the French police.

They all climbed back into the truck; the driver drove off at a sensible speed, until they reached the first road block. He told them to remove their balaclavas.

"I'll do all the talking," the driver said, as they came to a halt in front of the barrier.

"Papers!" the guard ordered, as he gesticulated with his automatic rifle pointing at the driver. They each handed them over in turn.

"You saw us all last Thursday," the driver said, hoping it might make a difference and hurry things up.

The guard looked at each person's papers, looked at the person concerned and back to the list that was on a board.

"What is the nature of your business in Luxemburg?"

"We are builders working on the repair of a building near St Michael's Church, in the centre of the city. We've been coming through for the last few weeks," the driver replied calmly.

Deliberations between the guard and the officer in charge seemed to go on for a long time. Just as the driver was going to say something, the guard handed back their papers and raised the barrier.

"Heil Hitler!" they all said, as the guard gave the Nazi salute and waved them through.

"They don't normally take that long," the driver said. "Maybe they've been given information from an informant that materials were dropped from a plane a few days ago," the driver said, as he looked over at Artur and smiled.

Once they had been driving for a while in the city, they looked for the sign pointing east to the German border. Control at the border was easier than expected so, after only a very little delay, they drove at a reasonable pace for the next hour until the driver pulled into a garage for fuel. Artur offered to pay, but the driver turned him down.

Once they were on their way again, there was some conversation between them all that seemed to be quite relaxed.

"As we get nearer to Koblenz," the driver said, "we will be coming in from the west to turn right over the bridge that crosses the Mosel. Heidi has an uncle who lives in a street that is off Simmerner Strasse that will be used as a safe house for you two people. His name is Friedrich; he has lived in Koblenz for

208

many years and is familiar with the main locations of the German hierarchy in Koblenz. You must be very careful in this city as there is a large presence of the *Wehrmacht* located mainly on the other side of the Rhine. Please understand that I know nothing about what you are here for, I am only expected to bring you here safely."

Nothing needed to be said by either of the other two after the driver's words, although Heidi looked at Artur and smiled once again.

"We are now heading down Simmerner Strasse," the driver said after about twenty minutes. "I will pass the road you need and drop you off about one hundred metres further on; you are then on your own."

The driver pulled up, Arthur gave him the other man's papers that he had been using; he and Heidi stepped out on to the pavement. Within moments, the truck was gone. Heidi and Artur walked up a sideroad past two streets, turned right, then right again after passing three roads. They crossed the road and after twenty metres, Heidi stopped and knocked on the door. An older man opened the door, saw it was his niece and beckoned them to quickly come inside.

"How was your journey?" he asked as he shook Artur's hand and embraced Heidi.

"It was fine uncle Friedrich, thank you. Please call me Heidi, this man's name is Artur, but he is also known as 'Stingray'."

"You are slightly earlier than I expected; come inside to the kitchen. Would you like something to drink or eat?" he asked, as he looked at his watch. "I have a nice bottle of Mosel on the floor of the larder? It should be quite cool."

Heidi said they would like that very much. She put her rather oversized handbag on one of the kitchen chairs, Artur put his kitbag next to the same chair. They stood in their dark blue overalls when Heidi laughed at how they looked. She undid the buttons, slipped out of the overalls and suggested Artur did the same.

"Here we are," Friedrich said, as he poured out three glasses of the pale liquid. "It is good to see you after all these years, Monique: sorry, I must remember to call you Heidi." They touched glasses and took a sip of the well-balanced, slightly dry wine.

"Out of interest, uncle Friedrich, have you spoken to my aunt Vivienne, your sister-in-law, recently?"

"No, I haven't, but I understand she keeps in quite regular contact with some of her friends south of Hamburg. One or two of them are strong Nazi supporters which makes me think that she might be like-minded.

"Now, Heidi, you haven't really told me why the two of you want to stay here. As you might know, however, I have good contacts in the *Wehrmacht* and the SS in Koblenz. I'm not a member of the Nazi party, but they don't interfere with my life: they probably think I'm too old to get in their way!"

"What I'm going to tell you, uncle, is of a highly secret nature and is only for your ears."

"I fully understand, Heidi, you have my word," as he poured out more wine and touched their glasses.

"Artur, or 'Stingray' as he is known within the French Resistance, wants to get in touch with the main *Abwehr* office in the city. There is someone that he particularly wishes to meet. He used to know this woman when she worked for the British Secret Intelligence Service in London, but she now appears to be working in the German Intelligence Service. She is believed to be working at quite a senior level in the *Abwehr* office in Koblenz. We are hoping you will be able to help Artur."

"Tell me what you want and I'll see what I can do."

"The woman's name is Fraulein Marta Schwartzman. Artur needs to have it confirmed that she does work here and, if possible, the address of where she is living in Koblenz."

"I know where the office is, I have a distant unmarried relative working as a secretary there. She has an apartment not far from here and I see her from time to time; she won't be surprised if I go to see her this evening. I don't want to phone her in case her line is bugged.

"Heidi, we'll leave you in the kitchen to make something to eat, I'm sure you must be hungry after your journey. I will entertain Artur over another glass of wine in the lounge."

After some twenty-five minutes, Heidi came in from the kitchen to say that lunch was now ready. They left the lounge for the kitchen to find she had cooked a delicious piece of meat with fried potatoes and a green salad. Friedrich fetched another bottle of wine whereupon they all settled down to a much-needed meal that lasted for well over an hour.

"That was the most delicious meal I have had for a long time, Heidi; thank you very much," Friedrich said. "Please follow me so I can take you to your rooms."

They went up to the first floor to Heidi's and then the second floor to Artur's, having shown them where the bathroom was on the first floor. Artur said he would like to have a rest so Heidi and Friedrich returned downstairs to the lounge: Artur could hear them talking, but couldn't make out what they were saying. He didn't really need a sleep, he wanted to write up some notes about what had happened since leaving Newmarket airfield. After the best part of an hour, he lay on his bed thinking about his mission: he knew it was very risky.

"Artur, do you want to join us downstairs?" Heidi said as she gently knocked on his door. "Uncle Friedrich will be leaving for his distant relative's apartment soon."

"I'll be right down," he replied, as he slipped off the bed and put on his shoes.

"I'll be leaving in a few minutes," Friedrich said when Artur came into the lounge. "I've written down the woman's name," he said, as he showed Artur a piece of paper to make sure he had remembered it correctly.

"That's her name," Artur said.

Friedrich left his house indicating that he may not be back for over an hour; they were to make themselves comfortable in his absence.

"I'm sorry," Artur said, "we haven't had the chance to talk since you collected me from Madelaine's house early this morning. It really is good to see you; you are looking well. Are you happy working for the Resistance?"

"I would have preferred it if France hadn't signed the armistice so readily last June, but there are many people around the country—in the German occupied zone, as well as the Vichy controlled area—who are actively trying to make life as difficult as they can for the Nazis. You may not know it, but I have been assigned to escort you out of Germany, maybe into Belgium or the Netherlands, or even back into France, once you have completed your assignment."

"Did you know it was me you were to be escorting?"

"I had no idea; I only knew the name 'Stingray', the fewer the people who know the real identity of agents, the better. Heidi Schmidt is my name within the group I work for and I have papers that were prepared by someone known to the DOME cell."

They continued to discuss the possible exit routes and other matters for over fifty minutes, by which time they had finished the second bottle of wine and had had a cup of coffee.

"You seem different somehow," Heidi remarked. "What's going through your mind with this mission? Is it because you are working on your own?"

"I suppose it's because I'm now in real enemy territory and I am going to do something that my bosses are not expecting me to be successful in achieving. Originally, I was to persuade the *Abwehr* that I should become a German agent, but at the last moment they changed their mind. I have to remove someone who is a traitor to my country and is working as a senior operative for the enemy. If I'm successful, everyone who has helped me will be on the wanted list of the Gestapo; that is what is worrying me, especially as you will be one of those people on the list. I had no idea you had joined the Resistance; to me, this might be the first time that your life will be in danger: it's because of my presence here in Koblenz."

Heidi moved to sit next to Artur on the sofa, she held his hands in hers and kissed him. She could feel the tension in his body.

"You must understand, Artur, that I am not afraid of what might happen to me; my duty is to make sure that you get back to England safely, and in one piece."

At that moment, they heard the key turn in the front door so Heidi quickly returned to her chair. She smiled as she remembered being a young teenager when she was caught in a huddle with a boy from her school by her parents.

"I'm back, Heidi," her uncle called out. He came into the lounge smiling like a Cheshire cat.

"Hopefully I have all the information you need, Artur. The young woman was very helpful. Apparently, Fraulein Schwartzman returned from a meeting in Berlin only yesterday; she will be in Koblenz for the rest of the week."

He handed a piece of paper to Artur on which were the addresses of the *Abwehr* office in Koblenz plus Marta's home address.

"That's really very helpful, Friedrich," Artur said. "May I keep it, please?"

"Of course, I got it for you anyway; it's of no use to me."

"Where abouts in Koblenz is the home address?"

Friedrich went over to his desk, opened a drawer, brought out a map of the city and laid it out on the table. Heidi and Artur got up, stood on either side of

Friedrich and watched Friedrich's finger follow Simmerner Strasse up towards the Mosel, then over to the Kaiser Wilhelm memorial.

"Here," he said, "this is the road where Fraulein Marta lives. My young relative says that the Fraulein leaves her office on most days at 5:30 p.m. and never seems to see anybody after office hours, but goes straight home. Does that give you enough details, Artur?"

"That's excellent," he said as he looked at his watch. "It's too early for her to be going home, so I would like to go to where Marta's apartment is and then return here. Will you come with me, Heidi? We will pretend to be a courting couple just out for a stroll," Artur said with a smile.

Artur went up to his room to fetch his satchel containing his German identification papers that the Service had made for him, leaving the ones he didn't need in his kitbag. He took out his pistol, checked that the magazine was full and pushed it down the belt on his left side. He put on his jacket and returned to the lounge. Within a few minutes, Heidi appeared having brushed her hair wearing bright lipstick and rouge on her cheeks.

"We shouldn't be out too long, Friedrich. If we're not back by 7 o'clock, you can assume we have a problem, so phone a friend for assistance."

Chapter 31
Monday, 2 June 1941

Heidi had her arm linked through Artur's as they casually walked up the Simmerner Strasse: just as Artur had said to her. After some minutes, they were heading for the statue and came to a building on their left: Marta's flat was on the second floor. Artur looked down the list of names living there; he saw her name, just as Friedrich had told them.

"I don't want to hang around too long, Heidi, but let's cross over the road. It's just coming up to 5:30 p.m. so she should be returning home very soon."

They went across the road, walked for about forty metres and stood by a tree: they waited. They saw some German soldiers walking towards them so Artur leant against the tree, gently brought Heidi to him taking her in his arms. He kissed her passionately on her lips just as the soldiers passed them. The soldiers smiled at the couple, making comments about them being lovers.

The couple stayed close until the soldiers were more than thirty metres away from them. Artur turned his head just in time to see Marta walking up the road to her house: he recognised her immediately. He looked at his watch: it was 5:40 p.m. He watched her every move as she placed the key in the main door and went inside. She looked behind her, up and down the road then closed the door. It seemed as though she was nervous or wary about something, *perhaps she always behaves like this*, Artur thought to himself.

"Did you see her?" he asked Heidi.

"Yes, I did. Why do you think she's behaving that way?"

"I have been involved in many situations since I left you at that station in France at the end of March last year. One particular mission was to Norway where I had to kill a woman who was trying to prevent the king of Norway from taking up exile in London. She worked with a small group of German agents in London some of whom reported to Fraulein Marta Schwartzman here in

Koblenz. I believe she was briefed by someone who gave the identity of the person that shot that woman. I believe she knows I'm in Germany; I need to get to her before she lets her hounds loose on me.

"If I get caught by her mob, I will be interrogated like no other agent before and if I say nothing or not admit my involvement in the shooting in Norway, I will be executed by firing squad."

Artur felt Heidi shiver at what he had just said, but she needed to know what he was up against. He continued to watch the building that Marta had gone in to, particularly the windows on the second floor: no noticeable movement.

"I think we should start to wander back to your uncle's place," he said to Heidi, as he turned to walk towards the memorial and go the long way back. She linked her arm through his as they set off. Within twenty-five minutes, they were back at the house: it was just before 6:30 p.m.

"Well done, you two, I was starting to get worried about your safety; you can't be too careful in this part of Germany, or any part for that matter. What are your plans for tomorrow, Artur?"

"We will go out at about the same time to make sure Fraulein Marta sticks to the same schedule. Until then, we shall just have to stay in your house, if that's alright with you?"

"Of course, it is; just make yourselves feel at home," Friedrich replied, as he went into the kitchen. He came back with three glasses and a bottle of red wine.

"I get the impression that you probably will prefer red to white," he said, as he opened the bottle, sniffed the cork and poured out two glasses. "I take it you would prefer some white, Heidi?" She replied that she would.

They toasted each other's health and grinned as they took a large sip of the liquid.

"That is a particularly pleasing wine," Artur said.

"It's a French wine from Bordeaux that I bought a few years before the war; I only have three more bottles left so take it easy: we don't want to finish it before tomorrow," he said with a loud laugh.

The evening went well, Heidi prepared a meal for them all under Friedrich's supervision. They finished off with coffee and a French brandy that Friedrich brought from a cupboard in the hall. At about 10 o'clock, Friedrich said he was going to retire to bed as he had a few important things to do in the morning. He thanked them for a very enjoyable evening and went upstairs to his bedroom on the first floor. After he had gone into his room, Heidi went and sat next to Artur on the sofa.

"I wish we didn't always have to use German all the time, Artur, I'm much more comfortable speaking French and in particular using that language with you; it's what we have always spoken when we are together."

"I fully understand, Heidi," he replied in a whisper in French; "I also much prefer using the name Monique: it's a much more beautiful name than Heidi.

"We have to remember, however," as he reverted back to German, "that we are here in Germany. I am on a special mission, our papers are forgeries, our identities are false; we have to act out the parts we have been instructed to play, or we could find ourselves in serious trouble."

He put his arms around her, drew her close to him, looking lovingly into her eyes.

"We both have ideas of wanting each other tonight, but we must be patient, at least until we are out of Germany." They then kissed for a number of minutes, before Artur moved his face away from hers and smiled.

"The next few days are extremely important to my mission, so I need to get a good night's sleep; after all, I haven't slept properly for two days."

They had a final lengthy kiss; Artur stood up, lifted Heidi to her feet and touched her gently on the cheek. He left the room and went up to his bedroom after visiting the bathroom on the first floor.

It was the sun shining brightly through the curtains in his room that woke him. He couldn't believe it was already 8:30 a.m., nobody had come to wake him. He lay there and was aware of voices—probably coming from the kitchen. He wondered what Friedrich was going out for in the morning, but then his mind turned to Heidi: what a coincidence that she would be helping him escape yet again.

Artur went to the bathroom, returning afterwards to his room to get dressed. He was aware of someone knocking on the front door, so he opened his bedroom door. He strained to hear what was being said, but he was too far away, although he knew the visitor was a male. After a few exchanges, he heard Friedrich appear to go back to the kitchen, presumably to speak to Heidi. He then returned to the front door and left the house. Artur went to his window that overlooked the road, but, as they were walking away from the house, he couldn't see the face of the man who was with Friedrich. He came away from the window rather puzzled and went downstairs.

"Good morning, Heidi. I knew your uncle was going out, but I thought it would be later in the morning."

"So did I, but as his friend arrived at the time that he did, he had to go."

"Do you happen to know what they were going to be doing?"

"I believe they were going to meet some other people and then all go for a meeting in the town hall. Would you like some breakfast, Artur? There's not a lot of choice, but there is rye bread, cheese, ham and hard-boiled eggs. Please sit over there, I'll bring a coffee to you."

Artur did as he was told, realizing he was quite hungry; the coffee was good too.

"What are we going to do until we leave for Marta's at 5 o'clock? It wouldn't really be wise to walk anywhere, would it?"

"If we go down to Simmerner Strasse, we could catch a train from the main station to Cologne. It should only take just over an hour and a half and, for the most part, it is very picturesque as the line follows the Rhine. We could have a light lunch there and be back again in good time to be at Marta's home. What do you think?"

"It would be better than just sitting around in doors, I agree. Come on then, let's just do it. Make sure you've got all the relevant papers. Leave a note for Friedrich so he knows roughly what time we'll be back."

After they had completed everything, they used the spare key to lock up and walked to the station. The weather was warm, they only waited for fifteen minutes for a train to Cologne. They went into the cathedral, had a snack lunch in a nice bar and caught the train back to Koblenz at 2:30 p.m.

"Anybody at home, Heidi said, as she entered the hallway. There was no reply and it was obvious that Friedrich had not come back yet.

"We've got half an hour before we set off for Marta's; do you want anything to drink?" Heidi asked.

"Just a coffee will be fine for me, thanks."

Once he'd finished his coffee, Artur packed his kitbag in the same way as the day before, checked his papers and they were ready to leave just after 5 o'clock.

They chose a tree that was a bit further away from the entrance to Marta's apartment this time. They thought it was strange that—just like the day before— a small group of soldiers came along the pavement. Heidi and Artur went into a romantic clinch with Artur able to keep an eye on the soldiers coming towards them. As they got next to them, one of the corporals tapped Artur on the shoulder, telling him that he and his girlfriend had to move on and not linger in this part of the city.

"But we like it here; we were here yesterday without being a problem to a different group of soldiers."

"Show me your papers," the corporal demanded.

Artur wanted to argue with the soldier, but Heidi suggested they should do as they were asked. They slowly presented their papers that were very carefully scrutinised, their names and ID numbers being written on to a pad held by one of the other soldiers.

"Why are you in Koblenz?" the corporal demanded.

"We've come to visit a relative who lives here," Heidi replied with a smile, touching him gently on the hand, using all her charm. The soldier smiled and suggested she would be better off being with him.

"Possibly," Heidi replied as she gently touched his face. "Maybe next week if you're passing this way."

"I'll be off duty next Monday, so I'll come by this way at the same time."

Heidi smiled; the soldiers moved on with the corporal turning around several times to see Heidi waving at him. Artur suddenly realised that he had been distracted by the soldiers and thought he might have missed seeing Marta. He looked at his watch: it was 5:35 p.m. He told Heidi he was going across the road, for her to stay by the tree, but to keep her eyes skinned; if he wasn't back in fifteen minutes, she was to return to her uncle's and wait for him there. He took out his pistol, put it in his jacket pocket at the same time giving her his kitbag.

He had seen a tree not far from the entrance to Marta's apartment block that he headed for. He got there just as she came around the corner. He waited for her to reach the door of her apartment block before he walked up to her just as she opened the door. She hadn't noticed him as he put his hand across her mouth and frog-marched her into the hallway, closing the door behind them.

"Don't try anything or you're a dead woman, Marta," he said directly into her ear in German as he dragged her up the stairs to the second floor—she had recognised his voice immediately and was now concerned for her safety. She knew she had to unlock the door of her flat so she fumbled with her keys to try and gain some time to think. They went into the flat with Artur closing the door behind them with his foot.

For the first time, he let Marta see who it was that had hold of her, but he didn't release his hand from the back of her neck. He found a handkerchief in his left pocket and he slipped his right hand across her throat to prevent any sound coming out. In one swift movement, he quickly brought the handkerchief over her mouth bringing it tight round the back of her head and tied it so that she could only make a few sounds.

Artur pushed Marta into a chair next to a desk, brought out his pistol from his jacket pocket and pointed it at her head.

"I have many questions to ask you, Marta. I don't need you to try and say anything, but give your answers by just nodding or shaking your head. I will know when you are not telling the truth.

"Are you expecting anyone else in the next two hours?" she nodded: no.

"Do you know the name Schwartz in London?"

She indicated 'yes'.

Artur went through a number of other questions and he was satisfied with the answers given by her. With his pistol still pointing at her head, he managed to release the handkerchief, at the same time telling her not to shout out or try to jump out of the chair.

"As you will recall," he said, as he sat down in a chair opposite to her, "you were badly injured when you were at that meeting with me in Munich. How is it that you didn't die on the operating theatre, as everyone in London was led to believe?"

"In a way, Sparks was my saviour," she replied, "and I wasn't as badly injured as was first thought. The surgeons did a wonderful job and I was released after a week as long as I had someone to care for me: Sparks was there for me. I stayed at his house for over four weeks until I was strong enough to fend for myself. I didn't want to return to England so, as he had connections within the *Abwehr*, they took me on as one of their team. He dealt with all the paperwork: my death certificate, my phoney burial and so on."

"Do you know why I'm here, Marta?"

"I heard that someone from the SIS called Artur Selmer was in Germany and had come to Koblenz; I suspected it was you and that you would want to find me. I don't really know what else you want," she said very calmly.

"My instructions from London are that you should help me to be taken on by the *Abwehr*, as one of your agents. If that proves to be an impossibility, I have an alternative mission."

"I can guess what the alternative might be: either you take me back to London for interrogation, or you execute me for treason right here. I don't have the power or the seniority to take you on as an agent of the Reich and, even if I did, I don't believe you would have the commitment to the cause."

All of a sudden when Artur was looking about the room, Marta jumped out of the chair, pulled open the drawer nearest to her and anxiously searched inside with her right hand. Artur immediately leapt at Marta from behind just as she was about to pull out a pistol. He slammed the drawer shut with a great deal of force putting his other hand over her mouth. She tried to scream, but he was strong and determined so that her scream was only a muffled sound. He now no longer held the drawer's handle, but brought his hand across her head and with all his strength, he twisted it while he kept her shoulders straight. Her body went tense, she knew what was about to happen to her, but she hadn't the strength to resist. There was a crack as he broke her neck. She went limp and he let her fall gently to the floor. He placed his fingers on her neck: there was no pulse.

Artur lifted her over his shoulder, walked to the hallway and entered what he guessed was her bedroom. With one hand, he pulled back the bedclothes, laid her down on the bed, took off her shoes and covered her so she looked as though she were sleeping. He returned to the lounge to make sure that everything was back in its place, just as it was when they first had entered the room. He felt sick: bile rose up in the back of his throat so he swallowed hard. He collected his pistol from the chair, went out of the flat and down the stairs to the street. He knew he had to get back to Friedrich's house; he hoped nobody had seen him enter or leave Marta's place.

Chapter 32

Tuesday, 3 June 1941

Artur had walked purposefully, but calmly back to Friedrich's house; he knocked on the door. Heidi opened it; she could see that he was troubled by something. He rushed inside and told her to close the door quickly.

"Has your uncle returned home yet?" he said in German.

"No, he hasn't, but I don't think he'll be very long. What's the matter, you look as though you've seen a ghost?"

"I'll tell you the details in a minute, but we have to leave here as soon as we can. Does your uncle have a car?"

"Yes, he does. He keeps it in a locked garage in the next road. The keys are on a hook on the inside of the door in the hall." Heidi knew what Artur was thinking of doing so she went to fetch the keys.

"We must leave before your uncle gets back. Have you got everything you need in your handbag?"

She said she would go and get it and also bring his kitbag from the lounge while he went to the toilet. After not many minutes, they were standing at the front door.

"My uncle usually comes up from Simmerner Strasse so it would be best if we went left to the top of the road then right; the garage is on the right of that street."

They arrived outside the garage; Heidi unlocked the door, gave the car's keys to Artur, they went inside. Artur was so surprised to see a shiny, black BMW, probably only a couple of years old. He walked around examining the car, he saw it was a model 327 in immaculate condition; he remembered reading about this model in one of the English motoring magazines. He told Heidi to open both garage doors whereupon the evening sunlight shone in accentuating the car's beauty. Artur unlocked the driver's door, put his kitbag in the well of the passenger seat and examined the dials and switches. He inserted the key in the ignition and pulled the choke out a short distance: it started first time. The straight-6 engine purred into life. After a few moments, he reduced the choke completely, engaged first gear and drove out slowly into the street, with Heidi indicating it was clear to do so. He brought the car to a halt by the pavement.

"It would be best if you drove, Heidi," he said as he got out of the car. He got into the passenger seat once he had closed and locked the garage doors.

"Where are we going to, Artur?"

Artur didn't reply, but looked in the glove compartment for a map; he was sure Friedrich would keep one in there: he was right.

"Turn right somewhere convenient and follow the Rhine to the south in the direction of Mainz."

"Before we start, Artur, I want to know what has happened to Marta and why we're leaving so suddenly?"

"Once we are out of Koblenz, I will tell you. We need to be on our way so we can find somewhere to stay; it's already 7 o'clock."

Heidi thought it would be unwise to ask about Marta again so she set off for the road following the river. Artur studied the map very intently, but he couldn't stop his hands from shaking.

"After about twenty kilometres, the road will follow the Rhine for nearly another twenty kilometres. I'm sure we'll find a small hotel somewhere along that stretch."

Sure enough, Artur pointed out a *Gasthaus* sign as they entered Spay.

"That looks promising, Heidi; stop here while I go and ask."

Artur went up to the reception desk and rang the bell. A pretty young lady came out of the office. He asked if she had two single rooms for one night, to which she said that there were two available. He signed the register for him and Heidi; he returned to the car.

"We can stay here tonight; the receptionist said we can park the car at the side of the hotel, making it less visible to a passer-by."

Heidi drove the car across to the side of the hotel, parking it with another car between it and the road. Artur opened the passenger door, got in, undid the glove compartment and drew out a number of papers and maps, he rolled them up, put them in his jacket pocket and picked up his kitbag. Heidi collected her handbag and walked into the reception area with Artur. They showed their identity cards with the receptionist writing down the relevant details in the register. She handed the keys for the second-floor rooms to Artur telling them that supper would be served up to 8:30 p.m.

Artur unlocked Heidi's door and invited her to go in first. Once the door was locked, Heidi turned to face Artur with a stern look on her face.

"It is time you told me what's going on, Artur; what has happened to Marta? Why did we need to leave Koblenz so quickly without saying goodbye to my uncle?"

"Marta drew a gun on me after we had got into her apartment. I had no alternative than to silence her. She was a traitor to her country of birth; after working for the British Service, she went over to the enemy and was plotting against the allies."

"So, you killed her?"

"As I said, I had no alternative. It is highly likely that I was seen either entering or leaving her apartment so we had to get out of Koblenz very quickly. Fortunately, your uncle had a car, otherwise we would have had to go by train."

Heidi relaxed a little once she heard what Artur had told her; she half suspected Marta had been silenced.

"Regarding my uncle's car, you'll be pleased to hear that I left a short note saying that we needed to borrow it for a few days."

"That was a very good idea, Heidi," he said, smiling at her for the first time in a long while. He walked over to her and held her tight in his arms; they stood together for several minutes.

"Where do we go from here, Artur? Do you really think we can get out of Germany when we don't have any papers for the vehicle?"

"Have a look at these: I found a number of papers in the car," he informed her as he laid them out on the bed.

"We could be in luck," he said as he put the registration document and the insurance certificate to one side. "I suppose your uncle keeps these papers in the car as, by law, he has to have them with him when driving in case he's stopped. Fortunately, as the Service knew I was going to Germany, I was provided with a German driving licence, so at least we can drive legally.

"But, for the moment, I need a quick bath and a change of some of my clothes," he said, touching her arms. "We'll have some supper and discuss our next move in my room after that."

Artur hugged Heidi again, picked up his kitbag, collected the maps and papers, and went to his room on the opposite side of the corridor. Once he had

had a bath, he put on a different sweater and pair of trousers: he could no longer smell Marta's strange perfume.

They had a pleasant supper together before going up to Artur's room at around 10 o'clock. He chose a large-scale map of Germany that covered Luxemburg, as well as NE France; he laid it on top of the chest of drawers.

"I believe we need to get back into France where we can try to contact some of the members of DOME. Do you know if any of them live near the place I was dropped? Wasn't it called Jeandelize?"

"I seem to remember that one of them, Emile, lives near Bar-le-Duc; I have his address in my handbag. Two of the others live south of there, near Chaumont, with the fourth living near me in Pesmes. Emile is the person who owns the truck."

Artur studied the maps and wrote down some details. He had chosen a route that followed minor roads with the first stage reaching close to the border with France at Orscholz.

"By my rough reckoning, it will be about 160 kilometres. I had a look at the fuel gauge in your uncle's car and it would appear to be over three quarters full so we should be able to get to Orscholz before buying more fuel. I would suggest, however, that if we find a petrol station in Morbach, we fill it up and have some lunch at the same time."

"Artur, how are we going to get the car back to my uncle, or are you planning to leave it somewhere in France?"

"Look, Heidi, I'm sorry to say this, but using your uncle's car is the best option we have for getting out of Germany and for me to get back to England. One suggestion might be that you drive it back to him, once my route out of France is decided."

Heidi didn't like the idea of driving back to Koblenz on her own, but at the moment she couldn't think of any alternative.

"So that's the plan, Heidi. We'll leave after breakfast and hopefully be in Morbach in time for lunch."

"You seem to be so sure the journey will be easy and straightforward; have you forgotten there's a war on and we are in enemy territory with false identifications and forged papers?"

"You are quite right, Heidi, it could be a very tricky run to the border. Not only that, sooner or later Marta's body will be found and all the border posts will be on high alert for anyone appearing suspiciously or doing anything irregular. I suggest we get a good night's sleep so we are in good form for tomorrow."

Artur took Heidi in his arms, kissed her and took her to her room. On his return to his room, he collected all the papers up, put his notes with the map and got ready for bed; he was satisfied that the plans were as good as they could be.

They had arranged to have breakfast at 8:30 a.m., but Artur had been awake from 6 o'clock. As he reviewed his planned route, he couldn't help thinking about what might or might not happen in the next two days. He was dressed and ready to go down stairs by 8:20 a.m. so he left his room, knocked on Heidi's door and went down to the breakfast room without waiting for Heidi to appear at her door.

"You might have waited for me, Artur," she remarked, as she reached the table that Artur was sitting at. "Did you have a sleepless night as well?"

"Sorry, I should have stayed by your door till you were ready," he said, as he stood up and assisted Heidi to her place.

They had an enjoyable breakfast, but Artur noticed it had started to rain just before they had finished.

"I'll go to reception to settle the account so I'll see you by the main entrance in fifteen minutes. Is that enough time for you, Heidi?" She nodded and smiled.

Once he had finished paying the bill, he returned to collect all his papers—most of which he placed in his kitbag—and went down to the entrance.

"Have you got the car keys as it would be best if I drove this morning?"

Heidi handed over the keys as they went out to the car. They left the *Gasthaus* and after some minutes, they passed through Boppard and were on their way to Kirchberg having left the Rhine behind them. The rain had stopped as they were about to enter Kirchberg around 10:30 a.m. when a road block came into view, but there was no barrier.

"This will be our first test of the day," Artur commented, as he slowed, "but probably not the last."

Artur greeted the guard politely only to be told very gruffly for their papers. Artur took his papers out of his satchel which he had organised soon after he had woken up that morning; he had suggested Heidi should do the same during breakfast.

The guard asked the usual questions and he seemed to be satisfied with the answers until the officer came forward to ask Artur about the car.

"Is this your car? Show me the car's documents."

Heidi opened Artur's kitbag that was in the well of the passenger seat and handed the papers to him, he passed them to the officer.

"This car is not registered in your name, so why are you driving it?" the officer said aggressively after a few moments.

Artur nearly always felt it was safer to stick reasonably close to the truth, so he told the officer that his passenger's uncle had lent it to them for a few days.

"Show me the letter that gives you permission to use it."

Artur decided not to reply, but to see what would happen next. The officer repeated the question.

"We didn't think we needed one: a Germen car, driven by a German in his own country."

The officer handed the documents back to Artur telling him to proceed, but next time have a letter with him from the owner.

"Heil Hitler," they all said with the officer and his guards giving the Nazi salute.

"That was a close call," Artur said, once they were on their way again; "I hadn't thought about a letter; I suppose we could create a forgery," he said as he looked at Heidi with a smile.

Chapter 33

Wednesday, 4 June 1941

The journey to Morbach was uneventful, so they decided not to stop until Orscholz where they hoped they could get fuel. They made good progress to Orscholz, filled up with fuel and found a small restaurant that was still serving food at 2:30 p.m. Over half a dozen German soldiers were also having a snack, but they couldn't keep their eyes off Heidi.

"I think we should go to the bar across the road," Artur suggested; "it might be a bit quieter."

The bar didn't serve food, so they just had a drink before returning to the car. Artur examined the map for their best route across the border.

"When we leave Orscholz there is a very small road going through the forest to a village. If we are lucky, there might be a small *Gasthaus* where we could stay the night. I suggest we book in, pay for the night's stay, but leave in the middle of the night to cross the border; we then continue to Verdun and Bar-le-Duc, all in the dark. How does that sound to you, Heidi?"

"But what about the curfew in France?"

"We'll have to hope we get lucky. So, you're happy to give it a try?"

Heidi nodded.

After some minutes, he was aware of noisy conversation coming from outside the restaurant over the road; he saw that the soldiers had come out into the street. He started the car and drove away from the bar, but he noticed the officer amongst them appeared to be writing something down: probably the car's registration number; Heidi hadn't noticed.

It wasn't far to the village, but there was no sign suggesting accommodation so Artur drew up outside the shop and went inside. He was told that he could find a small *Gasthaus* a few kilometres down the road opposite. He thanked the shop assistant, went back to the car and drove down the road. After a few minutes, he saw a small sign outside a house offering accommodation. He left Heidi in the car and went up the front path to the house.

"Is it possible," he said to the person who came to the door, "that you have two single rooms for tonight?"

The elderly woman replied that she only had two rooms and that they were both doubles. He followed the woman upstairs where she showed him both rooms that overlooked a well-proportioned and tidy back garden.

"I would like both of them, please," he said.

"Are you able to provide us with a light supper tonight?"

"Yes, I can," she said, "but it will have to be early, about 6:30 p.m., as I like to be in bed before 9 o'clock these days."

Artur thanked her as they went back down to the hallway. He was told he could park the car at the end of the driveway to the side of the house.

"All organised, Heidi," he told her as he returned to the car; it was now 3:30 p.m.

"Before we go to our rooms, I want to take a short drive along the road we will be using tonight to cross the border; to see how rough it is and look out for any possible hazards."

The road was indeed narrow—more like a farm track—with ruts and puddles, some of which were quite deep such that the car bottomed-out every now and again. As they started to go up a slight rise and then down the other side, they stopped at a junction with another dirt road.

"I think we are now in France," he said with some surprise in his voice, "and there's no border post," he continued with a joyous laugh.

"I'm going to turn right to see where it goes to."

He drove for only a kilometre and reached another T-junction. His sense of direction told him to turn left so that he was going further away from the border. After only one kilometre, they passed the sign for the village of Merschweiller.

"That wasn't as bad as I expected: no border post or guards is a real surprise," Artur said, as he brought the car to a stop in the centre of the village.

"I'm just going to ask a few questions in the village shop over there; I'll be back in a moment."

When he got inside, and the other customer had left, he asked the young woman a few questions in French about whether or not German soldiers—or the Gestapo—had been in the neighbourhood or near the border recently. She told him that people had seen them come through the village going to the border, but that it was not a regular occurrence. The last time they had come through the village was two days ago from the south and were going to Orscholz; they had stopped at the shop to buy cigarettes.

"Do they then come back this way a few days later?" Artur asked, to which she replied that it usually happened that way.

"Sorry to keep asking you, but I have one last question: when they return, is it during the day or at night?"

"During the day," she replied.

Artur thanked the woman and went back to the car. He told Heidi everything the woman had told him, after which he said that it was essential to cross the border during the night.

"I suggest we return to where we will be staying, we'll go back the way we came." Heidi agreed.

"Hang on a minute, Artur," she suddenly said, "what's the point of going back into Germany only to return here tonight, or have I missed something?"

"You are quite right; I haven't been thinking straight. I didn't leave anything in our rooms, so we can continue on our way?"

"Fine by me," Heidi said.

"The things we have to look out for are the fortresses of the Maginot Line. One of the largest was at Hackenberg and another near Cattenom, but I'm assuming that, soon after France signed the armistice, the French forces in those forts would have surrendered and become prisoners of war. They could, however, now be used by the Wehrmacht or the Gestapo for any purpose."

Artur got out the map and ran his finger along a road going to Malling then on to Audun, Ētain and Verdun.

"We need to cross the Mosel somewhere near here," he said, pointing at the bridge at Malling. "So, let's get going. One thing that might be in our favour is that we're driving a German registered car in German occupied France."

They went over the bridge at Malling, followed the road north of Thionville, ending up in Audun after about forty minutes.

"We have to keep going," Artur insisted, "as we must get to Emile's place by 6:30 p.m.; hopefully he can put us up for the night, or tell us where we can stay."

"Emile's home is in a village called Chaumont-sur-Aire which is about twenty kilometres north of Bar-le-Duc," Heidi said, as she produced a piece of paper with an address on it from her handbag.

"Look at the map, Heidi, and give me a rough guide on the distance to Emile's place; we have just gone through Landers."

"By my reckoning, we have another eighty kilometres to go."

Artur was silent, but he was quite positive about reaching Emile's around 6 o'clock as he increased the car's speed a little. The road from Verdun went almost due south as it followed the Meuse River until Artur took a turn to the left down a secondary road.

"Do you have any directions for Emile's place or just an address?" he asked Heidi.

"Only that the road is next to a bar in the centre of the village."

They proceeded along the secondary roads all the way to Bar-le-Duc, Heidi looked out for the bar.

"There it is," she exclaimed excitedly. "There's a narrow road going up the side of it."

Artur drove slowly up the road with Heidi looking for a house number.

"Stop, Artur; that's his house to my right. I'll go to the door while you wait in the car. I must remember to start speaking French," she said with a grin.

Artur watched her knock on the door; it was opened after a few moments by a woman. Some words were exchanged and Heidi was invited inside. It seemed to be an age before the door opened again, but it was probably only a couple of minutes. Heidi came out with a man who Artur recognised as Emile from a few days ago, so he got out of the car to meet them.

"I'm glad to see you again, Artur," as the two men shook hands. "Heidi told me a little about what you've been up to and that you would like to stay the night. That's fine with us, but we need to take your car to a barn on my brother François' farm a few kilometres from here. We can decide what to do with it later on, but for the moment we must keep it out of sight. My car is parked in the centre of the village so you will need to back down this road and follow me," Emile said, as he walked towards the bar and waved Artur into the street; they had left Heidi by the front gate.

"I'm parked over there," he said, pointing to a small black saloon car parked under a tree.

Chapter 34
Wednesday, 4 June 1941

Artur followed Emile out of the village in a northerly direction for a few kilometres then turned right up a long farm track towards some farm buildings. They pulled up outside the house; Emile got out of his car and knocked on the door before going inside. Artur heard him calling his brother's name, but after a few minutes nobody came out.

As an agent, Artur was trained to follow his instincts and he was now very suspicious of something not being right. He took his pistol from his kitbag, got out of the car as silently as he could and ran down the side of the house to where he hoped to find a back door. He ducked out of view as he went past a large window to find the back door open. He carefully went inside holding his pistol at the ready. He heard German being spoken by one man to another—neither was Emile's voice—from a room to his right. When he reached the doorway, he saw the backs of two German soldiers standing behind two chairs with two men sitting on them: one was Emile; *the other must be Emile's brother* Artur thought to himself.

"Don't even think of doing anything," Artur said very calmly, but firmly, in German as he entered the room, "or I'll shoot you both."

Artur went around in front of the chairs to see that Emile and his brother had been gagged and tied to the chairs with rope; François had been badly beaten up and looked in a bad way.

"What right do you have to enter this man's house and beat him up?" Artur said loudly to the two soldiers. They didn't reply.

"Unfasten these men immediately, but don't try any funny business," Artur said, as he waved his pistol in front of them.

"Emile, take the soldiers rifles off their arms and tie their arms behind their backs with the rope," Artur said in French once they had been released. As

Emile's brother was in a bad way, Artur told him to remain sitting on the chair: he was also obviously very badly shaken by the experience.

Artur squatted down next to François:

"How did these men get in here?"

"I was in the kitchen when they came in through the back door; I was taken by surprise. I was asked many questions about the Resistance group called DOME, but as I knew nothing and couldn't therefore tell them anything, they beat me up, gagged me, then tied me to the chair. I think they would have shot me, had you and Emile not arrived when you did."

"The problem now is what to do with them; have you any ideas?" Artur asked.

"There is a well at the back of the house, we could throw them down there; they don't deserve anything better."

Artur went over to Emile to help him tie up the soldiers who weren't offering much resistance.

"What we should do next," Artur said in French to Emile, "is to ask these men a few questions, then shoot them and throw them down the well that's in the back garden. It seems to me," he continued, "it was a case of mistaken identity by the soldiers, but they don't need to know that. Seeing that you and your brother are identical twins, it's not surprising, but I wonder who told them where your brother lived and that he was a member of the Resistance? Do you know of a collaborator in the area?"

"It's very difficult to think of someone even though my brother and I have lived in this vicinity since we were born. Let's ask the soldiers to see if they will reveal their source."

Emile told the soldiers, in German, to go out through the back door and to stand against the wall, which they did rather nervously.

"Why did you come to my brother's farm?"

They made no reply.

"Where did you get information about my brother and why did you need to beat him up so severely?"

"We are aware of resistance to the Reich's occupation in this part of France," one of them replied.

"You beat up my brother so badly and he still told you nothing, is that correct?"

The same soldier nodded.

"Would you have eventually shot him?"

"Those were our orders," the soldier said.

"Where is the officer who gave you the orders?"

"We are based just north of Bar-le-Duc?"

"Do you expect any of your group to follow you up here if you don't arrive back at base by a given time?"

"Yes," the soldier replied.

Artur then decided to enter the interrogation as time might be running out and they needed to get François back for treatment:

"You are aware that for the protection of French lands and her people, we will have no option than to shoot you, just as you would have done to this man's brother? Do you have anything else to say?"

Both the soldiers shook their heads.

Artur raised his cocked pistol, shot the first soldier, then the next, in the head. The soldiers were both large men, so it required both Emile and Artur to take each of them to the well in turn and heave them over the low wall. They didn't hear the splash for many seconds. They went into the kitchen, locked the backdoor leaving the house through the front door that they also locked.

"Let's quickly put your car in that barn over there," Emile said, "then help me put François in the back of my car."

Once the BMW was parked in the barn, Artur collected his kitbag, picked up all the registration papers and got into the front seat of Emile's car.

"We'll have to hope we don't get caught by the *Wehrmacht*, even if there isn't a curfew in this part of France at present," Emile said, as he drove quickly back to his village.

He drove up the narrow road, parked outside his house and ran inside to tell his wife, Isabelle, about François. She came outside to find him with his arm over Artur's shoulder being assisted up the garden path.

"He's in quite a bad way," Artur said; "not sure if he needs hospital treatment. Emile will no doubt tell you what has happened."

"That's alright, Artur, I am a qualified nurse so I should have most things that François might need. Heidi can help me, but if I feel he needs a doctor, I can always contact my brother as he lives in the village too."

Artur now needed to speak to Emilie about how he can get back to England. He was hopeful that someone in the DOME Resistance cell will have a shortwave radio. François had been taken into the kitchen by the women to assess the damage and to attend to his wounds; Artur found Emile in the lounge lighting a cigarette.

"Emile, I need to ask if anyone near here in your Resistance group has access to a shortwave radio?"

"There's a man called Jean living near Épernay who has one and is in regular contact with London. I have been there a couple of times in the last three months, he usually tunes in every other day at 6 o'clock in the evening. He listens in and, when necessary, he sends a coded Morse message back; the last time I was there, he was making contact on Tuesdays, Thursdays and Saturdays. We could drive over to him tomorrow; you might even be able to stay the night to hear the transmission as I would like to be back here before 8 o'clock."

"That would be brilliant, Emile, but isn't it a long way from here?"

"It takes less than two hours, unless we get held up for some reason. Heidi could come as well so that, if you stay there, she could come back here with me. After all the excitement of today, it calls for a drink. I trust you'll have a glass of red, Artur?"

"Nothing could be better, thank you," he replied.

They talked about the day's events as the women were still dealing with François' injuries. They heard later that he only sustained a couple of broken ribs, the rest being mainly superficial wounds and a couple of black eyes: he was a lucky man, everyone thought.

While Isabelle was applying the final dressings to François' wounds, Heidi followed instructions for the evening meal that they sat down for at about 9 o'clock. Much wine flowed, but nobody talked about the fate of the German soldiers; after all, they were at war.

Artur slept on the sofa in the lounge and was woken up at 8:30 a.m. by a lively Emile.

"What's got into you today?" Artur said, as Emile poured nearly half a glass of water over him.

"The weather is fine and we have a nice excursion to Épernay. I don't expect to find any champagne to purchase as the Gestapo have all the cellars of the major producers closely guarded: they are obliged to send thousands of their very best to Berlin for the Führer and his cronies.

"Anyway, get up Artur, the bathroom is free; breakfast will be in the kitchen; we must try to leave by 10 o'clock."

Artur did as he was told. After breakfast, he went up to see François; he was cheerful enough, but Artur thought he looked worse today than yesterday—he didn't say so, of course.

They waved to Isabelle as they left the house, with Heidi sitting in the back. Emile took the road through Vitry-le-François, then on to a minor road south of Châlons: Jean lived in Avize, south of Épernay.

"That's his house over there," Emile said. "We're in luck, his car is there in the driveway."

Emile got out of the car; as he reached the front door, it was opened before he had a chance to knock; it was quite comical as he almost fell in side. A burly, bearded man came out and embraced Emile. They talked for a short while then walked over to the car. Artur got out and was introduced to Jean.

"You had better come inside," Jean said as he opened the door for Heidi, who grabbed her handbag and Artur's kitbag from the back seat.

They went into the kitchen where Emile explained about Artur's mission and his need to get back to England.

"I am expecting to get a coded message from London this evening," Jean explained, "after the BBC French news service bulletin. There is a strong possibility that one of de Gaulle's men will be brought to France in the next few days; his job is to set up another Resistance group in the Compiègne area. There is a full moon on Monday, but, depending on the weather forecast, the plane might come up to two days either side.

"I have a radio upstairs in the loft so I will listen to the broadcast at 6 o'clock tonight. If you are hoping to be on the plane going back to England, you can stay here or come back on Saturday."

"It would probably be better for everybody if you would let me stay here," Artur commented. "The weather here is warm and it looks quite settled for a day or two; this makes me think that the plane will come on Saturday night. The only question is: what is the weather like on the other side of La Manche?"

"Instead of standing around trying to be weather forecasters," Jean said with a smile, "who would like a glass of red wine?"

All of them put up their hands and burst out laughing as they looked like they were back at school responding to their teacher.

Jean fetched four glasses, brought out bread and cheeses and poured out the wine.

"Santé," they all said, as they raised their glasses.

"Tell me, Emile, how does this lovely young woman, Heidi, fit into the group?" Jean enquired.

Artur said he would explain some of the background to Heidi's involvement, also saying that her real name is Monique. He mentioned that when he leaves for England, she will return to carry out her work with the French Resistance.

Before any of them knew it, they had finished the second bottle of wine as well as most of the five varieties of cheese: it was 3:30 p.m.

"What have you decided to do?" Jean asked Artur.

"As you have already mentioned, it would be best if I stayed here. My gut feeling is that the flight will take place on Saturday night and, if I'm right, I will be in the best place to catch the plane back to England."

"That's fine with me," Jean said, "but are you happy for Monique to go back with Emile, or have you another idea?"

"I know what I would prefer, but why don't you let Monique answer the question of what she would like to do."

Monique mentioned quite calmly that, if it was alright with Jean, she would prefer to be with Artur until he leaves French soil; she said that she would then find her own way back to Briey, perhaps by way of Emile.

Their preferences were agreed by Jean; he jokingly said that with Heidi around for a few days, he would get some really enjoyable meals.

Chapter 35
Thursday, 5 June 1941

They all went down to Emile's car to wish him a good journey back to Bar-le-Duc. Most specifically, they hoped François' injuries would soon be healed.

When they had returned to the house, Jean took them to their rooms upstairs.

"As I wasn't expecting any visitors, I'm sorry to tell you that the beds have not been made up and the rooms are in a bit of mess. I'll fetch some clean sheets, pillow cases and towels and will be back in a moment."

Artur smiled at Heidi and he thought she was on the same wavelength: *perhaps we will only need one set of sheets and pillows cases.*

The items duly arrived so Heidi made up one bed and Artur the other. They went downstairs to find Jean looking through the kitchen window to the back garden.

"Is something on your mind, Jean?"

"A few weeks ago, when my wife went to the Saturday market in Château-Thierry, she was picked up with a lot of other people by the Gestapo—she and the others are Jewish. They were flung into a large open-backed truck and, by all accounts, were taken away to Rheims where they were put on a train bound for a concentration camp in eastern Germany. I've heard nothing since so to help me through, I have committed myself to the French Resistance with even greater resolve."

"That's terrible news, Jean. Is there really no news of your wife and the others, apart from what you have told us?" Artur asked, as Heidi went over and put her arms around Jean.

"No, I fear for the worst," he said as tears rolled down his face into his moustache and beard. "I haven't shaved since the day that I heard the news."

"Anyway, enough of me. Why don't you walk down to the village and be back here just after 5:30 p.m.? If you turn right at the end of the drive, there's a small bar up on the right, but watch out for the Bosch as they sometimes go there; as you know, we are in the heart of the champagne area."

Artur and Heidi went upstairs to their rooms; Heidi unpacked her large handbag of most things, whereas Artur took out his pistol and put it into his inside jacket pocket.

When they returned downstairs to the lounge, Jean was sitting on the sofa clasping a framed photo to his chest.

"Are you happy for us to go out, Jean?" Heidi asked. He just waved his hand dismissively with a slight smile.

Instead of turning right, they turned left out of the village towards the vineyards. They walked for nearly twenty minutes in the warm summer air before turning back. Artur said that they ought to visit the bar that Jean had mentioned, even though it was coming up to 5 o'clock. As they walked in, they mostly saw elderly people, but there were a few German soldiers at the back in the corner. Artur greeted the lady behind the bar, ordered two glasses of red wine and sat at the table by the window next to the door.

"Your very good health, Monique," he said, much to her surprise. "I've been wanting to say that for a long time, but the opportunity hadn't arisen before. Anyway, I don't want the soldiers over there to hear me say your agent name."

Monique smiled, put her hand on his leg and touched his glass with hers. They sat talking for a while, but they were aware of the soldiers looking over at them from time to time. They had finished their drinks within fifteen minutes and felt they should be back to Jean's house in good time for the broadcast.

"We're back," Artur said as he walked into the hallway. He heard a noise from upstairs so they went up to find Jean had brought the steps down from the loft and that there was a light on inside.

"Come up when you're ready, Artur, but I want Heidi to be on lookout from the lounge window. The Gestapo sometimes drive their radio detector vans along the road trying to pick up signals from anyone who might be tuning in to a radio; they're particularly wanting to find people listening to the BBC's French broadcasting service."

Heidi went to the lounge as Artur climbed the ladder up to the loft. It was a large area with considerable height; Jean was sitting on a box facing Artur as he came up the ladder. The receiver was on another box with its lid open; Jean had earphones on as he tuned in to the frequency for a Thursday 6 o'clock news bulletin. Artur could hear faint, squeaky sounds as Jean passed over the stations he didn't need. Artur looked at his watch: there were five minutes to go. Jean put a clipboard on his knee and looked at the pencil to make sure it was sharp and ready for use. Artur carefully walked around Jean so that he was standing behind him. After a few minutes, Jean raised his left hand and then dropped it.

Artur couldn't make out all that was being said, but he got the gist of it. At the end of the bulletin, there was a slight pause before a few messages were issued. They seemed quite innocent and unimportant, but Jean scribbled down everything as quickly as he could.

"Was that it?" Artur asked with surprise.

"It certainly was. From what I understand, the flight will arrive on Saturday night: these are the coordinates of the field," he said, as he showed the piece of paper to Artur that he had decoded.

"I assume there was no detector in the road as there was no warning from Heidi?"

Jean switched off the equipment, closed down the lid and furled up the aerial wire. He pushed everything to the back of the loft and placed a blanket over it all.

Down on the landing, Jean closed the hatch to the loft, folded up the ladder and took it to his bedroom where he hid it in the wardrobe behind his wife's clothes.

Once in the hallway, Jean asked Heidi if she had seen anything suspicious, but she replied that she hadn't.

"Well, now that's done, we ought to go and have something to eat. There's a nice little place in Montmort where we can get a very respectable meal, considering it is wartime. Are you two ready or do you need five minutes to prepare?"

Artur looked at Heidi and they both said they were ready to go.

They drove out of the village in the direction that they had walked for a kilometre then turned right with vineyards on both sides of the road. Within a few minutes, they entered the centre of Montmort with the small restaurant half right of them. They parked in the small square next to a German army truck.

"Hopefully, the enemy are in the bar down there," Jean remarked, pointing to his left.

"Ah, monsieur Jean, how nice to see again," said the senior waiter. "And you have brought a lovely couple with you," as he took Heidi's hand and kissed it gently.

"I'm sorry to say that your usual table is not available, but is this one near the window acceptable?"

Jean agreed so they sat down at the table given to them.

"As you might realise, we don't have so much choice available at present, but we hope you will still enjoy what we do offer."

The waiter brought a complimentary bottle of champagne as they looked at the selection on the menu. At the end, Artur and Heidi agreed that the meal was very good and tasty, bearing in mind the circumstances. They drove back to Jean's house without incident, had a coffee and a brandy before Jean excused himself for retiring to bed early at 10:30 p.m. as he was feeling very tired: he also seemed very thoughtful and quiet.

Artur and Heidi agreed to sleep in their own rooms, but might consider sharing a room for the last night at Jean's place on Friday night.

The next day started off fine and sunny, but it began to rain in the afternoon continuing well into the late evening. Artur was starting to wonder if the forecast for Saturday was going to be favourable. They had planned to go for a walk again in the afternoon to give Jean time to himself, but the rain changed that idea. Neither Artur nor Heidi could stop talking, and thinking, about what might be the outcome of Saturday night; it did them no good whatsoever such that they lost their appetite for an evening meal.

They all went to bed early with Artur going into Heidi's room; he was sure from the snoring coming from Jean's room that he had fallen asleep soon after he had got into bed. Artur held on to Heidi, but was unable to bring himself to a love-making situation, however hard she tried to encourage him. So many questions flew around in his mind: will the plane get to the landing field; will the pilot get them off the ground before the Germans shoot at it; will they avoid being hit by enemy ground fire; if they are hit, will they have enough fuel to get over the Channel; will they survive the landing; will he ever have the chance to see Heidi again?

Artur worried himself to sleep in Heidi's arms, she was having similar thoughts as she too fell asleep. Artur woke at 7:15 a.m., slipped out of Heidi's bed and looked out of his bedroom window. It was starting to get light, there were a few cottonwool clouds to the south, but otherwise a clear sky; it seemed to augur well for the night.

"Did you sleep well, Artur?" Jean said, as he came into Artur's room, having found the door open. "I suppose you have been thinking about tonight's flight?

It's quite understandable as for once everything will be outside your control; you'll be in the hands of the pilot and your God. You may not be a religious man, but at least look to the future. You will have done your best under very dangerous conditions; I believe you to be a survivor."

Artur turned away from the window, wished Jean a good morning and smiled at him.

"You are probably right on all counts, but it doesn't stop me thinking about a few 'what might be' situations."

"You are right, of course, Artur. The main problem, as I see it, is that you have had too much time on your hands to think between arriving here on Thursday and boarding the plane tonight.

"Anyway, when the two of you are ready, we'll have some breakfast; I'll then go through the details of what we will be doing this evening and tonight."

Jean left and Artur went to Heidi's room where he told her of the plan. She still wasn't happy that she would be saying farewell to Artur: who knows when their paths will cross again.

They all enjoyed a very relaxed breakfast which they finished by 9:30 a.m. Heidi cleared everything from the table just as Jean fetched his maps and notes from the Thursday evenings broadcast and brought them to the table.

"This map is just about the right scale for the Compiègne-Soissons area and we can easily see the village of Vic-sur-Aisne almost midway between the two towns, it is about 120 kilometres from here; we need to be there before dark at about 9:30 p.m. The coordinates given to us show a mid-point of this field here," he said, pointing to a place on a map of a much larger scale.

"Is it going to be wide enough for the plane to turn and take off again?"

"The men in London think so. What we have to bear in mind is that if the wind is blowing from the south, the pilot will land downwind; after turning, depositing his man and the cargo, he will then take off into the wind giving him a much better chance of being airborne before he reaches the ditch and the hedge.

"You will see here that the road from Vic is quite narrow, but at least it's straight. We will stop in the wooded area that is next to the landing area. We are to rendezvous with the Resistance group at 9:30 p.m. in the woods; the leader will have brought a truck with three other armed people. The new Resistance man will be put in the back of the truck hidden under a large tarpaulin together with one other person whose job it is to protect him if they are attacked."

The mention of a truck with a tarpaulin reminded Artur of the time he was picked up by the DOME group near Briey and taken to Koblenz.

They continued to discuss possible situations that might arise before reaching the landing place, as well as after, for over one and half hours when Jean suddenly stopped:

"I'm not being very hospitable to you: I've forgotten to get you a drink." He jumped up from the table, collected wine glasses from the cupboard and went to the pantry for some wine.

"To a successful mission," he said, as they all raised their glasses.

"Now, where were we?"

"I think you have covered everything, Jean," Artur replied, "except for our departure time from here."

"Ah, yes; 6:30 p.m. sharp."

Heidi looked at her watch and couldn't believe that it was well after 12 o'clock.

"Would you like me to make some lunch, Jean?"

"Yes, please, but keep it simple."

Jean and Artur retreated to the lounge to discuss the mission further, leaving Heidi to prepare the lunch.

Heidi called them into the kitchen and by 1:30 p.m. they had finished the meal. Artur told Jean that he would like to take a rest for a few hours; Heidi wished to do the same.

Chapter 36
Saturday, 7 June 1941

Artur heard a knock on his door to hear Jean saying that it was already 5:30 p.m. He jumped out of bed, took his small washbag from the top of the dresser and went to the bathroom. He passed Heidi's room on the way and heard movement inside so he knew she was up.

They all gathered in the lounge just after 6 o'clock, so, as there was no point in hanging around any longer, Jean reckoned they should leave, just in case they encountered any delays, such as road blocks.

As usual, Artur sat in the passenger seat, his pistol between his legs and his kitbag in the footwell. Heidi was in the back and Artur had lent her the Luger. They drove to Château Thierry and on towards Soissons, all on minor roads. At the junction with the road from Rheims, they came to a road block, but there was no barrier; three armed soldiers stood in the middle of the road.

"Papers," one of the guards demanded. Jean slowly reached over, took the papers from the glove box and passed them through the window to the guard.

"Where are you going?" the guard asked in German. Jean replied slowly in French that he didn't understand him, but pretended to have a guess.

"We are going to my mother's place in St Quentin," he said, again slowly in French. The guard handed them back to Jean and came around to the passenger side asking for Artur's papers. He handed them to him. The guard tried to take them away to show the other two, but Artur snatched them back from his hands. All three raised their rifles pointing them at Artur, who, by this time had had enough. In one swift movement, he raised his pistol and shot the guard nearest to him. The other two tried to shoot Artur, but their safety catches were on. Heidi had wound down her window and shot one of the other guards, the third one ran to the roadside and jumped into the ditch.

"Drive away as fast as you can to Vic-sur-Aisne," Artur shouted to Jean.

After the turning to Vic, Jean asked Artur why he felt it necessary to shoot the guard.

"You didn't see, but he had a notice marked URGENT, CONFIDENTIAL with a description of me and my name as someone wanted for killing German soldiers and the stealing of a *Wehrmacht* truck on a previous mission; I couldn't take any chances. Thank you for supporting me, Heidi," he said as he turned around to smile at her.

Jean said no more as he drove carefully through Vic, up the track and into the forest. Artur looked at his watch: it was 9:15 p.m. Jean entered a clearing on their left, he turned the car around at the far end for a speedy getaway and stopped the engine. There was still some light in the woods, everything was eerily quiet.

"I'm going to take a walk to the field," Artur said, as he got out of the car, closely followed by Heidi. They reached the edge of the field, looked up and down and across to the wooded area on the other side.

"I wonder if the one guard that is still alive will send out a platoon of soldiers to look for us?" Heidi asked. Artur didn't reply, he was imagining the plane landing, the quick changing of agents and the take off. He was excited at the thought of leaving, but anxious for Jean and Heidi's return to Avize. Heidi took Artur's arm as they stood together, staring ahead, each with their own thoughts.

"Believe it or not," Artur said, as he saw the time, "it's nearly zero hour."

They went back to the car and, to their surprise, nobody was in it. Artur took out his pistol and crept closer only to find Jean asleep on the back seat. They both laughed rather nervously, tapped on the window and pointed their pistols at him. He immediately sat up, put his hands in the air in submission until the penny dropped. He jumped out of the car and grabbed Artur, but he was laughing so much that they fell to the ground in a heap.

"You really startled me, Artur. At first glance, you looked like the enemy."

"Sorry old man, it was only meant to be a joke."

At that moment, they heard a vehicle coming up the track so they squatted behind their car and listened. It stopped about fifty metres further on. They heard voices of several people, but, to their relief, not speaking German. They heard one of them say that he would switch on the radio receiver for two minutes in case the plane's pilot said anything. Another person said that the pilot would only give a coded message on the hour, the next time being 11 o'clock.

Jean was keen to make contact with the other group as he knew a few of them. He told Artur to guard the car as he would be away for twenty minutes. If he should hear any other vehicle or voices, he should blow the whistle that he gave him once only, as a warning.

Time seemed to go by very slowly. Artur told Heidi that Jean had been away for nearly half an hour.

"Perhaps he has waited for them to pick up the pilot's message," Heidi suggested. "After all, it's now 11:05 p.m."

They waited for a further ten minutes when suddenly they heard a noise from the woods to their right, the opposite direction to where the other vehicle was parked. Artur didn't think it warranted the whistle to be blown, but he said he would go and have a look. He crept from one tree to another to where he thought the noise had come from. Suddenly from behind him, there was a shout to halt in German. Artur stopped, turned around only to find Jean laughing outrageously at the expression on Artur's face.

"I think I have just got my own back to your prank on me in the car."

They walked towards each other, embraced and laughed joyously, but quietly. They went back to Heidi and the car where they told her what had happened: she too laughed.

"Seriously now for a moment, I heard the pilot's short coded message: he has the new man with him, he is only fifteen minutes behind schedule. That means he should be landing at around 12:15 a.m. The other group will put out the lamps at midnight so we have been asked to go and join them by their vehicle."

Artur collected his kitbag and they all walked along the track and then up to the group of five where the truck was parked. They greeted each one warmly, but quietly, with the leader taking Artur to one side to explain what will happen in detail. He also explained that all the other three occasions had been successful, as neither the Gestapo nor the *Wehrmacht* had any prior knowledge of the missions. He said they were now getting cleverer and getting information from collaborators.

"I'm not trying to worry you, Artur, but we have to keep being more careful, particularly as the agent arriving has been especially selected by de Gaulle."

"I understand fully," Artur replied.

"The wind is gentle, but it is coming up the field. That means the plane will turn up there," he said, as he pointed to his right. "The agent will run from the plane to here; you will run towards the plane once he is here and safe with us in the woods. You must run fast and straight to the plane unless the enemy open fire, at which point you run in a zigzag fashion. Any enemy fire is likely to come from the woods on the other side or from the top right. Don't stop to shoot at the enemy, that will be our job."

"Let's hope we don't get any enemy fire," Artur said.

They concluded their discussions and went back to join the others at the truck. Somebody said it was midnight, the leader told those responsible to light the lamps to give guidance to the pilot.

"I hear the noise of a plane," Artur said in a whisper. They all listened intently and they agreed. They went to the edge of the woods, saw the lamps were lit and looked left. Artur could just make out the plane before anyone else. At the last moment, as it was coming about forty feet above the hedge, the pilot put on the landing lights and landed halfway up the field. Everyone wanted to cheer, but they were excited inside. As the plane made its way to the end of the field it turned through 180 degrees, stopping after about twenty metres and switching off the landing lights. The pilot unhitched the ladder from the side of the fuselage and fastened it upright. The pilot came out of the plane followed by the agent—leaving the engine still ticking over—as they ran to the welcoming group.

"My name's Miles and I desperately need a pee," the pilot said, and went behind a tree.

Artur embraced Jean, thanked all the group members and went over to Heidi.

"I have to leave you for the time being, but I must call you Monique," he said, as he took her in his arms and kissed her fondly on her lips; he felt a few tears run down onto his face.

"We will meet again, I'm sure. Take good care of yourself," he said, as he took her hands.

He turned and ran with Miles to the plane. Artur climbed in first, squeezed himself into the place behind the pilot's seat. The pilot got into his seat, took up the ladder and secured it lengthways to the fuselage. He brought the engine up to full revs, turned on the landing light, put on full flaps and started down the field. Just as the plane left the ground, there was rifle fire from the far side of the field: he thought the plane had been hit, he turned the lights off. He knew the engine of a Lysander was not very powerful, but he did all he could to avoid being hit a second time which could be fatal. By this time, the group with the agent had opened fire on the enemy which drew their attention away from the plane.

Artur could just about stretch his legs out where he was, but before he settled down, he just managed to congratulate Miles on his avoidance tactics.

The pilot took the plane to 7,000 feet for the first hour, then came down to 800 feet as they neared the Channel. There was light cloud over the water, but the anti-aircraft fire was rather wayward even with the searchlights.

Before too long, the pilot contacted traffic control and they were cleared to land at Tangmere. As they descended, someone in the tower noticed that the right-hand undercarriage and a tyre had been blown off. The man in the tower told the pilot suggesting he should do another circuit while the fire engine and ambulance were in position near the grass runway. The pilot acknowledged and told Artur to brace himself for a possible bumpy landing.

The plane came around on to finals and everyone held their breath. The pilot used full flaps to reduce the speed as much as possible and with the nose high, the stall indicator made itself heard continuously. At the very last moment before touching down, the pilot raised the right wing so that the left wheel and undercarriage took all the force of the landing. He cut the engine and turned the rudder at the same time. The force was too much for the left undercarriage so it collapsed; all forward movement immediately stopped as the plane lurched forward onto its nose.

"Welcome to England, Artur," the pilot said. "Sorry about the landing."

The fire engine was quickly beside the plane with the ladder reaching out to the cockpit. The pilot collected his things and descended the ladder, followed by Artur with his kitbag.

"Well done," Artur said to Miles, "I'm sure nobody could have done a better job than you with that landing. If the NAAFI's open, let me buy you a beer."

The ambulance man quickly checked the pilot and Artur when they were on the ground: nothing broken, just a few bruises. A staff car brought the station commander out to the plane where he jumped down to welcome them both.

"A well-earned drink is called for on these chaps' safe return to our shores."

Miles and Artur stepped into the car and they were driven off at high speed to the bar; beers were consumed and many stories were told until well after dawn.

CPSIA information can be obtained
at www.ICGtesting.com
Printed in the USA
BVHW031010251122
652759BV00013B/473